A COLLECTION OF
NURSING
STORIES

A COLLECTION OF
NURSING
STORIES

HAMLYN

First published in 1979
Revised edition published in 1988
This revised edition published in 1991 by
Hamlyn Children's Books, part of Reed International Books,
Michelin House, 81 Fulham Road, London SW3 6RB

This arrangement copyright © 1979, 1988, 1991
Octopus Books Limited

Line illustrations by Lawrence Taylor
Cover artwork by Julie Dodd (represented by Artist Partners)

ISBN 0 600 57095 9

Printed in England

Contents

CHRISTMAS ON DUTY

Monica Dickens

Just before Christmas, Sister went on holiday, and a temporary woman called Sister Oates took charge. She was a snob of the highest order, so superior that she could never bother to learn anybody's right name. She had been relieving on the private wards, where apparently she had spent most of the time bridling and smoking cigarettes in the middle of her mouth in the room of Lady Mondsley, who was in hospital for hypochondria.

I was not looking forward to Christmas. It was the first I had ever spent away from home and I didn't think I would be very good at communal jollity. 'Christmas is such fun here,' people kept telling me.

'What do you do?'

'Well, for one thing, the nurses all have a Christmas dinner and the doctors wait on us. It's a scream, my dear, we all throw the food about. Last year we had wine.'

'What, Graves?' She nodded, awed.

'What else do you do?'

'Oh, everyone goes perfectly *mad*, you know. We do the daftest things . . . we all throw the food about!' That seemed to be her criterion of wassail.

Because I could not be at home, I pig-headedly determined not to enjoy myself, but as the preparations advanced I began to be drawn in. You can't live in a place that takes up your whole time and interest without absorbing some of the current atmosphere. The men were out to have a good time: they accepted the situation in which they found themselves and determined to make the most of it. They had been getting out of hand for some time—ever since Sister Martin removed her velvet-gloved control. They mocked Sister Oates behind her back and called her 'Wild Oats,' because she was so proper. There were quite a lot of them at this time who were allowed up, and it was the hardest thing in the world to get them into bed at all.

They were not allowed up between nine and twelve in the morning. 'Nurse Dickinson,' Sister would say, 'get all those men into bed. I'm going to have my coffee now and I don't want to see anyone running about when I get back.' Having her coffee was a morning ritual which took place in the sitting-room. No one must disturb this sacred rite, but Nurse Sowerby was graciously admitted to discuss the day's work, rather as if she were a cook coming up to settle the meals.

I managed to hound some of the meeker men into bed, but others would only say: 'Come orf it, Blondie, can't a chap get shaved in peace?'

'Well, mind you get into bed as soon as you've finished, and for heaven's sake don't smoke till she's inspected the ashtrays.'

I tried to chivvy them back by the time Sister came to do her stately morning round. She would be half-way round the beds, with her 'And how are you this morning, Jenkins?' or Fox, or Stuart, or whatever the name might *not* be, when a wild pyjamaed figure would scuffle across the floor and bound into bed, emerging above the sheets with an innocent air, while Sister Oates would stop in her tracks, staring as if she had found bugs in her kitchen.

There was a man called Toller, a railwayman who had lost an arm in a shunting accident. He had only three fingers on the remaining hand, but he could do more for himself than a lot of the patients did with ten. After a few days of drinking through a straw, he demanded a cup and taught his fingers to hold it. He would not even use a spoon for his meals, but managed to manipulate a fork like an American. It was agony sometimes to watch him struggling to strike a match,

7

missing time after time, but it was as much as your life was worth to try to help him. He would deliver some goods-yard language that sent you away red to the ears. He had a vital Latin appearance—black hair, brown skin and very white teeth, and his eyes were always up to something. He kept the whole ward alive, and his cheek was colossal. On Christmas Day he kissed Sister Oates, smack on the lips, which must have needed some courage.

'Nurse Dickinson and Nurse Bunter,' she said, on the day before Christmas Eve, 'this afternoon we will decorate the ward.' Mounds of holly and miles of coloured paper-chains were stacked in readiness in the splint cupboard, and there was a Christmas tree and a whole boxful of balloons. Sister began to blow one up, her pigeon chest poutering alarmingly. The whole ward was watching open-mouthed wondering which would burst first—she or the balloon.

'There,' she said at last, panting and holding her hand to her heaving apron, 'that's the way to do it. I mustn't do any more, because of my heart.' Soon after that, she retired to her room to eat tea and buttered toast, leaving Gunter and me to cope with the decorations, and emerging when we had finished to say: 'Oh, no, I don't fancy that at *all*.' Fortunately, she couldn't make us rearrange them, because two of the results of a motor-cycle accident came in and kept us busy. So she was able to spend the rest of the Christmas days saying: 'Now if only we'd had the Christmas tree at this end of the ward—,' and 'If you'd put those balloons where I wanted them, the men wouldn't have been able to reach them with their cigarettes.'

On Christmas Eve there was a dress rehearsal of the concert that we were to give to the patients—as if their sufferings were not enough. Chris and Barney and I had been asked to go to a dance at the aerodrome that night, and as the other two were not in the concert they refused to let me make us all late by staying on for the rehearsal.

'No one'll notice if you're not there,' said Barney.

'But I daren't not go. What'll Beaver say?'

'Oh—her,' said Chris, and Barney said: 'Anyone would think you were the flaming princ. boy, the way you go on.' Actually, I was in the back row of the chorus: 'The Redwood Juveniles', in knee-length operating gowns and big white bows of bandage in our hair.

After a day of running about after Wild Oats like a negro slave, I was as keen to get out of the hospital as the others. I had just decided to cut the rehearsal and was going into my room to change, when Beaver, the Senior Staff Nurse, gave me a slap on the back that pitched me through the doorway. 'That's right, old thing,' she said bursting with Christmas Cheer, 'don't be late for rehearsal. I'm going to give you a line to say, as Jones is off sick,' she added, as if bestowing a colossal treat. I would have to go to the rehearsal now. Chris and Barney went on to the dance without me, as Arthur was champing outside, but he promised to come back for me later.

The rehearsal was held in the Common Room. Some people turned up in the strange garments that were their idea of a policeman or a soldier or a black minstrel; others, under the delusion that it would be All Right on the Day, had not yet thought about their costumes. Everyone talked the entire time.

Beaver kept telling us that a bad dress rehearsal made a good first night.

The House Surgeons were in the concert, too. They strolled in after dinner, guffawed their way through the sketches, but soon got bored with it and strolled out again. Miss Llewellyn, one of the female Housemen, stayed on till the bitter end, her spectacles and teeth flashing with keenness. She had been an awful nuisance all along, always having some ambitious idea about a thing long after it had been settled and wanting to argue it out. She kept urging us to have part songs, although none of us could sing in tune, much less keep a part.

'We always used to do them at the Royal Free,' she would say, with that nervous, pecking movement of her woolly head. 'They were a tremendous go, I can tell you.'

I escaped as soon as I could, and changed my silly operation gown and did something to the face which had obviously not been attended to since six o'clock that morning. On my way out, I ran into one of the Sisters and had to pretend that I was just going out to post a letter.

'There's no post out on Christmas Eve,' she said, eyeing my clothes suspiciously.

'Yes, there is Sister,' I lied. 'Special wartime arrangement.'

'Well, in that case, you can post some for me.' I toiled up to her

9

room with her to get the letters, which I forgot all about and found in my pocket weeks later.

When I reached the usual meeting place, out of sight of the hospital, there was no sign of Arthur and his biscuit tin on wheels. A large black car was waiting a little farther up, however, and as I approached, a head looked out of the driver's window.

''Devening,' it said. 'Are you Nurse somebody-or-other?'

'I expect so.'

'Hooray. Climb into the pumpkin, sweetheart, and I'll take you to the ball,' said the head, disappearing inside. It was obviously rather drunk.

Even I could see, however, that it sat on top of a uniform with far more stripes than I was accustomed to.

'Are you a pilot?' I probed, as we shot dangerously downhill. He laughed so long and boisterously that I didn't dare enquire any farther, because it made the car lurch.

'Why did you come and fetch me?' I asked. We had left the dark deserted Victorian streets and were levelling out into the suburbs.

'Heard someone say they were coming to fetch a nurse,' he said. 'Marvellous party, by the way. Never could resist a nurse, so I said I'd come. Chap didn't mind—too busy with a cracking blonde.' This must be one of the evenings in which Chris was being nice to Arthur.

The hangar was gay with holly and flags and hordes of sweating, pushing people dancing to a band that was only audible at one end. The shuffle, shuffle of their feet on the concrete almost deafened you as you came in, but after a bit, you didn't notice it.

'Straight to the bar,' said my boy-friend. He turned out to be a large, well-fed man, with a great head of curly, greying hair, which he held very high, like a horse.

'What is it?' I whispered to Nigger, whom I found in the crowd round the bar. He giggled. 'It's a Wing-Commander. Doing well for yourself, aren't you?'

'Here you are, darling,' said the Wing-Commander, handing me a glass.

'Thank you angel,' I said, and he roared with laughter and kept telling me what a wit I was. He was easily amused.

'Look out,' said Nigger in my ear. 'There's its wife over there.'

Sitting at a table by the wall, hemmed in by the standing crowd, was a superior little party, with Mrs Wing-Commander in the middle, skinny and upright, with red hair piled on top of a face that seemed to go on for ever vertically. She sipped her drink as if it had been poured out for her by a Borgia. I danced with her husband and then escaped for a while, but he found me again and slapped me playfully.

'Naughty little girl to run away,' he said. 'I'll have to keep you on a collar and lead.' He was just as easily amused by his own wit as mine. He insisted that I should meet his wife, so that she could ask me to their house. He evidently didn't dare to ask me of his own accord. She was circling regally round the floor with a deferential young officer, who was under the delusion that he might thereby advance his career.

'This is Nurse What's-it, Mavis,' said the Wing-Commander—I hadn't yet discovered his name.

'Oh, yes?' she said, making inverted Vs of her eyebrows and looking at my swollen red nurse's hands as if she knew that I had corns on the soles of my feet.

'Yes,' he said, with his head higher than ever, not meeting her eye, 'she tells me they get God-awful food at the hospital, so I thought it would be fun if she came to dinner one night.' She was looking at him cannily, and he laughed uncomfortably, as much as to say: 'Yes, you're right, I am a bit tight.'

'So you're a nurse?' said his wife, and led me to a corner, where she questioned me with a kind of detached pity, as if I had been an unmarried mother. After a struggle between disinclination and her duty as a social worker, she fixed a date for me to dine on my evening off, and left me, her charitable conscience salved. I had no intention of going, but I thought it was simpler to accept now and cry off later.

Christmas Day. Noel. Sing Hey, the Holly, but I didn't feel like singing Hey anything when the Senior Night Nurse bawled: 'Six o'clock, Nurse,' maliciously across my sleep. One couldn't even go to church, to make it seem more like Christmas, because on Christmas and Boxing Day we had no off duty at all.

All the essential work of the ward, the dressing and treatments, had to be got through in the morning, so as to leave the afternoon free for jollity. Fortunately, we had only one very ill patient, but I didn't see how he was going to last out the day, with the noise that the men were already making. They had started the morning by dressing up and playing charades. Jackson, who could get about at a great rate on his crutches, had chased Gunter into the bathroom and relieved her of her cap and apron. I found her sitting resignedly on the edge of the bath, reading a two–days–old paper. She looked funny without her cap; her head was quite flat, like a boiled egg with the top sliced off.

In the middle of Toller's famous impersonation of herself, Wild Oats arrived on duty, with a majestic hangover from the Sister's Christmas Eve party, at which they had had Empire Burgundy and Bagatelle. We had to tell her he was being Douglas Byng.

We had all to subscribe to a present for her, and Sowerby now presented it in the sitting-room, with much clearing of the throat. It was a tooled copy of Shakespeare's Comedies, which Ross had picked up cheap because it had a page missing. It was only one of the last pages and there was no reason, anyway, to suppose that she would ever read the book, and it looked handsome and expensive. She was pleased with it. She visualized it sitting behind a glass-fronted bookcase when her ex-patients came to tea with her.

Then she fished in the cupboard where she kept the tea and sugar locked away from us, and surprisingly presented us each with a bottle of eau-de-Cologne. 'A happy Christmas to you all,' she said, her gold back tooth glittering.

When she went for her elevenses later in the morning, we gathered in the kitchen to distribute our own gifts. To save having to buy five presents, we had each bought one, and we jumbled them up in the bread bin and drew in turn. I had bought a bottle of complexion milk that I wanted myself. I thought I'd be able to recognize its shape. To my fury, who should draw it but Ross, whose face obviously had no dealings with such things. She unwrapped it in silence and went away to her work. I drew a beastly little memo book, with 'Lest I Forget' stamped across the cover. I was pretty sure it was Ross's contribution. Gunter drew a bit of bread the first time, but tried again and got a powder compact. Powder and scent—her young man would have had a fit if he had known. She had told me all about him. He was a male nurse in the RAMC who thought that clothes were for utility, not adornment. 'He likes women to be as God made them,' she said.

After the present-giving, she drew me into the linen cupboard. 'Something for you,' she said, fumbling under her apron and producing a very nice screw pencil. 'A Merry Xmas,' she said, taking my arm. She had a passion for touching you. Luckily she had not seen me draw the memo book, so I was able to say: 'And I've got something for *you*!' and produce it proudly.

The men's Christmas dinner was the high spot of the day. There was a huge turkey and a plum pudding, and a crate of bottled beer. The surgeons had to dress up in chef's caps and carve the turkeys. We had Mr Harvey Watkins, who wore a small frilly apron round his non-existent waist and was full of bonhomie. He carved the turkey on a table in the middle of the ward, and we all stood round him with trays, saying 'Ha-ha' to whatever he said. Sister ladled out the vegetables and sauces as if she were presiding at an East End soup kitchen, and we carried the plates round and opened the beer. There was big eating, and a certain amount of cheating among those who were on special diet. I got mixed up and gave a Gastric a leg of turkey and three roast potatoes, but it didn't seem to do him any harm, and he was very difficult afterwards about his normal diet of flaked fish and purée.

The shattered turkey and the remains of the excellent rich dark plum pudding were taken out to the ward kitchen, and when Sister had taken Mr Harvey Watkins into her sitting-room for a glass of sherry and the men were busy pulling crackers, a disgraceful scene took place. All the nurses rushed for the kitchen, as fast as their various degrees of foot trouble allowed, and with silent accord we fell on the broken meats. You can get far more turkey and plum pudding by snatching it from the dish with your fingers than you ever could at table. Goodness knows how long we would have gone on stuffing if it had not been for the frenzied shouts of: 'Nurse!' from the ward. Old McGilligan had fallen out of bed and was sitting happily on the floor in his nightshirt, singing 'Come Back, Paddy Riley to Ballyjamesduff.'

Seeing that there were enough people to deal with him, Gunter hurried back to the kitchen, before the porter should come and take away the dishes.

The visitors came after lunch, bringing presents and strewing the ward with paper and string. I had to go off and get ready for the concert. I was feeling tired now, but I remembered that Chris's Maternity Ward had some bottles of port going in the Labour Ward. It was queer to find the hospital regulations so suddenly relaxed. Ordinarily, it was an appalling crime to go to another ward without a very good reason, but today, one could wander about anywhere and nobody even said: 'Where are your cuffs?'

By the time we had done the concert on all the five big wards, it seemed to be getting very stale, but the audience lapped it up. They enjoyed seeing the doctors and nurses, in whose power they normally were, making fools of themselves. The House Surgeons dashed off in between every performance to fortify themselves, taking some of the more attractive nurses with them. Poor Nurse Beaver was perpetually hunting for people, and when they didn't turn up in time to go on, Miss Llewellyn, who was anti-fortification, leaped into the breach and understudied, mouthing her words and doing a great deal of miming at the side of the stage when someone else was talking. After I had said my one line: 'But look, Princess, see who's coming!' I lost interest and used to go and sit in the audience. There was never room for all the Redwood Juveniles in the space at the end of the ward, anyway. Some of them would be going through the motions right out of sight, but quite happy.

Some of the Night Nurses had stayed up as it was Christmas and were sitting yawning, their eyes bright with lack of sleep. Andrews told me she had followed us round and seen the concert on every ward. She was in love with Mr Briant, and was torturing herself with the sight of him in a borrowed battledress, with a bandage round his head.

The Nurses' dinner party was as promised, except that it was cider, not Graves. There was plenty of food, both eaten and thrown about, and Mr Vavasour, the gynaecologist, was very giddy with a bit of mistletoe. Matron looked in to see how we were getting on, and we all had to give three cheers for her, goodness knows why, as she was not even responsible for the food. She had probably had a row with the Housekeeper about providing too much. Afterwards, there was dancing in the Common Room, with five times as many women as men. Etiquette decreed that the doctors should dance principally with the Sisters, and when one of them danced with a nurse, there was much jealous whispering: 'Look at Harrison. Isn't she soft? *I* wouldn't dance with Johnny Briant—conceited ass.' If a couple were so rash as to sit out somewhere, the Assistant Matron, a cushiony woman with abundant hair, would search for them and manoeuvre them back into the ballroom. With the nurses' bedrooms so close, you see. . . . One never knew. These modern girls. . . .

I enjoyed Boxing Day more than Christmas Day. Sister went off in the afternoon, and the men produced some beer from their lockers. Robins brought up her gramophone, and we moved the desk and cupboards from the centre of the ward and danced. Toller could rumba. 'This is the other thing you don't need two arms for,' he grinned.

The ill patient had fortunately been given an injection of morphia after lunch, and slept like a log, even through the singing of the patients who couldn't get up to dance. Even Sow's varicose veins took the floor and she polka'd with old Daddy Masters, who might never have heard of such a thing as Hernia. Jackson and I had discovered the delightful game of filling with water balloons for unsuspecting people to burst. I can't quite remember how it happened, but it ended in a rugger scrum with me underneath. I was lying on my face, screaming, when all the bodies on top of me suddenly melted away, and I rolled over to see Wild Oats looming above me in perspective. At the time, she only said: 'Put your cap on at once and go and change your apron,' but the next day she had me into the sitting-room.

'You see, Nurse Dixon, it isn't so much a question of bad behaviour. We won't go into that—that's your parents' responsibility. It's a question of your dignity as a Nurse. You're letting down the whole Profession, don't you see?'

I mumbled and shuffled my feet.

'It's playing for popularity, Nurse,' she went on, her eyes bulging like a Hyper-Thyroid, 'and it won't do. The men don't like you any the better for it—don't imagine that for a moment.'

'But, Sister—'

'I'm speaking, Nurse. I say they don't think any the more of you; they merely lose their respect for you. They remember, and they'll take advantage of you another time.'

'But, Sister, they wouldn't. After all, they are sensible.'

'They are not sensible, Nurse.' She looked up at me in surprise. 'And remember: whatever class a patient may be, and some of them may be very good class—*quite* good class—you must always keep yourself just that little bit above them. Dignity, Nurse—without it, you may be a nurse, but you'll never be a good nurse, Nurse.' I edged towards the door, and she held up her hand. 'One more thing,' she said impressively. 'There might not always be other nurses there to back you up. Night Duty, for example. You might easily find yourself one day in a *very embarrassing position*.' She pronounced the last words with a ponderous horror, and I left her, slightly out of breath, to contemplate this interesting possibility.

The aftermath of Christmas was as might be expected. Two days of thirteen hours apiece without a break had left everyone tired and irritable, and the patients were inclined to be whiny, like children over-tired by a party. There was all the clearing up to do, a lot of extra cleaning, and all the decorations to take down.

'How about leaving them up for next year, Sister?' asked Robins, from the top of a step-ladder. 'It would save an awful lot of trouble.'

'I can't hear a word you say, Nurse Dobbin,' said Sister Oates, who was in no mood for joking. 'Mind what you're doing with that holly.' Robins dropped it on the upturned face of a sleeping man, and he sat up with a yell.

'I don't know how Sister Martin puts up with such girls. Ah, there's Mr Harvey Watkins!' She steamed towards him, the badges and medals on her apron arriving long before she did. 'Good morning, Mr Harvey Watkins,' I heard her say. 'Just clearing away the traces of merriment, you see.'

The surgeon rubbed his hands and ha-ha'd, throwing out his legs as he walked. The House Surgeon lagged behind, looking as if he could have done with more sleep and less liquor.

This reaction was general, it seemed. One would not have thought Redwood to be a town of unbridled licence, nor of the temptation or facility to make a beast of oneself. Yet into the Out-patients' Department there poured a stream of black eyes, broken heads and acute abdominal disorders. One man, who was admitted to our ward as a query concussion, was found to be merely sleeping in the comfortable lap of Bacchus, and was fetched home, as soon as he had stopped being sick, by a harridan in a hard hat.

We also had an old man who had been knocked down by a car, and a couple of motor-cycle accidents. One of these was a Canadian soldier, whose right leg was amputated soon after he came in. He was a fine man in his prime, about thirty-five, weathered and independent, a man to lean on in a crisis. And now he was leaning on me, asking me whether his leg was there, for of course he could still feel it.

I didn't know what to say. He was only just round from the anaesthetic and very shocked. They were going to give him a blood transfusion as soon as Mr Briant could get down. I hedged. 'You'll be all right. All you've got to do is just not to worry. Try and get some sleep.'

The words sounded trite and silly as I said them. He was not a man to be fobbed off with glib hospital jargon.

He gave me a look that he had probably given a lot of brainless women, and said: 'Come on now, Honey. Don't stall. I can take it.'

'We're not allowed to tell patients anything. You have to ask Sister, or a doctor.'

'They've chopped it off, then,' he said fixing a cold blue eye on me. I nodded.

'Yeah.' It was more a long-drawn expiration than a word. 'Yeah. Thanks for telling me.'

In spite of his ability to bear pain, he was a difficult patient. He was autocratic and grumbled about everything except his leg. He had the aggressive Canadian conviction of supremacy and was quick to criticize anything that displeased him. Wild Oats mistrusted him because she felt he had got her number, and I think all the nurses except Ross were a little afraid of him. He made one feel somehow pettily feminine, and rather ridiculous for being occupied most of the day with trifling details. Unlike the other men, he would not accept a rule because it was a rule, unless he approved of it.

'If he wants to have things his own way,' Sister kept saying, 'he ought to go into a private ward. But I don't suppose even the Canadian Army is mad enough for that. The man's only a Private, after all.'

Laurence Cowley—that was the Canadian's name—had had a knock on the head that wiped out all recollection of the accident or what led up to it. The police had been to see him once with notebooks, and boots that resounded through the ward, but he had been unable to tell them anything. He was very tactless with them, and started to quote the Canadian highway laws and they went away, their boots a little subdued by pique.

It was more than a week after his operation before something clicked in Cowley's brain and he remembered part of what he had forgotten. I was feeding him his dinner, for one of his wrists was broken and the other hand bandaged. We had got beyond the preliminary 'Hell, where do they get this stuff, anyway?' stage, and he was taking the spoonfuls sulkily and abstractedly, as if he were trying to keep his mind on more pleasant things. Feeding somebody is very boring. Because you are impatient to be finished you try to make them take the food faster than they want, and they either choke or take it slower than ever—on purpose, I believe. Cowley had two teeth knocked out, which did not help matters much. I shovelled in as large a mouthful as he would take without protest, and while he dealt with it, shifted my weight from foot to foot, leaned against the bed and gazed round the ward with ennui. I was watching old Daddy James trying to retrieve a piece of meat that had fallen down the front of his nightshirt, when Cowley suddenly gave the impression of having leapt six feet in the air, although he was actually unable to move.

'Jumping Jesus!' he said, 'I knew there was something!'

'What—'

'Maisie!' he almost shouted. 'What happened to her? Why in Hell didn't they tell me what happened to her?'

'What happened to who? Who's Maisie?'

'Why the kid who was riding pillion on the bike. I forgot she was with me till just now. I guess that bang on the head—but they could have told me about her, they could have told me what happened.'

'Perhaps she wasn't hurt,' I suggested.

'She must have been. She'd have come around to see me. Listen, maybe she's hurt bad. Maybe she's even dead—Jeeze, poor little Mais. Poor Kid—'

'If she was hurt, she's probably in this hospital. I'll ask Sister if I can ask the Secretary's office.'

'Keep that old battleship out of this, will you? She'd have the inquiry scheduled in triplicate and sent up to the Ministry of Information. Find out yourself—it'll be much quicker. Jeeze, I'm going to feel badly if—'

'I'll try, but we're not supposed to give information about patients, you know.'

'Don't pull that on me,' he said, magnetizing me with an eye.

'All right,' I said. 'I'll find out at teatime. Look, you haven't had your pudding. I'll go and get it.'

'If you do,' he said, 'I'll sling it in your pan. Listen, Honey, it's not pudding I want, it's Mais.'

Maisie was in Jane English Ward, with compound fractures of both legs. At first they had thought she would not live, and it was nature, not she herself, who had made the effort and proved them wrong. She had been told about Cowley, though not yet about the amputation. Evans, one of the Welsh girls who had come with me, was on Jane English, and she told me all I wanted to know while we squatted in front of the gas fire making toast. Above the fire, a notice in a looping hand was pinned to the wall with drawing pins:

'Owing to damage to the Asbestos
No Nurse may Make Toast at the Gas Fire
Bread is more nourishing than toast
E. Harriman, Ass. Mat.'

There were dozens of these little texts, all over the hospital and nurses' hostel. Sister Harriman's duties seemed to be wholly deterrent, but she was evidently of the school that thinks children should be told Why, and nearly every one improved the occasion with a little free information. One of the notices in the bathroom read:

'Do Not Use Too Much Hot Water
There are others to come after you

also
Too hot a bath lowers the vitality
and reduces resistance to infection'

and another on the board in the entrance hall read:

'NURSES ARE RESPONSIBLE FOR THEIR OWN BLACKOUT
ALSO FOR ANY FINE INCURRED IN CONNECTION WITH SAME
Carelessness in such matters is more than unpatriotic
IT IS TREACHEROUS'

After I had found out all I could about Maisie, I sounded Sister
Oates. I was helping her to put away the clean linen—at least, she
was telling me where to put it and I was running up and down the
step-ladder to reach the top shelves.

'Sister,' I said casually, with my face in the linen basket, 'does
Cowley know about that girl who was injured with him?'

'No,' she said. 'He remembers nothing about her, and Sir Curtis
Rowntree doesn't want him told yet. How many pillowcases have you?'

'Forty-two.' Sister ticked it off on her list. 'How did you know
about the girl, Nurse Dixon?' she asked. 'He hasn't said anything about
her, has he?'

'No,' I said. 'One of the nurses on Jane English was talking about her
at tea.'

'There's a great deal too much shop talked at meals, in my opinion,'
said Wild Oats. 'When I was doing my training, one of the Sisters
used to listen to our talk and anyone who mentioned the wards was
sent away from table. We used to have some very interesting con-
versations, I remember.' She sighed. 'But girls these days have no social
manners at all.'

'I make that twenty-four drawsheets altogether,' I said coldly.

'Correct,' she said. 'Up on that top shelf, please.'

'Sister,' I pursued, when I was at the top of the steps, making piles of
the fragrant-smelling linen, 'supposing Cowley remembers about the
girl and asks, will you tell him?'

'I should certainly do nothing without Sir Curtis's permission, Nurse.
He has given his orders and it is my duty to see that they are
carried out. Surely there was a great deal of laundry this week. I shall

have to see about making the nurses wash some of the things in future.'

When she was safely away at her supper, I told Cowley what Evans had told me. He considered the information, acclimatizing himself to the idea of Maisie with a bruise on her forehead and both legs in plaster casts up to the hip.

'You won't tell anyone I told you, will you?' I said.

'Hell, no. You were great to do it. Listen, do one thing more for me, will you? Write a little note and have them give it her.'

'Quick, then,' I said, 'before Sister comes back.'

I got a bit of paper and he dictated to me:

'HULLO, MAIS,

Sorry I busted you up. Keep your chin up, kid, and get well quick. Am feeling fine, but afraid I'll have to use cork on my right leg from now on.

Be seeing you soon, Honey.

LARRY.'

I took the note round when I went off duty, and had to dodge in the shadows out of Sister Porter's way until Evans came out of the ward. She made some excuse to go back again, and came out after a while with another bit of paper, folded very small. 'She's crying,' said Evans.

I sneaked back to Herbert Waterlow, and gave the note to the Junior Night Nurse, who was making Horlicks in the kitchen. As I came out, Sister was just coming off duty with a great bunch of chrysanthemums that I could almost have sworn were the ones Mrs Lockyer had brought for Lockyer.

'I sent you off duty hours ago, Nurse Dickinson,' she said. 'What on earth are you doing?'

'I forgot my lecture book, Sister,' I answered. 'I was just asking Nurse Andrews if she'd seen it, because I want to do some work to-night.' I did not want to have to walk majestically to the hostel with her, so I hurried on ahead to get dressed for the Police Dance at the 'Rowan Arms'.

It strikes me now how very often I failed to obey Sister Fairchild's injunction to 'cultivate scrupulously the habit of accurate statement'. Unless it meant harm to anyone else, it was always much simpler to make an excuse, if you had a convincing one, than to go through the fatigue of another row. I probably never deviated from the accurate statement so often in my life before, not even at school. But in hospital you have got to look after your own interests. Nobody else will.

I carried several notes backwards and forwards for Larry before Sir Curtis Rowntree decreed that the taboo subject might be broached. Larry put up a very good pantomime of surprise and gradually dawning memory, and immediately began to make himself a nuisance. He wanted to be put on a trolley and wheeled round to call on Maisie. He could see no reason why it should not be allowed. If it came to that, nor could I, but I realized that it could not be done. It was just one of those things that weren't.

'I came over here to fight for liberty,' he told Sir Curtis, who stood over him with his elegant length and proud face, his black hair flicked carefully up over each ear. 'For liberty,' continued Larry aggressively, 'and what do I get? First thing I know, I'm in a prison camp. Don't talk to me of the Motherland. When can I get up, Doc?'

'Take it easy, son,' said Sir Curtis, whose daughter sometimes took him to the cinema, 'we've got to get you a new leg first.'

'Say, do I have to wait for a cork leg before I can see Maisie? Now see here, Doc—'

Across the bed, Sister Oates threw a glance which said: 'What can one do with such a man?' but the Surgeon ignored her and turned round to ask me politely to bring screens.

Sister Martin came back at the end of that week, much to the relief of everyone, including Sister Oates, who was going to the Maternity Ward, where she hoped to find some high-class babies. She had despaired of ever finding any high-class Surgical Men.

Sister Martin made a brisk tour of the premises on the first day and announced that we had been slacking, which was true, but somehow one felt that she blamed Wild Oats as much as us. There were indigestion tablets loose in her desk drawer and a ring from a hot coffee jug on her sitting-room table. Once one got used to the idea of working harder, it was nice to see the ward return to its old efficiency and the stimulating air of enthusiasm come creeping back. Even Larry noticed the difference and became more amenable. Then, just when I had got to the stage of waking each day with anticipation instead of distaste, my happiness was neatly whisked away.

There was only one announcement after roll-call at breakfast. 'Nurse Dickens to go on Night Duty tonight. For what we have received, the Lord make us truly thankful.'

MARK OF THE BEAST

Rudyard Kipling

East of Suez, some hold, the direct control of Providence ceases; Man being there handed over to the power of the Gods and Devils of Asia, and the Church of England Providence only exercising an occasional and modified supervision in the case of Englishmen.

This theory accounts for some of the more unnecessary horrors of life in India: it may be stretched to explain my story.

My friend Strickland of the Police, who knows as much of natives of India as is good for any man, can bear witness to the facts of the case. Dumoise, our doctor, also saw what Strickland and I saw. The inference which he drew from the evidence was entirely incorrect. He is dead now; he died in a rather curious manner, which has been elsewhere described.

When Fleete came to India he owned a little money and some land in the Himalayas, near a place called Dharmsala. Both properties had been left him by an uncle, and he came out to finance them. He was a big, heavy, genial, and inoffensive man. His knowledge of natives was, of course, limited, and he complained of the difficulties of the language.

He rode in from his place in the hills to spend New Year in the station, and he stayed with Strickland. On New Year's Eve there was a big dinner at the club, and the night was excusably wet. When men foregather from the uttermost ends of the Empire, they have a right to be riotous. The Frontier had sent down a contingent o' Catch-'em-Alive-O's who had not seen twenty white faces for a year, and were used to ride fifteen miles to dinner at the next Fort at the risk of a Khyberee bullet where their drinks should lie. They profited by their new security, for they tried to play pool with a curled-up hedgehog found in the garden, and one of them carried the marker round the room in his teeth. Half a dozen planters had come in from the south and were talking 'horse' to the Biggest Liar in Asia, who was trying to cap all their stories at once. Everybody was there, and there was a general closing up of ranks and taking stock of our losses in dead or disabled that had fallen during the past year. It was a very wet night, and I remember that we sang 'Auld Lang Syne' with our feet in the Polo Championship Cup, and our heads among the stars, and swore that we were all dear friends. Then some of us went away and annexed Burma, and some tried to open up the Soudan and were opened up by Fuzzies in that cruel scrub outside Suakim, and some found stars and medals, and some were married, which was bad, and some did other things which were worse, and the others of us stayed in our chains and strove to make money on insufficient experiences.

Fleete began the night with sherry and bitters, drank champagne steadily up to dessert, then raw, rasping Capri with all the strength of whisky, took Benedictine with his coffee, four or five whiskies and sodas to improve his pool strokes, beer and bones at half-past two, winding up with old brandy. Consequently, when he came out, at half-past three in the morning, into fourteen degrees of frost, he was very angry with his horse for coughing, and tried to leapfrog into the saddle. The horse broke away and went to his stables; so Strickland and I formed a Guard of Dishonour to take Fleete home.

Our road lay through the bazaar, close to a little temple of Hanuman, the Monkey-god, who is a leading divinity worthy of respect. All gods have good points, just as have all priests. Personally, I attach much importance to Hanuman, and am kind to his people—the great gray apes of the hills. One never knows when one may want a friend.

25

There was a light in the temple, and as we passed, we could hear voices of men chanting hymns. In a native temple, the priests rise at all hours of the night to do honour to their god. Before we could stop him, Fleete dashed up the steps, patted two priests on the back, and was gravely grinding the ashes of his cigar-butt into the forehead of the red, stone image of Hanuman. Strickland tried to drag him out, but he sat down and said solemnly:

'Shee that? Mark of the B—beasht! *I* made it. Ishn't it fine?'

In half a minute the temple was alive and noisy, and Strickland, who knew what came of polluting gods, said that things might occur. He, by virtue of his official position, long residence in the country, and weakness for going among the natives, was known to the priests and he felt unhappy. Fleete sat on the ground and refused to move. He said that 'good old Hanuman' made a very soft pillow.

Then, without any warning, a Silver Man came out of a recess behind the image of the god. He was perfectly naked in that bitter, bitter cold, and his body shone like frosted silver, for he was what the Bible calls 'a leper as white as snow.' Also he had no face, because he was a leper of some years' standing, and his disease was heavy upon him. We two stooped to haul Fleete up, and the temple was filling and filling with folk who seemed to spring from the earth, when the Silver Man ran in under our arms, making a noise exactly like the mewing of an otter, caught Fleete round the body and dropped his head on Fleete's breast before we could wrench him away. Then he retired to a corner and sat mewing while the crowd blocked all the doors.

The priests were very angry until the Silver Man touched Fleete. That nuzzling seemed to sober him.

At the end of a few minutes' silence one of the priests came to Strickland and said, in perfect English, 'Take your friend away. He has done with Hanuman, but Hanuman has not done with him.' The crowd gave room and we carried Fleete into the road.

Strickland was very angry. He said that we might all three have been knifed, and that Fleete should thank his stars that he had escaped without injury.

Fleete thanked no one. He said that he wanted to go to bed. He was gorgeously drunk.

26

We moved on, Strickland silent and wrathful, until Fleete was taken with violent shivering fits and sweating. He said that the smells of the bazaar were overpowering, and he wondered why slaughter-houses were permitted so near English residences. 'Can't you smell the blood?' said Fleete.

We put him to bed at last, just as the dawn was breaking, and Strickland invited me to have another whisky and soda. While we were drinking he talked of the trouble in the temple, and admitted that it baffled him completely. Strickland hates being mystified by natives, because his business in life is to overmatch them with their own weapons. He has not yet succeeded in doing this, but in fifteen or twenty years he will have made some small progress.

'They should have mauled us,' he said, 'instead of mewing at us. I wonder what they meant. I don't like it one little bit.'

I said that the Managing Committee of the temple would in all probability bring a criminal action against us for insulting their religion. There was a section of the Indian Penal Code which exactly met Fleete's offence. Strickland said he only hoped and prayed that they would do this. Before I left I looked into Fleete's room, and saw him lying on his right side, scratching his left breast. Then I went to bed cold, depressed, and unhappy, at seven o'clock in the morning.

At one o'clock I rode over to Strickland's house to inquire after Fleete's head. I imagined that it would be a sore one. Fleete was breakfasting and seemed unwell. His temper was gone, for he was abusing the cook for not supplying him with an underdone chop. A man who can eat raw meat after a wet night is a curiosity. I told Fleete this and he laughed.

'You breed queer mosquitoes in these parts,' he said. 'I've been bitten to pieces, but only in one place.'

'Let's have a look at the bite,' said Strickland. 'It may have gone down since this morning.'

While the chops were being cooked, Fleete opened his shirt and showed us, just over his left breast, a mark, the perfect double of the black rosettes—the five or six irregular blotches arranged in a circle—on a leopard's hide. Strickland looked and said, 'It was only pink this morning. It's grown black now.'

Fleete ran to a glass.

'By Jove!' he said, 'this is nasty. What is it?'

We could not answer. Here the chops came in, all red and juicy, and Fleete bolted three in a most offensive manner. He ate on his right grinders only, and threw his head over his right shoulder as he snapped the meat. When he had finished, it struck him that he had been behaving strangely, for he said apologetically, 'I don't think I ever felt so hungry in my life. I've bolted like an ostrich.'

After breakfast Strickland said to me, 'Don't go. Stay here, and stay for the night.'

Seeing that my house was not three miles from Strickland's, this request was absurd. But Strickland insisted, and was going to say something when Fleete interrupted by declaring in a shamefaced way that he felt hungry again. Strickland sent a man to my house to fetch over my bedding and a horse, and we three went down to Strickland's stables to pass the hours until it was time to go out for a ride. The man who has a weakness for horses never wearies of inspecting them; and when two men are killing time in this way they gather knowledge and lies the one from the other.

There were five horses in the stables, and I shall never forget the scene as we tried to look them over. They seemed to have gone mad. They reared and screamed and nearly tore up their pickets; they sweated and shivered and lathered and were distraught with fear. Strickland's horses used to know him as well as his dogs; which made the matter more curious. We left the stables for fear of the brutes throwing themselves in their panic. Then Strickland turned back and called me. The horses were still frightened, but they let us 'gentle' and make much of them, and put their heads in our bosoms.

'They aren't afraid of *us*,' said Strickland. 'D' you know, I'd give three months' pay if *Outrage* here could talk.'

But *Outrage* was dumb, and could only cuddle up to his master and blow out his nostrils, as is the custom of horses when they wish to explain things but can't. Fleete came up when we were in the stalls, and as soon as the horses saw him, their fright broke out afresh. It was all that we could do to escape from the place un-kicked. Strickland said, 'They don't seem to love you, Fleete.'

'Nonsense,' said Fleete; 'my mare will follow me like a dog.'

He went to her; she was in a loose-box; but as he slipped the bars she plunged, knocked him down, and broke away into the garden. I laughed, but Strickland was not amused. He took his moustache in both fists and pulled at it till it nearly came out. Fleete, instead of going off to chase his property, yawned, saying that he felt sleepy. He went to the house to lie down, which was a foolish way of spending New Year's Day.

Strickland sat with me in the stables and asked if I had noticed anything peculiar in Fleete's manner. I said that he ate his food like a beast; but that this might have been the result of living alone in the hills out of the reach of society as refined and elevating as ours for instance. Strickland was not amused. I do not think that he listened to me, for his next sentence referred to the mark on Fleete's breast, and I said that it might have been caused by blister-flies, or that it was possibly a birth-mark newly born and now visible for the first time. We both agreed that it was unpleasant to look at, and Strickland found occasion to say that I was a fool.

'I can't tell you what I think now,' said he, 'because you would call me a madman; but you must stay with me for the next few days, if you can. I want you to watch Fleete, but don't tell me what you think till I have made up my mind.'

'But I am dining out to-night,' I said.

'So am I,' said Strickland, 'and so is Fleete. At least if he doesn't change his mind.'

We walked about the garden smoking, but saying nothing—because we were friends, and talking spoils good tobacco—till our pipes were out. Then we went to wake up Fleete. He was wide awake and fidgeting about his room.

'I say, I want some more chops,' he said. 'Can I get them?'

We laughed and said, 'Go and change. The ponies will be round in a minute.'

'All right,' said Fleete. 'I'll go when I get the chops—underdone ones, mind.'

He seemed to be quite in earnest. It was four o'clock, and we had had breakfast at one; still, for a long time, he demanded those underdone chops. Then he changed into riding clothes and went out into the verandah. His pony—the mare had not been caught—would not let him come near. All three horses were unmanageable—mad with fear—and finally Fleete said that he would stay at home and get something to eat. Strickland and I rode out wondering. As we passed the temple of Hanuman, the Silver Man came out and mewed at us.

'He is not one of the regular priests of the temple,' said Strickland. 'I think I should particularly like to lay my hands on him.'

There was no spring in our gallop on the racecourse that evening. The horses were stale, and moved as though they had been ridden out.

'The fright after breakfast has been too much for them,' said Strickland.

That was the only remark he made through the remainder of the ride. Once or twice I think he swore to himself; but that did not count.

We came back in the dark at seven o'clock, and saw that there were no lights in the bungalow. 'Careless ruffians my servants are!' said Strickland.

My horse reared at something on the carriage drive, and Fleete stood up under its nose.

'What are you doing, grovelling about the garden?' said Strickland.

But both horses bolted and nearly threw us. We dismounted by the stables and returned to Fleete, who was on his hands and knees under the orange-bushes.

'What the devil's wrong with you?' said Strickland.

'Nothing, nothing in the world,' said Fleete, speaking very quickly and thickly. 'I've been gardening—botanising you know. The smell of the earth is delightful. I think I'm going for a walk—a long walk—all night.'

Then I saw that there was something excessively out of order somewhere, and I said to Strickland, 'I am not dining out.'

'Bless you!' said Strickland. 'Here, Fleete, get up. You'll catch fever there. Come into dinner and let's have the lamps lit. We'll all dine at home.'

Fleete stood up unwillingly, and said, 'No lamps—no lamps. It's much nicer here. Let's dine outside and have some more chops—lots of 'em and underdone—bloody with gristle.'

Now a December evening in Northern India is bitterly cold, and Fleete's suggestion was that of a maniac.

'Come in,' said Strickland sternly. 'Come in at once.'

Fleete came, and when the lamps were brought, we saw that he was literally plastered with dirt from head to foot. He must have been rolling in the garden. He shrank from the light and went to his room. His eyes were horrible to look at. There was a green light behind them, not in them, if you understand, and the man's lower lip hung down.

Strickland said, 'There is going to be trouble—big trouble—to-night. Don't change your riding-things.'

We waited and waited for Fleete's reappearance, and ordered dinner in the meantime. We could hear him moving about his own room, but there was no light there. Presently from the room came the long-drawn howl of a wolf.

People write and talk lightly of blood running cold and hair standing up and things of that kind. Both sensations are too horrible to be trifled with. My heart stopped as though a knife had been driven through it, and Strickland turned as white as the tablecloth.

The howl was repeated, and was answered by another howl far across the fields.

That set the gilded roof on the horror. Strickland dashed into Fleete's room. I followed, and we saw Fleete getting out of the window. He made beast-noises in the back of his throat. He could not answer us when we shouted at him. He spat.

I don't quite remember what followed, but I think that Strickland must have stunned him with the long bootjack or else I should never have been able to sit on his chest. Fleete could not speak, he could only snarl, and his snarls were those of a wolf, not of a man. The human spirit must have been giving way all day and have died out with the twilight. We were dealing with a beast that had once been Fleete.

The affair was beyond any human and rational experience. I tried to say 'Hydrophobia,' but the word wouldn't come, because I knew that I was lying.

We bound this beast with leather thongs of the punkah-rope, and tied its thumbs and big toes together, and gagged it with a shoe-horn, which makes a very efficient gag if you know how to arrange it. Then we carried it into the dining-room, and sent a man to Dumoise, the doctor, telling him to come over at once. After we had despatched the messenger and were drawing breath, Strickland

31

said, 'It's no good. This isn't any doctor's work.' I, also, knew that he spoke the truth.

The beast's head was free, and it threw it about from side to side. Any one entering the room would have believed that we were curing a wolf's pelt. That was the most loathsome accessory of all.

Strickland sat with his chin in the heel of his fist, watching the beast as it wriggled on the ground, but saying nothing. The shirt had been torn open in the scuffle and showed the black rosette mark on the left breast. It stood out like a blister.

In the silence of the watching we heard something without mewing like a she-otter. We both rose to our feet, and, I answer for myself, not Strickland, felt sick—actually and physically sick. We told each other, as did the men in *Pinafore*, that it was the cat.

Dumoise arrived, and I never saw a little man so unprofessionally shocked. He said that it was a heart-rending case of hydrophobia, and that nothing could be done. At least any palliative measures would only prolong the agony. The beast was foaming at the mouth. Fleete, as we told Dumoise, had been bitten by dogs once or twice. Any man who keeps half a dozen terriers must expect a nip now and again. Dumoise could offer no help. He could only certify that Fleete was dying of hydrophobia. The beast was then howling, for it had managed to spit out the shoe-horn. Dumoise said that he would be ready to certify to the cause of death, and that the end was certain. He was a good little man, and he offered to remain with us; but Strickland refused the kindness. He did not wish to poison Dumoise's New Year. He would only ask him not to give the real cause of Fleete's death to the public.

So Dumoise left, deeply agitated; and as soon as the noise of the car-wheels had died away, Strickland told me, in a whisper, his suspicions. They were so wildly improbable that he dared not say them aloud; and I, who entertained all Strickland's beliefs, was so ashamed of owning to them that I pretended to disbelieve.

'Even if the Silver Man had bewitched Fleete for polluting the image of Hanuman, the punishment could not have fallen so quickly.'

As I was whispering this the cry outside the house rose again, and the beast fell into a fresh paroxysm of struggling till we were afraid that the thongs that held it would give way.

'Watch!' said Strickland. 'If this happens six times I shall take the law into my own hands. I order you to help me.'

He went into his room and came out in a few minutes with the barrels of an old shot-gun, a piece of fishing line, some thick cord, and his heavy wooden bedstead. I reported that the convulsions had followed the cry by two seconds in each case, and the beast seemed perceptibly weaker.

Strickland muttered, 'But he can't take away the life! He can't take away the life!'

I said, though I knew that I was arguing against myself, 'It may be a cat. It must be a cat. If the Silver Man is responsible, why does he dare to come here?'

Strickland arranged the wood on the hearth, put the gun-barrels into the glow of the fire, spread the twine on the table and broke a walking stick in two. There was one yard of fishing line, gut, lapped with wire, such as is used for *mahseer*-fishing, and he tied the two ends together in a loop.

Then he said, 'How can we catch him? He must be taken alive and unhurt.'

I said that we must trust in Providence, and go out softly with polo-sticks into the shrubbery at the front of the house. The man or animal that made the cry was evidently moving round the house as regularly as a night-watchman. We could wait in the bushes till he came by and knock him over.

Strickland accepted this suggestion, and we slipped out from a bath-room window into the front verandah and then across the carriage drive into the bushes.

In the moonlight we could see the leper coming round the corner of the house. He was perfectly naked, and from time to time he mewed and stopped to dance with his shadow. It was an unattractive sight, and thinking of poor Fleete, brought to such degradation by so foul a creature, I put away all my doubts and resolved to help Strickland from the heated gun-barrels to the loop of twine—from the loins to the head and back again—with all tortures that might be needful.

The leper halted in the front porch for a moment and we jumped out on him with the sticks. He was wonderfully strong, and we were afraid that he might escape or be fatally injured before we

He was literally plastered with dirt from head to foot.

caught him. We had an idea that lepers were frail creatures, but this proved to be incorrect. Strickland knocked his legs from under him and I put my foot on his neck. He mewed hideously, and even through my riding-boots I could feel that his flesh was not the flesh of a clean man.

He struck at us with his hands and feet-stumps. We looped the lash of a dog-whip round him, under the armpits, and dragged him backwards into the hall and so into the dining-room where the beast lay. There we tied him with trunk-straps. He made no attempt to escape, but mewed.

When we confronted him with the beast the scene was beyond description. The beast doubled backwards into a bow as though he had been poisoned with strychnine, and moaned in the most pitiable fashion. Several other things happened also, but they cannot be put down here.

'I think I was right,' said Strickland. 'Now we will ask him to cure this case.'

But the leper only mewed. Strickland wrapped a towel round his hand and took the gun-barrels out of the fire. I put the half of the broken walking stick through the loop of fishing line and buckled the leper comfortably to Strickland's bedstead. I understood then how men and women and little children can endure to see a witch burnt alive; for the beast was moaning on the floor, and though the Silver Man had no face, you could see horrible feelings passing through the slab that took its place, exactly as waves of heat play across red-hot iron—gun-barrels for instance.

Strickland shaded his eyes with his hands for a moment and we got to work. This part is not to be printed.

The dawn was beginning to break when the leper spoke. His mewings had not been satisfactory up to that point. The beast had fainted from exhaustion and the house was very still. We unstrapped the leper and told him to take away the evil spirit. He crawled to the beast and laid his hand upon the left breast. That was all. Then he fell face down and whined, drawing in his breath as he did so.

We watched the face of the beast, and saw the soul of Fleete coming back into the eyes. Then a sweat broke out on the forehead and the eyes—they were human eyes—closed. We waited for an hour but Fleete still slept. We carried him to his room and bade the leper go, giving him the bedstead, and the sheet on the bedstead to cover his nakedness, the gloves and the towels with which we had touched him, and the whip that had been hooked round his body. He put the sheet about him and went out into the early morning without speaking or mewing.

Strickland wiped his face and sat down. A night-gong, far away in the city, made seven o'clock.

'Exactly four-and-twenty hours!' said Strickland. 'And I've done enough to ensure my dismissal from the service, besides permanent quarters in a lunatic asylum. Do you believe that we are awake?'

The red-hot gun-barrel had fallen on the floor and was singeing the carpet. The smell was entirely real.

That morning at eleven we two together went to wake up Fleete. We looked and saw that the black leopard-rosette on his chest had disappeared He was very drowsy and tired, but as soon as he saw us, he said, 'Oh! Confound you fellows. Happy New Year to you. Never mix your liquors. I'm nearly dead.'

'Thanks for your kindness, but you're over time,' said Strickland. 'To-day is the morning of the second. You've slept the clock round with a vengeance.'

The door opened, and little Dumoise put his head in. He had come on foot, and fancied that we were laying out Fleete.

'I've brought a nurse,' said Dumoise. 'I suppose that she can come in for . . . what is necessary.'

'By all means,' said Fleete cheerily, sitting up in bed. 'Bring on your nurses.'

Dumoise was dumb. Strickland led him out and explained that there must have been a mistake in the diagnosis. Dumoise remained dumb and left the house hastily. He considered that his professional reputation had been injured, and was inclined to make a personal matter of the recovery. Strickland went out too. When he came back, he said that he had been to call on the Temple of Hanuman to offer redress for the pollution of the god, and had been solemnly assured that no white man had ever touched the idol and that he was an incarnation of all the virtues labouring under a delusion. 'What do you think?' said Strickland.

I said, '"There are more things . . ."'

But Strickland hates that quotation. He says that I have worn it threadbare.

One other curious thing happened which frightened me as much as anything in all the night's work. When Fleete was dressed he came into the dining-room and sniffed. He had a quaint trick of moving his nose when he sniffed. 'Horrid doggy smell, here,' said he. 'You should really keep those terriers of yours in better order. Try sulphur, Strick.'

But Strickland did not answer. He caught hold of the back of a chair, and, without warning, went into an amazing fit of hysterics. It is terrible to see a strong man overtaken with hysteria. Then it struck me that we had fought for Fleete's soul with the Silver Man in that room, and had disgraced ourselves as Englishmen for ever, and I laughed and gasped and gurgled just as shamefully as Strickland, while Fleete thought that we had both gone mad. We never told him what we had done.

Some years later, when Strickland had married and was a church-going member of society for his wife's sake, we reviewed the incident dispassionately, and Strickland suggested that I should put it before the public.

I cannot myself see that this step is likely to clear up the mystery; because, in the first place, no one will believe a rather unpleasant story, and, in the second, it is well known to every right-minded man that the gods of the heathen are stone and brass, and any attempt to deal with them otherwise is justly condemned.

THE PAPER-CHASE

E. Nesbit

Roberta, Peter and Phyllis move to the country with their mother while their father is away. The family is poor, but the children find new entertainment at the nearby railway station. Their days are filled with adventures and new friends, including an old gentleman they wave to each time he passes on the train.

One day the local school holds a paper-chase along the railway line. The children decide to go and watch the schoolboys as they charge through the tunnel. However, one of the boys gets very left behind, and, in fact, does not emerge from the tunnel. Peter insists that they go down to the tunnel to investigate and while doing so nearly get run over by a passing train.

So the three went on into the deeper darkness of the tunnel. Peter led, holding his candle end high to light the way. The grease ran down his fingers, and some of it right up his sleeve. He found a long streak from wrist to elbow when he went to bed that night.

It was not more than a hundred and fifty yards from the spot where they had stood while the train went by that Peter stood still, shouted 'Hullo' and then went on much quicker than before. When the others caught him up, he stopped. And he stopped within a yard of what they had come into the tunnel to look for. Phyllis saw a gleam of red, and shut her eyes tight. There, by the curved, pebbly down line, was the red-jerseyed hound. His back was against the wall, his arms hung limply by his sides, and his eyes were shut.

'Was the red, blood? Is he all killed?' asked Phyllis, screwing her eyelids more tightly together.

'Killed? Nonsense!' said Peter. 'There's nothing red about him except his jersey. He's only fainted. What on earth are we to do?'

'Can we move him?' asked Bobbie.

'I don't know; he's a big chap.'

'Suppose we bathe his forehead with water. No, I know we haven't any, but milk's just as well. There's a whole bottle.'

'Yes,' said Peter, 'and they rub people's hands, I believe.'

'They burn feathers, I know,' said Phyllis.

'What's the use of saying that when we haven't any feathers!'

'As it happens,' said Phyllis, in a tone of exasperated triumph, 'I've got a shuttlecock in my pocket. So there!'

And now Peter rubbed the hands of the red-jerseyed one. Bobbie burned the feathers of the shuttlecock one by one under his nose, Phyllis splashed warmish milk on his forehead, and all three kept on saying as fast and as earnest as they could:

'Oh, look up, speak to me! For my sake, speak!'

    ★   ★   ★   ★

'Oh, look up! Speak to me! For *my* sake, speak!' The children said the words over and over again to the unconscious hound in a red jersey, who sat with closed eyes and pale face against the side of the tunnel.

'Wet his ears with milk,' said Bobbie. 'I know they do it to people that faint—with eau-de-Cologne. But I expect milk's just as good.'

So they wetted his ears, and some of the milk ran down his neck under the red jersey. It was very dark in the tunnel. The candle end Peter had carried, and which now burned on a flat stone, gave hardly any light at all.

'Oh, *do* look up,' said Phyllis. 'For *my* sake! I believe he's dead.'

'For *my* sake,' repeated Bobbie. 'No, he isn't.'

'For *any* sake,' said Peter; 'come out of it.' And he shook the sufferer by the arm.

And then the boy in the red jersey sighed, and opened his eyes, and shut them again and said in a very small voice, 'Chuck it.'

'Oh, he's *not* dead,' said Phyllis. 'I *knew* he wasn't,' and she began to cry.

'What's up? I'm all right,' said the boy.

'Drink this,' said Peter, firmly, thrusting the nose of the milk bottle into the boy's mouth. The boy struggled, and some of the milk was upset before he could get his mouth free to say:

'What is it?'

'It's milk,' said Peter. 'Fear not, you are in the hands of friends. Phil, you stop bleating this minute.'

'Do drink it,' said Bobbie gentle; 'it'll do you good.'

So he drank. And the three stood by without speaking to him.

'Let him be a minute,' Peter whispered; 'he'll be all right as soon as the milk begins to run like fire through his veins.'

He was.

'I'm better now,' he announced. 'I remember all about it.' He tried to move, but the movement ended in a groan. 'Bother! I believe I've broken my leg,' he said.

'Did you tumble down?' asked Phyllis, sniffing.

'Of course not—I'm not a kiddie,' said the boy, indignantly; 'it was one of those beastly wires tripped me up, and when I tried to get up again I couldn't stand, so I sat down. Gee whillikins! It does hurt though. How did *you* get here?'

'We saw you all go into the tunnel and then we went across the hill to see you all come out. And the others did—all but you, and you didn't. So we are a rescue party,' said Peter, with pride.

'You've got some pluck, I will say,' remarked the boy.

'Oh, that's nothing,' said Peter with modesty. 'Do you think you could walk if we helped you?'

'I could try,' said the boy.

He did try. But he could only stand on one foot; the other dragged in a very nasty way.

'Here, let me sit down. I feel like dying,' said the boy. 'Let go of me— let go, quick—' He lay down and closed his eyes. The others looked at each other by the dim light of the little candle.

'What on earth!' said Peter.

'Look here,' said Bobbie quickly, 'you must go and get help. Go to the nearest house.'

'Yes, that's the only thing,' said Peter. 'Come on.'

'If you take his feet and Phil and I take his head, we could carry him to the manhole.'

They did it. It was perhaps as well for the sufferer that he had fainted again.

'Now,' said Bobbie, 'I'll stay with him. You take the longest bit of candle, and, oh—be quick, for this bit won't burn long.'

'I don't think Mother would like me leaving you,' said Peter, doubtfully. 'Let me stay, and you and Phil go.'

'No, no,' said Bobbie, 'you and Phil go—and lend me your knife. I'll try to get his boot off before he wakes up again.'

'I hope it's all right what we're doing,' said Peter.

'Of course it's right,' said Bobbie, impatiently. 'What else *would* you do? Leave him here all alone because it's dark? Nonsense. Hurry up, that's all.'

So they hurried up.

Bobbie watched their dark figures and the little light of the little candle with an odd feeling of having come to the end of everything. She knew now, she thought, what nuns who were bricked up alive in convent walls felt like. Suddenly she gave herself a little shake.

'Don't be a silly little girl,' she said. She was always very angry when anyone else called her a little girl, even if the adjective that went first was not 'silly' but 'nice' or 'good' or 'clever'. And it was only when she was very angry with herself that she allowed Roberta to use that expression to Bobbie.

She fixed the little candle end on a broken brick near the red-jerseyed boy's foot. Then she opened Peter's knife. It was always hard to manage—a halfpenny was generally needed to get it open at all. This time Bobbie somehow got it open with her thumbnail. She broke the nail, and it hurt horribly. Then she cut the boy's bootlace, and got the boot off. She tried to pull off his stocking, but his leg was dreadfully swollen, and it did not seem to be the proper shape. So she cut the stocking down, very slowly and carefully. It was a brown knitted stocking, and she wondered who had knitted it, and whether it was the boy's mother, and whether she was feeling anxious about him, and how she would feel when he was brought home with his leg broken. When Bobbie got the stocking off and saw the poor leg, she felt as though the tunnel was growing darker, and the ground felt unsteady, and nothing seemed quite real.

'*Silly* little girl!' said Roberta to Bobbie, and felt better.

'The poor leg,' she told herself; 'it ought to have a cushion—ah!'

She remembered the day when she and Phyllis had torn up their red flannel petticoats to make danger signals to stop the train and prevent an accident. Her flannel petticoat today was white, but it would be quite as soft as a red one. She took it off.

'Oh, what useful things flannel petticoats are!' she said; 'the man who invented them ought to have a statue directed to him.' And she said it aloud, because it seemed that any voice, even her own, would be comfort in that darkness.

'*What* ought to be directed? Who to?' asked the boy, suddenly and very feebly.

'Oh,' said Bobbie, 'now you're better! Hold your teeth and don't let it hurt too much. Now!'

She had folded the petticoat, and lifting his leg laid it on the cushion of folded flannel.

'Don't faint again, *please* don't,' said Bobbie, as he groaned. She hastily wetted her handkerchief with milk and spread it over the poor leg.

'Oh, that hurts,' cried the boy, shrinking. 'Oh—no, it doesn't—it's nice, really.'

'What's your name?' said Bobbie.

'Jim.'

'Mine's Bobbie.'

'But you're a girl, ain't you?'

'Yes, my long name's Roberta.'

'I say—Bobbie.'

'Yes?'

'Wasn't there some more of you just now?'

'Yes, Peter and Phil—that's my brother and sister. They've gone to get someone to carry you out.'

'What rum names. All boys.'

'Yes—I wish I was a boy, don't you?'

'I think you're all right as you are.'

'I didn't mean that—I meant don't you wish *you* were a boy, but of course you are without wishing.'

'You're just as brave as a boy. Why didn't you go with the others?'

'Somebody had to stay with you,' said Bobbie.

'Tell you what, Bobbie,' said Jim, 'you're a brick. Shake.' He reached out a red-jerseyed arm and Bobbie squeezed his hand.

'I won't shake it,' she explained, 'because it would shake *you*, and that would shake your poor leg, and that would hurt. Have you got a hanky?'

'I don't expect I have.' He felt in his pocket. 'Yes, I have. What for?'
She took it and wetted it with milk and put it on his forehead.
'That's jolly,' he said; 'what is it?'
'Milk,' said Bobbie. 'We haven't any water—'
'You're a jolly good little nurse,' said Jim.
'I do it for Mother sometimes,' said Bobbie—'not milk, of course,
but scent, or vinegar and water. I say, I must put the candle out now,
because there mayn't be enough of the other one to get you out by.'
'By George,' said he, 'you think of everything.'
Bobbie blew. Out went the candle. You have no idea how black-
velvety the darkness was.
'I say, Bobbie,' said a voice through the blackness, 'aren't you afraid
of the dark?'
'Not—not—very, that is—'
'Let's hold hands,' said the boy, and it was really rather good of him,
because he was like most boys of his age and hated all material tokens of
affection, such as kissing, and holding of hands. He called all such things
'pawing', and detested them.
The darkness was more bearable to Bobbie now that her hand was
held in the large rough hand of the red-jerseyed sufferer; and he, holding
her little smooth hot paw, was surprised to find that he did not mind it so
much as he expected. She tried to talk, to amuse him, and 'take his mind
off' his sufferings, but it is very difficult to go on talking in the dark, and
presently they found themselves in a silence, only broken now and then
by a—
'You all right, Bobbie?'
Or an—
'I'm afraid it's hurting you most awfully, Jim. I *am* so sorry.'
And it was very cold.

★   ★   ★   ★

Peter and Phyllis tramped down the long way of the tunnel towards
daylight, the candle-grease dripping over Peter's fingers. There were no
accidents unless you count Phyllis's catching her frock on a wire, and
tearing a long, jagged slit in it, and tripping over her bootlace when it

came undone, or going down on her hands and knees, all four of which were grazed.

'There's no end to this tunnel,' said Phyllis—and indeed it did seem very, very long.

'Stick to it,' said Peter; 'everything has an end, and you get to it if you only keep on.'

Which is quite true, if you come to think of it, and a useful thing to remember in seasons of trouble—such as measles, arithmetic, impositions, and those times when you are in disgrace, and feel as though no one would ever love you again, and you could never—never again—love anybody.

'Hurray,' said Peter, suddenly, 'there's the end of the tunnel—looks just like a pin-hole in a bit of black paper, doesn't it?'

The pin-hole got larger—blue lights lay along the sides of the tunnel. The children could see the gravel way that lay in front of them; the air grew warmer and sweeter. Another twenty steps and they were out in the good glad sunshine with the green trees on both sides.

Phyllis drew a long breath.

'I'll never go into a tunnel again, as long as ever I live,' said she, 'not if there are twenty hundred thousand million hounds inside with red jerseys and their legs broken.'

'Don't be a silly cuckoo,' said Peter, as usual. 'You'd *have* to.'

'I think it was very brave and good of me,' said Phyllis.

'Not it,' said Peter; 'you didn't go because you were brave, but because Bobbie and I aren't skunks. Now where's the nearest house, I wonder? You can't see anything here for the trees.'

'There's a roof over there,' said Phyllis, pointing down the line.

★   ★   ★   ★

Thus it happened that Mother, writing away for dear life at a story about a Duchess, a designing villain, a secret passage, and a missing will, dropped her pen as her work-room door burst open, and turned to see Bobbie hatless and red with running.

'Oh, Mother,' she cried, 'do come down. We found a hound in a red jersey in the tunnel, and he's broken his leg and they're bringing him home.'

'They ought to take him to the vet,' said Mother, with a worried frown; 'I really *can't* have a lame dog here.'

'He's not a dog, really—he's a boy,' said Bobbie, between laughing and choking.

'Then he ought to be taken home to his mother.'

'His mother's dead,' said Bobbie, 'and his father's in Northumberland. Oh, Mother, you will be nice to him? I told him I was sure you'd want us to bring him home. You always want to help everybody.'

Mother smiled, but she sighed, too. It is nice that your children should believe you willing to open house and heart to any and every one who needs help. But it is rather embarrassing sometimes, too, when they act on their belief.

'Oh, well,' said Mother, 'we must make the best of it.'

When Jim was carried in, dreadfully white and with set lips whose red had faded to a horrid bluey violet colour, Mother said:

'I am glad you brought him here. Now, Jim, let's get you comfortable in bed before the Doctor comes!'

And Jim, looking at her kind eyes, felt a little, warm, comforting flush of new courage.

'It'll hurt rather, won't it?' he said. 'I don't mean to be a coward. You won't think I'm a coward if I faint again, will you? I really and truly don't do it on purpose. And I do hate to give you all this trouble.'

'Don't you worry,' said Mother; 'it's you that have the trouble, you poor dear—not us.'

And she kissed him just as if he had been Peter. 'We love to have you here—don't we, Bobbie?'

'Yes,' said Bobbie—and she saw by her Mother's face how right she had been to bring home the wounded hound in the red jersey.

★   ★   ★   ★

Mother did not get back to her writing all that day, for the red-jerseyed hound whom the children had brought to Three Chimneys had to be put to bed. And then the Doctor came, and hurt him most horribly. Mother was with him all through it, and that made it a little better than it would have been, but 'bad was the best,' as Mrs Viney said.

The children sat in the parlour downstairs and heard the sound of the

Doctor's boots going backwards and forwards over the bedroom floor. And once or twice there was a groan.

'It's horrible,' said Bobbie. 'Oh, I wish Dr Forrest would make haste. Oh, poor Jim!'

'It *is* horrible,' said Peter, 'but it's very exciting. I wish Doctors weren't so stuck-up about who they'll have in the room when they're doing things. I should most awfully like to see a leg set. I believe the bones crunch like anything.'

'Don't!' said the two girls at once.

'Rubbish!' said Peter. 'How are you going to be Red Cross Nurses, like you were talking of coming home, if you can't even stand hearing me say about bones crunching? You'd have to *hear* them crunch on the field of battle—and be steeped in gore up to the elbows as like as not, and—'

'Stop it!' cried Bobbie, with a white face; 'you don't know how funny you're making me feel.'

'Me, too,' said Phyllis, whose face was pink.

'Cowards!' said Peter.

'I'm not,' said Bobbie. 'I helped Mother with your rake-wounded foot, and so did Phil—you know we did.'

'Well, then!' said Peter. 'Now look here. It would be a jolly good thing for you if I were to talk to you every day for half an hour about broken bones and people's insides, so as to get you used to it.'

A chair was moved above.

'Listen,' said Peter, 'that's the bone crunching.'

'I do wish you wouldn't,' said Phyllis. 'Bobbie doesn't like it.'

'I'll tell you what they do,' said Peter. I can't think what made him so horrid. Perhaps it was because he had been so very nice and kind all the earlier part of the day, and now he had to have a change. This is called reaction. One notices it now and then in oneself. Sometimes when one has been extra good for a longer time than usual, one is suddenly attacked by a violent fit of not being good at all. 'I'll tell you what they do,' said Peter; 'they strap the broken man down so that he can't resist or interfere with their doctorish designs, and then someone holds his head, and someone holds his leg—the broken one, and pulls it till the bones fit in—with a crunch, mind you! Then they strap it up and—let's play at bone-setting!'

'Oh, no!' said Phyllis.

But Bobbie said suddenly: 'All right—*let's!* I'll be the doctor, and Phil can be the nurse. You can be the broken boner; we can get at your legs more easily, because you don't wear petticoats.'

'I'll get the splints and bandages,' said Peter; 'you get the couch of suffering ready.'

The ropes that had tied up the boxes that had come from home were all in a wooden packing-case in the cellar. When Peter brought in a trailing tangle of them, and two boards for splints, Phyllis was excitedly giggling.

'Now, then,' he said, and lay down on the settle, groaning most grievously.

'Not so loud!' said Bobbie, beginning to wind the rope round him and the settle. 'You pull, Phil.'

'Not so tight,' moaned Peter. 'You'll break my other leg.'

Bobbie worked on in silence, winding more and more rope round him.

'That's enough,' said Peter. 'I can't move at all. Oh, my poor leg!' He groaned again.

'*Sure* you can't move?' asked Bobbie, in a strange tone.

'Quite sure,' replied Peter. 'Shall we play it's bleeding freely or not?' he asked cheerfully.

'*You* can play what you like,' said Bobbie, sternly, folding her arms and looking down at him where he lay all wound round and round with cord. 'Phil and I are going away. And we shan't untie you till you promise never, never to talk to us about blood and wounds unless we say you may. Come, Phil!'

'You beast!' said Peter, writhing. 'I'll never promise, never. I'll yell, and Mother will come.'

'Do,' said Bobbie, 'and tell her why we tied you up! Come on, Phil. No, I'm not a beast, Peter. But you wouldn't stop when we asked you and—'

'Yah,' said Peter, 'it wasn't even your own idea. You got it out of Stalky!'

Bobbie and Phil, retiring in silent dignity, were met at the door by the Doctor. He came in rubbing his hands and looking pleased with himself.

'Well,' he said, '*that* job's done. It's a nice clean fracture, and it'll go on all right, I've no doubt. Plucky young chap, too—hullo! What's all this?'

His eye had fallen on Peter who lay mousey-still in his bonds on the settle.

'Playing at prisoners, eh?' he said; but his eyebrows had gone up a little. Somehow he had not thought that Bobbie would be playing while in the room above someone was having a broken bone set.

'Oh, no!' said Bobbie, 'not at *prisoners*. We were playing at setting bones. Peter's the broken boner, and I was the doctor.'

'I was the nurse,' put in Phyllis cheerfully.

The Doctor frowned.

'Then I must say,' he said, and he said it rather sternly, 'that it's a very heartless game. Haven't you enough imagination even to faintly picture what's been going on upstairs? That poor chap, with drops of sweat on his forehead, and biting his lips so as not to cry out, and every touch on his leg agony and—'

'*You* ought to be tied up,' said Phyllis; 'you're as bad as—'

'Hush,' said Bobbie; 'I'm sorry, but we weren't heartless, really.'

'I was, I suppose,' said Peter, crossly. 'All right, Bobbie, don't you go on being noble and screening me, because I jolly well won't have it. It was only that I kept on talking about blood and wounds. I wanted to train for them Red Cross Nurses. And I wouldn't stop when they asked me.'

'Well?' said Dr Forrest, sitting down.

'Well—then I said, "Let's play at setting bones." It was all rot. I knew Bobbie wouldn't. I only said it to tease her. And then when she said "yes", of course I had to go through with it. And they tied me up. They got it out of Stalky. And I think it's a beastly shame.'

He managed to writhe over and hide his face against the wooden back of the settle.

'I didn't think that anyone would know but us,' said Bobbie, indignantly answering Peter's unspoken reproach. 'I never thought of your coming in. And hearing about blood and wounds does really make me feel most awfully funny. It was only a joke our tying him up. Let me untie you, Peter.'

'I don't care if you never untie me,' said Peter; 'and if that's your idea of a joke—'

'If I were you,' said the Doctor, though really he did not quite know what to say, 'I should be untied before your Mother comes down. You don't want to worry her just now, do you?'

'I don't promise anything about not saying about wounds, mind,' said Peter, in very surly tones, as Bobbie and Phyllis began to untie the knots.

'I'm very sorry, Pete,' Bobbie whispered, leaning close to him as she fumbled with the big knot under the settle; 'but if you only knew how sick you made me feel.'

'You've made *me* feel pretty sick, I can tell you,' Peter rejoined. Then he shook off the loose cords, and stood up.

'I looked in,' said Dr Forrest, 'to see if one of you would come along to the surgery. There are some things that your Mother will want at once, and I've given my man a day off to go and see the circus; will you come, Peter?'

Peter went without a word or a look to his sisters.

The two walked in silence up to the gate that led from the Three Chimneys field to the road. Then Peter said:

'Let me carry your bag. I say, it is heavy—what's in it?'

'Oh, knives and lancets and different instruments for hurting people. And the ether bottle. I had to give him ether, you know—the agony was so intense.'

Peter was silent.

'Tell me all about how you found that chap,' said Dr Forrest.

Peter told. And then Dr Forrest told him stories of brave rescues; he was a most interesting man to talk to, as Peter had often remarked.

Then in the surgery Peter had a better chance than he had ever had of examining the Doctor's balance, and his microscope, and his scales and measuring glasses. When all the things were ready that Peter was to take back, the Doctor said suddenly:

'You'll excuse my shoving my oar in, won't you? But I should like to say something to you.'

'Now for a rowing,' thought Peter, who had been wondering how it was that he had escaped one.

'Something scientific,' added the Doctor.

'Yes,' said Peter, fiddling with the fossil ammonite that the Doctor used for a paper-weight.

'Well,' said the Doctor, 'you know men have to do the work of the world and not be afraid of anything—so they have to be hardy and brave. But women have to take care of their babies and cuddle them and nurse them and be very patient and gentle.'

'Yes,' said Peter, wondering what was coming next.

'Well then, you see. Boys and girls are only little men and women. And *we* are much harder and hardier than they are'—(Peter liked the 'we'. Perhaps the Doctor had known he would.) – 'and much stronger, and things that hurt *them* don't hurt *us*. You know you mustn't hit a girl-'

'I should think not, indeed,' muttered Peter, indignantly.

'Not even if she's your own sister. That's because girls are so much softer and weaker than we are; they have to be, you know,' he added, 'because if they weren't, it wouldn't be nice for the babies. And that's why all the animals are so good to the mother animals. They never fight them, you know.'

'I know,' said Peter, interested; 'two buck rabbits will fight all day if you let them, but they won't hurt a doe.'

'No; and quite wild beasts—lions and elephants—they're immensely gentle with the female beasts. And we've got to be, too.'

'I see,' said Peter.

'And their hearts are soft, too,' the Doctor went on, 'and things that we shouldn't think anything of hurt them dreadfully. So that a man has to be very careful, not only of his fists, but of his words. They're awfully brave, you know,' he went on. 'Think of Bobbie waiting alone in the tunnel with that poor chap. It's an odd thing—the softer and more easily hurt a woman is the better she can screw herself up to do what *has* to be done. I've seen some brave women—your Mother's one,' he ended abruptly.

'Yes,' said Peter.

'Well, that's all; excuse my mentioning it. But nobody knows everything without being told. And you see what I mean, don't you?'

'Yes,' said Peter. 'I'm sorry. There!'

'Of course you are! People always are—directly they understand. Everyone ought to be taught these scientific facts. So long!'

They shook hands heartily. When Peter came home, his sisters looked at him doubtfully.

'It's Pax,' said Peter, dumping down the basket on the table. 'Dr Forrest has been talking scientific to me. No, it's no use my telling you what he said; you wouldn't understand. But it all comes to you girls being poor, soft, weak, frightened things like rabbits, so us men have just got to put up with them. He said you were female beasts. Shall I take this up to Mother, or will you?'

'I know what *boys* are,' said Phyllis, with flaming cheeks; 'they're just the nastiest, rudest—'

'They're very brave,' said Bobbie, 'sometimes.'

'Ah, you mean the chap upstairs? I see. Go ahead, Phil—I shall put up with you whatever you say because you're a poor, weak, frightened, soft—'

'Not if I pull your hair you won't,' said Phyllis, springing at him.

'He said "Pax",' said Bobbie, pulling her away. 'Don't you see,' she whispered as Peter picked up the basket and stalked out with it, 'he's sorry, really, only he won't say so? Let's say we're sorry.'

'It's so goody-goody,' said Phyllis, doubtfully; 'he said we were female beasts, and soft and frightened—'

'Then let's show him we're not frightened of him thinking us goody-goody,' said Bobby; 'and we're not any more beasts than he is.'

And when Peter came back, still with his chin in the air, Bobbie said:

'We're sorry we tied you up, Pete.'

'I thought you would be,' said Peter, very stiff and superior.

This was hard to bear. But—

'Well, so we are,' said Bobbie. 'Now let honour be satisfied on both sides.'

'I did call it Pax,' said Peter, in an injured tone.

'Then let it *be* Pax,' said Bobbie. 'Come on, Phil, let's get the tea. Peter, you might lay the cloth.'

'I say,' said Phyllis, when peace was really restored, which was not till they were washing up the cups after tea, 'Dr Forrest didn't really say we were female beasts, did he?'

'Yes,' said Peter, firmly, 'but I think he meant we men were wild beasts, too.'

'How funny of him!' said Phyllis, breaking a cup.

★   ★   ★   ★

'May I come in, Mother?' Peter was at the door of Mother's writing-room, where Mother sat at her table with two candles in front of her. Their flames looked orange and violet against the clear grey blue of the sky where already a few stars were twinkling.

'Yes, dear,' said Mother, absently, 'anything wrong?' She wrote a few more words and then laid down her pen and began to fold up what she had written. 'I was just writing to Jim's grandfather. He lives near here, you know.'

'Yes, you said so at tea. That's what I want to say. Must you write to him, Mother? Couldn't we keep Jim, and not say anything to his people till he's well? It would be such a surprise for them.'

'Well, yes,' said Mother, laughing. 'I think it would.'

'You see,' Peter went on, 'of course the girls are all right and all that— I'm not saying anything against *them*. But I should like it if I had another chap to talk to sometimes.'

'Yes,' said Mother, 'I know it's dull for you, dear. But I can't help it. Next year perhaps I can send you to school—you'd like that, wouldn't you?'

'I do miss the other chaps, rather,' Peter confessed; 'but if Jim could stay after his leg was well, we could have awful larks.'

'I've no doubt of it,' said Mother. 'Well—perhaps he could, but you know, dear, we're not rich. I can't afford to get him everything he'll want. And he must have a nurse.'

'Can't you nurse him, Mother? You do nurse people so beautifully.'

'That's a pretty compliment, Pete—but I can't do nursing and my writing as well. That's the worst of it.'

'Then you *must* send the letter to his grandfather?'

'Of course—and to his schoolmaster, too. We telegraphed to them both, but I must write as well. They'll be most dreadfully anxious.'

'I say, Mother, why can't his grandfather pay for a nurse?' Peter suggested. 'That would be ripping. I expect the old boy's rolling in money. Grandfathers in books always are.'

'Well, this one isn't in a book,' said Mother, 'so we mustn't expect him to roll much.'

★   ★   ★   ★

'Bobbie,' called Mother's voice.

They opened the kitchen door, and Mother leaned over the stair railing.

'Jim's grandfather has come,' she said; 'wash your hands and faces and then you can see him. He wants to see you!' The bedroom door shut again.

'There now!' said Peter; 'fancy us not even thinking of that! Let's have some hot water, Mrs Viney. I'm as black as your hat.'

The three were indeed dirty, for the stuff you clean brass candlesticks with is very far from cleaning to the cleaner.

They were still busy with soap and flannel when they heard the boots and the voice come down the stairs and go into the dining-room. And when they were clean, though still damp—because it takes such a long time to dry your hands properly, and they were very impatient to see the grandfather—they filed into the dining-room.

Mother was sitting in the window-seat, and in the leather-covered arm-chair that Father always used to sit in at the other house sat—

THEIR OWN OLD GENTLEMAN!

'Well, I never did,' said Peter, even before he said, 'How do you do?' He was, as he explained afterwards, too surprised even to remember that there was such a thing as politeness—much less to practise it.

'It's our own old gentleman!' said Phyllis.

'Oh, it's you!' said Bobbie. And then they remembered themselves and their manners and said, 'How do you do?' very nicely.

'This is Jim's grandfather, Mr—' said Mother, naming the old gentleman's name.

'How splendid!' said Peter; 'that's just exactly like a book, isn't it, Mother?'

'It is, rather,' said Mother, smiling; 'things do happen in real life that are rather like books, sometimes.'

'I am so awfully glad it is you,' said Phyllis; 'when you think of the lots of old gentlemen there are in the world—it might have been almost anyone.'

'I say, though,' said Peter, 'you're not going to take Jim away, though, are you?'

'Not at present,' said the old gentleman. 'Your Mother has most kindly consented to let him stay here. I thought of sending a nurse, but your Mother is good enough to say that she will nurse him herself.'

'But what about her writing?' said Peter, before anyone could stop him. 'There won't be anything for him to eat if Mother doesn't write.'

'That's all right,' said Mother hastily.

The old gentleman looked very kindly at Mother.

'I see,' he said, 'you trust your children, and confide in them.'

'Of course,' said Mother.

'Then I may tell them our little arrangement,' he said. 'Your Mother, my dears, has consented to give up writing for a little while and to become a Matron of my Hospital.'

'Oh!' said Phyllis, blankly; 'and shall we have to go away from Three Chimneys and the Railway and everything?'

'No, no, darling,' said Mother, hurriedly.

'The Hospital is called Three Chimneys Hospital,' said the old gentleman, 'and my unlucky Jim's the only patient, and I hope he'll continue to be so. Your Mother will be Matron, and there'll be a hospital staff of a housemaid and a cook—till Jim's well.'

'And then will Mother go on writing again?' asked Peter.

'We shall see,' said the old gentleman, with a swift, slight glance at Bobbie; 'perhaps something nice may happen and she won't have to.'

'I love my writing,' said Mother, very quickly.

'I know,' said the old gentleman; 'don't be afraid that I'm going to try to interfere. But one never knows. Very wonderful and beautiful things do happen, don't they? And we live most of our lives in the hope of them. I may come again to see the boy?'

'Surely,' said Mother, 'and I don't know how to thank you for making it possible for me to nurse him. Dear boy!'

DEMONSTRATION PATIENT

P.D. James

She bestowed on students and teacher her brief smile of reassurance and encouragement and perched herself on one of the four chairs placed ready at the side of the room. Matron Taylor and Miss Rolfe seated themselves on either side of her as quietly and unobtrusively as possible in the face of Mr Courtney-Briggs's determination to be fussily gallant over pulling out the ladies' chairs. The arrival of the little party, however tactfully arranged, seemed temporarily to have disconcerted the nurse tutor. An inspection was hardly a natural teaching situation, but it was always interesting to see how long it took a tutor to re-establish *rapport* with her class. A first-class teacher, as Miss Beale knew from personal experience, could hold a class's interest even through a heavy bombing raid let alone the visit of a General Nursing Council Inspector; but she did not feel that Mavis Gearing was likely to prove one of that rare and dedicated band. The girl—or woman rather—lacked authority. She had a propitiatory air; she looked as though she might easily simper. And she was a great deal too heavily made up for a woman who should have her mind on less ephemeral arts. But she was, after all, merely the clinical instructor, not a qualified nurse tutor. She was taking the session at short notice and under difficulties. Miss Beale made a mental resolution not to judge her too harshly.

The class, she saw, were to practise feeding a patient by intra-gastric tube. The student who was to act as patient was already in one of the demonstration beds, her check dress protected by a mackintosh bib, her head supported by the back rest and a bank of pillows. She was a plain girl with a strong, obstinate and oddly mature face, her dull hair drawn back unbecomingly from a high nobbly forehead. She lay there immobile under the harsh strip lighting, looking a little ridiculous but strangely dignified as if concentrating on some private world and dissociating herself from the whole procedure by an effort of will. Suddenly it occurred to Miss Beale that the girl might be frightened. The thought was ridiculous but it persisted. She found herself suddenly unwilling to watch that resolute face. Irritated by her own unreasonable sensitivity, she turned her attention to the nurse tutor.

Sister Gearing cast an apprehensive and interrogative glance at the Matron, received a confirmatory nod and resumed her lesson.

'Nurse Pearce is acting the part of our patient this morning. We have just been going through her history. She is Mrs Stokes, the fifty-year-old mother of four children, wife of a council refuse collector. She has had a larynectomy for the treatment of cancer.' She turned to a student sitting on her right.

'Nurse Dakers, will you please describe Mrs Stokes's treatment so far.'

Nurse Dakers dutifully began. She was a pale, thin girl who blushed unbecomingly as she spoke. It was difficult to hear her but she knew her facts and presented them well. A conscientious little thing, thought Miss Beale, not outstandingly intelligent, perhaps, but hard working and reliable. It was a pity that no one had done anything about her acne. She retained her air of bright professional interest whilst Nurse Dakers propounded the fictional medical history of Mrs Stokes and took the opportunity of a close look at the remaining students in the class, making her customary private assessment of their characters and ability.

The influenza epidemic had certainly taken its toll. There was a total of seven girls only in the demonstration room. The two who were standing one on each side of the demonstration bed made an immediate impression. They were obviously identical twins, strong, ruddy-faced girls, with copper-coloured hair clumped in a thick fringe above remarkable blue eyes. Their caps, the pleated crowns as saucers, were perched well forward, the two immense wings of white linen jutting behind. Miss Beale, who knew from her own student days what could be done with a couple of white-tipped hat pins, was nevertheless intrigued by the art which could so firmly attach such a bizarre and unsubstantial edifice on such a springing bush of hair. The John Carpendar uniform struck her as interestingly out of date. Nearly every hospital she visited had replaced these old-fashioned winged caps with the smaller American-type which were easier to wear, quicker to make up, and cheaper to buy and launder. Some hospitals, to Miss Beale's regret, were even issuing disposable paper caps. But a hospital's nurse uniform was always jealously defended and changed with reluctance and the John Carpendar was obviously wedded to tradition. Even the uniform dresses were slightly old fashioned. The twins' plump and speckled arms bulged from sleeves of check pink gingham which reminded Miss Beale of her own student days. Their skirt lengths paid no concession to modern fashion and their sturdy feet were planted in low-heeled black lace-up shoes.

She glanced quickly at the remaining students. There was a calm, bespectacled girl with a plain intelligent face. Miss Beale's immediate reaction was that she would be glad to have her on any ward. Next to her sat a dark, sulky-looking girl, rather over-made-up and assuming an air of careful disinterest in the demonstration. Rather common, thought Miss Beale. Miss Beale, to her superiors' occasional embarrassment, was fond of such unfashionable adjectives, used them unashamedly and knew precisely what she meant by them. Her dictum 'Matron recruits a very nice type of girl' meant that they came of respectable middle-class families, had received the benefit of grammar school education, wore their skirts knee length or longer, and were probably aware of the privilege and responsibilities of being a student nurse. The last student in the class was a very pretty girl, her blonde hair worn in a fringe as low as her eyebrows above a pert, contemporary face. She was attractive enough for a recruiting poster, thought Miss Beale, but somehow it was the last face one would choose. While she was wondering why, Nurse Dakers came to the end of her recital.

'Right, Nurse,' said Sister Gearing. 'So we are faced with the problem of a post-operative patient, already seriously under-nourished and now unable to take food by mouth. That means what? Yes, Nurse?'

'Intra-gastric or rectal feeding, Sister.'

It was the dark sulky-looking girl who answered, her voice carefully repressing any note of enthusiasm or even interest. Certainly not an agreeable girl, thought Miss Beale.

There was a murmur from the class. Sister Gearing raised an interrogative eyebrow. The spectacled student said:

'Not rectal feeding, Sister. The rectum can't absorb sufficient nourishment. Intra-gastric feeding by the mouth or nose.'

'Right, Nurse Goodale, and that's what the surgeon has ordered for Mrs Stokes. Will you carry on please, Nurse. Explain what you are doing at each step.'

One of the twins drew the trolley forward and demonstrated her tray of requirements: the gallipot containing sodium bicarbonate mixture for cleaning mouth or nostrils; the polythene funnel and eight inches of tubing to fit it; the connector; the lubricant; the kidney bowl with the tongue spatula, tongue forceps and gag. She held up the Jacques oesophageal tube. It dangled from her freckled hand obscenely like a yellow snake.

'Right, Nurse,' encouraged Sister Gearing. 'Now the feed. What are you giving her?'

'Actually, it's just warm milk, Sister.'

'But if we were dealing with a real patient?'

The twin hesitated. The spectacled student said with calm authority: 'We could add soluble protein, eggs, vitamin preparations and sugar.'

'Right. If tube feeding is to continue for more than forty-eight hours we must ensure that the diet is adequate in calories, protein and vitamins. At what temperature are you giving the feed, Nurse?'

'Body temperature, Sister, 38°C.'

'Correct. And as our patient is conscious and able to swallow we are giving her this feed by mouth. Don't forget to reassure your patient, Nurse. Explain simply to her what you are going to do and why. Remember this, girls, never begin any nursing procedure without telling your patient what is to happen.'

They were third-year students, thought Miss Beale. They should know this by now. But the twin, who no doubt would have coped easily enough with a real patient, found it embarrassingly difficult to explain her procedure to a fellow student. Suppressing a giggle she muttered a few words at the rigid figure in the bed and almost thrust the oesophageal tube at her. Nurse Pearce, still gazing fixedly ahead, felt for the tube with her left hand and guided it into her mouth. Then shutting her eyes she swallowed. There was a convulsive spasm of the throat muscles. She paused to take breath, and then swallowed again. The tube shortened. It was very silent in the demonstration room. Miss Beale was aware that she felt unhappy but was unsure why. It was a little unusual perhaps for gastric feeding to be practised on a student in this way but it was not unknown. In a hospital it might be more usual for a doctor to pass the tube but a nurse might well have to take the responsibility; it was better to learn on each other than on a seriously ill patient and the demonstration doll wasn't really a satisfactory substitute for a living subject. She had once acted as the patient in her own training school and had found swallowing the tube unexpectedly easy. Watching the convulsive movements of Nurse Pearce's throat and swallowing in an unconscious sympathy she could almost recall, after thirty years, the sudden chill as the tube slid over the soft palate and the faint shock of surprise at the ease of it all. But there was something pathetic and disturbing about that rigid white-faced figure on the bed, eyes tight closed, bibbed like a baby, the thin tube dragging and wriggling like a worm from the corner of her mouth. Miss Beale felt that she was watching gratuitous suffering, that the whole demonstration was an outrage. For a second she had to fight an urge to protest.

One of the twins was now attaching a 20-ml syringe to the end of the tube, ready to aspirate some of the gastric juices to test that the end of the tube had reached the stomach. The girl's hands were quite steady. Perhaps it was just Miss Beale's imagination that the room was preternaturally silent. She glanced across at Miss Taylor. The Matron had her eyes fixed on Nurse Pearce. She was frowning slightly. Her lips moved and she shifted in her seat. Miss Beale wondered if she were about to expostulate. But the Matron made no sound. Mr Courtney-Briggs was leaning forward in his chair, his hands clasping his knees. He was gazing intently, not at Nurse Pearce, but at the drip as if mesmerized by the gentle swing of the tubing. Miss Beale could hear the heavy rasp of his breathing. Miss Rolfe sat bolt upright, her hands folded loosely in her lap, her black eyes expressionless. But Miss Beale saw that they were fixed, not on the girl in the bed, but on the fair pretty student. And for a fleeting second the girl looked back at her, equally expressionless.

The twin who was administering the feed, obviously satisfied that the end of the oesophageal tube was safely in the stomach, lifted the funnel high over Nurse Pearce's head and began slowly to pour the milky mixture down the tube. The class seemed to be holding its breath. And then it happened. There was a squeal, high-pitched, horribly inhuman, and Nurse Pearce precipitated herself from the bed as if propelled by an irresistible force. One second she was lying, immobile, propped against her mound of pillows, the next she was out of bed, teetering forward on arched feet in a parody of a ballet dancer, and clutching ineffectually at the air as if in frantic search of the tubing. And all the time she screamed, perpetually screamed, like a stuck whistle. Miss Beale, aghast, had hardly time to register the contorted face, the foaming lips before the girl thudded to the floor and writhed there, doubled like a hoop, her forehead touching the ground, her whole body twitching in agony.

One of the students screamed. For a second no one moved. Then there was a rush forward. Sister Gearing tugged at the tube and tore it from the girl's mouth. Mr Courtney-Briggs moved resolutely into the mêlée, his arms wide. Matron and Sister Rolfe bent over the twitching figure hiding her from view. Then Miss Taylor rose and looked round at Miss Beale.

'The students . . . could you look after them please? There's an empty room next door. Keep them together.'

She was trying to keep calm but urgency made her voice sharp. 'Quickly please.'

Miss Beale nodded. The Matron bent again over the convulsed figure. The screaming had stopped now. It was succeeded by a piteous moaning and a dreadful staccato drumming of heels on the wooden floor. Mr Courtney-Briggs took off his coat, threw it to one side, and began to roll up his sleeves.

Muttering gentle encouragement, Miss Beale shepherded the little group of students across the hall. One of them, she was not sure which, said in a high-pitched voice: 'What happened to her? What happened?

What went wrong?' But no one replied. They moved in a shocked daze into the room next door. It was at the back of the house, a small, odd-shaped room which had obviously been partitioned from the original high-ceilinged drawing-room and which now served as the Principal Tutor's office. Miss Beale's first glance took in a business-like desk, a bank of green steel filing cabinets, a crowded notice board, a small pegboard fitted with hooks from which hung a variety of keys, and a chart along the whole of one wall showing the teaching pro-gramme and the progress of each individual student. The partition wall cut the mullioned window in half so that the office, unpleasing in its proportions, was also inconveniently dark. One of the students clicked down the switch and the central bar of fluorescence began to flicker into light. Really, thought Miss Beale, her mind clutching desperately at the comfort of its normal preoccupations, it was a most unsuitable room for a Principal Tutor, or for any other tutor, come to that.

This brief remembrance of the purpose of her visit brought a second's comfort. But almost immediately the awful reality of the moment reasserted itself. The students—a pathetic and disorganized little bunch—had crowded together in the middle of the room as if incapable of action. Glancing quickly around, Miss Beale saw that there were only three chairs. For a moment she felt as embarrassed and nonplussed as a hostess who is not sure how she is going to seat all her guests. The concern wasn't altogether irrelevant. She would have to get the girls comfortable and relaxed if there were to be any chance of keeping their minds off what was happening next door; and they might be incarcerated for a long time.

'Come along,' she said brightly. 'Let's move Sister's desk back against the wall, then four of you can perch there. I'll take the desk chair and two of you can have the easy chairs.'

At least it was activity. Miss Beale saw that the thin, fair student was shaking. She helped her into one of the easy chairs and the dark, sulky-looking girl promptly took the other. Trust her to look after number one, thought Miss Beale. She busied herself helping the other students to clear the desk and push it back against the wall. If only she could send one of them to make some tea! Despite her intellectual assent to more modern methods of combating shock, Miss Beale still put her faith in warm strong sweet tea. But there wasn't a chance of any. It wouldn't do to upset and alert the kitchen staff.

'Now suppose we introduce ourselves,' she said encouragingly. 'My name is Miss Muriel Beale. There's no need to tell you I'm a GNC Inspector. I know some of your names but I am not really sure who is who.'

Five pairs of eyes gazed at her with startled incomprehension. But the efficient student—as Miss Beale still thought of her—quietly identified them.

'The twins are Maureen and Shirley Burt. Maureen is the elder by about two minutes and has the most freckles. Otherwise we don't find it easy to tell them apart. Next to Maureen is Julia Pardoe. Christine Dakers is in one armchair and Diane Harper in the other. I'm Madeleine Goodale.'

Miss Beale, never good at remembering names, made her customary mental recapitulation. The Burt twins. Bonny and bouncing. It would be easy enough to remember their name, although impossible to decide which was which. Julia Pardoe. An attractive name for an attractive girl. Very attractive if one liked that blonde, rather feline prettiness. Smiling into the unresponsive violet-blue eyes, Miss Beale decided that some people, and not all of them men, might like it very much indeed. Madeleine Goodale. A good sensible name for a good sensible girl. She thought she would have no difficulty in remembering Goodale. Christine Dakers. Something very wrong there. The girl had looked ill throughout the brief demonstration and now seemed close to collapse. She had a poor skin, unusually so for a nurse. It was now drained of colour so that the spots around the mouth and over the forehead stood out in an angry rash. She was huddled deep into the armchair, her thin hands alternately smoothing and plucking at her apron. Nurse Dakers was certainly the most affected of all the group. Perhaps she had been a particular friend of Nurse Pearce. Miss Beale superstitiously made a quick mental amendment of tense. Perhaps she was a particular friend. If only they could get the girl some hot reviving tea!

Nurse Harper, her lipstick and eye shadow garish on the whitened face said suddenly: 'There must have been something in the feed.'

The Burt twins turned to her simultaneously. Maureen said:

'Of course there was! Milk.'

'I mean something beside the milk.' She hesitated. 'Poison.'

'But there couldn't be! Shirley and I took a fresh bottle of milk out of the kitchen fridge first thing this morning. Miss Collins was there and saw us. We left it in the demo room and didn't pour it into the measuring jug until just before the demonstration, did we, Shirley?'

'That's right. It was a fresh bottle. We took it at about 7 o'clock.'

'And you didn't add anything by mistake?'

'Like what? Of course we didn't.'

The twins spoke in unison, sounding sturdily confident, almost unworried. They knew exactly what they had done and when, and no one, Miss Beale saw, was likely to shake them. They weren't the type to be tormented by unnecessary guilt or fretted by those irrational doubts which afflict less stolid, more imaginative personalities. Miss Beale thought that she understood them very well.

Julia Pardoe said: 'Perhaps someone else mucked about with the feed.'

She looked round at her fellow students from under lowered lids, provocative, a little amused.

Madeleine Goodale said calmly: 'Why should they?'

Nurse Pardoe shrugged and pursed her lips into a little secret smile. She said: 'By accident. Or it might have been a practical joke. Or perhaps it was done on purpose.'

'But that would be attempted murder!' It was Diane Harper who spoke. She sounded incredulous. Maureen Burt laughed.

'Don't be daft, Julia. Who would want to murder Pearce?'

No one replied. The logic was apparently unassailable. It was impossible to imagine anyone wanting to murder Pearce. Pearce, Miss Beale realized, was either of the company of the naturally inoffensive or was too negative a personality to inspire the tormenting hatred which can lead to murder. Then Nurse Goodale said drily: 'Pearce wasn't everyone's cup of tea.'

Miss Beale glanced at the girl, surprised. It was an odd remark to come from Nurse Goodale, a little insensitive in the circumstances, disconcertingly out of character. She noted, too, the use of the past tense. Here was one student who didn't expect to see Nurse Pearce alive again.

Nurse Harper reiterated stoutly: 'It's daft to talk about murder. No one would want to kill Pearce.'

Nurse Pardoe shrugged: 'Perhaps it wasn't meant for Pearce. Jo Fallon was supposed to act as patient today, wasn't she? It was Fallon's name next on the list. If she hadn't been taken ill last night, it would have been Fallon in that bed this morning.'

They were silent. Nurse Goodale turned to Nurse Beale.

'She's right. We take it in strict turn to act as patient; it wasn't really Pearce's turn this morning. But Josephine Fallon was taken into the sick bay last night—you've probably heard that we have an influenza epidemic—and Pearce was next on the list. Pearce was taking Fallon's place.'

Miss Beale was momentarily at a loss. She felt that she ought to put a stop to the conversation, that it was her responsibility to keep their minds off the accident, and surely it could only have been an accident. But she didn't know how. Besides, there was a dreadful fascination in getting at the facts. For her, there always had been. Perhaps, too, it was better that the girls should indulge this detached, investigatory interest, rather than sit there making unnatural and ineffective conversation. Already she saw that shock was giving way to that half-ashamed excitement which can follow tragedy, so long, of course, as it is someone else's tragedy.

Julia Pardoe's composed, rather childish voice went on: 'So if the victim was really meant to be Fallon, it couldn't have been one of us, could it? We all knew that Fallon wouldn't be acting the patient this morning.'

Madeleine Goodale said: 'I should think that everyone knew. Everyone at Nightingale House anyway. There was enough talk about it at breakfast.'

They were silent again, considering this new development. Miss Beale noted with interest that there were no protestations that no one would want to murder Fallon. Then Maureen Burt said:

'Fallon can't be all that sick. She was back here in Nightingale House this morning, just after eight-forty. Shirley and I saw her slipping out of the side door just before we went into the demo room after breakfast.'

Nurse Goodale asked sharply: 'What was she wearing?' Maureen was unsurprised at this apparently irrelevant question.

'Slacks. Her top coat. That red headscarf she wears. Why?'

Nurse Goodale, obviously shaken and surprised, made an attempt to conceal it. She said:

'She slipped those on before we took her to the sick bay last night. I suppose she came back to fetch something she wanted from her room. But she shouldn't have left the ward. It was stupid. She had a temperature of 103.8 when she was warded. Lucky for her that Sister Brumfett didn't see her.'

Nurse Pardoe said maliciously: 'Funny though, isn't it?' No one replied. It was indeed funny, thought Miss Beale. She recalled her long damp drive from the hospital to the nurse training school. The road was a winding one; obviously there would be a short cut through the trees. But it was a strange journey for a sick girl to make on an early January morning. There must have been some compelling reason to bring her back to Nightingale House. After all, if she did want something from her room there was nothing to prevent her asking for it. Any of the students would gladly have taken it across to the sick bay. And this was the girl who should have played the patient that morning, who should, logically, be lying next door among the tangle of tubes and linen.

Nurse Pardoe said: 'Well, there's one person who knew that Fallon wouldn't be acting patient this morning. Fallon herself.'

Nurse Goodale, white-faced, looked across at her.

'If you want to be stupid and malicious I suppose I can't stop you. But, if I were you, I would stop short of slander.'

Nurse Pardoe looked unconcerned, even a little pleased. Catching sight of her sly, gratified smile, Miss Beale decided that it was time this talking stopped. She was searching for a change of topic when Nurse Dakers said faintly from the depths of her chair: 'I feel sick.'

There was immediate concern. Only Nurse Harper made no move to help. The rest gathered around the girl, glad of the chance to be doing something. Nurse Goodale said: 'I'll take her to the downstairs cloakroom.'

She supported the girl out of the room. To Miss Beale's surprise Nurse Pardoe went with her, their recent antagonism apparently forgotten as they supported Nurse Dakers between them. Miss Beale was left with the Burt twins and Nurse Harper. Another silence fell.

65

But Miss Beale had learned her lesson. She had been unforgivably irresponsible. There was to be no more talk of death or murder. While they were here and in her charge they might as well work. She gazed sternly at Nurse Harper and invited her to describe the signs, symptoms and treatment of pulmonary collapse.

Ten minutes later the absent three returned. Nurse Dakers still looked pale but was composed. It was Nurse Goodale who looked worried. As if unable to keep it to herself, she said:

'The bottle of disinfectant is missing from the lavatory. You know the one I mean. It's always kept there on the little shelf. Pardoe and I couldn't find it.'

Nurse Harper interrupted her bored but surprisingly competent recital and said:

'You mean that bottle of milky-looking mixture? It was there after supper last night.'

'That's a long time ago. Has anyone been in that loo this morning?'

Apparently no one had. They looked at each other in silence.

It was then that the door opened. Matron came quietly in and shut it behind her. There was a creak of starched linen as the twins slipped from the desk and stood to attention. Nurse Harper rose gracelessly from her chair. All of them turned towards Miss Taylor.

'Children,' she said, and the unexpected and gentle word told them the truth before she spoke.

'Children, Nurse Pearce died a few minutes ago. We don't yet know how or why, but when something inexplicable like this happens we have to call the police. The Hospital Secretary is doing that now. I want you to be brave and sensible as I know you will be. Until the police arrive, I think it would be better if we don't talk about what has happened. You will collect your textbooks and Nurse Goodale will take you to wait in my sitting-room. I shall be ordering some strong hot coffee and it will be brought up to you soon. Is that understood?'

There was a subdued murmur of, 'Yes, Matron.'

Miss Taylor turned to Miss Beale.

'I'm so very sorry, but it will mean your waiting here too.'

'Of course, Matron, I quite understand.'

Across the heads of the students their eyes met in bewildered speculation and wordless sympathy.

STUDENT NURSE

Helen Dore Boylston

When the warm weather began in earnest Sue made a discovery. She found that it was very easy, on her free afternoons, or in the evenings, to get out into the country. During the autumn and winter the city had seemed vast and sprawling. There would have been nothing to do outside it except walk, and walking was one thing that no longer appealed to Sue as recreation. But now, seeing so many of the nurses hurrying away from the hospital on their afternoons off, dressed in old clothes and tennis shoes, she made inquiries. They were going canoeing. The blue distance that Sue could see from the roof of the Nurses' Home was veined with rivers.

All through the spring and early summer, with Kit and Connie, she explored the streams, drifting idly among the lily pads under the hot sun. They went, too, on moonlight nights, when the canoe pushed silently through curling mists, white under the moon, and the smell of damp earth and pine needles was achingly sweet after the stark cleanliness of the hospital. It was good to be away from the bustle and responsibility for a while, to loaf and talk and read.

The hot weather had brought other changes, too. Winter uniforms had been put away, and the nurses appeared in short sleeves and low collars. Classes had ceased with the final examinations in June. Two of the convalescent wards were moved out on to the lawns, in tents, and July found Connie on night duty there. Kit was still on the medical wards, but Sue had been sent to Skin, where she spent an interminable month smearing morose patients with vile-smelling ointments. The work was interesting, but Sue didn't like it as she had liked her other duty. The patients were gloomy and irritable, and the ward, in spite of open windows and electric fans, always seemed stuffy. Sue's best-fitting aprons collected strange spots which would not come out.

On Ward 2 she found herself in a different world. At least two-thirds of the patients had had bone deformities from birth. Ward 2 was no dreary hiatus in their lives. It brought them change, companionship—hope. Ever since they could remember they had been cripples. They had been stared at in the street. They had been pitied. Some had been laughed at. But here, on this friendly ward, they were not different from other people around them. So they lost their shyness and admired each other's little accomplishments, laughed at and with the nurses, made old jokes, were encouraged by each other. Pain did not make them irritable. They were accustomed to it. And each one hoped, some day, to leave the hospital greatly improved or quite cured. So they were gay and patient, submitting to the torture of dragging weights and heavy plaster casts without complaint.

The ward had a short corridor of private rooms and a nursery, with an open ward at either end, one for the men and another for the women. The ward had its own operating room in the basement. Nurse Rice, the staff nurse, was large and round-shouldered, with an amiable face and a uniform skirt that always sagged at the back. She had been staff nurse on Ward 2 for a long time, and ran it smoothly, without effort. The moment Sue came into the ward she knew that she would be happy there.

She was given five patients in the men's ward, but she occasionally helped the nurses who had private rooms. One of the patients in these rooms was a staff nurse. Sue read her case history with a mixture of horror and admiration. The nurse, whose name was Nurse Phelps, had been on private duty. Her patient, a young girl recovering from a nervous breakdown, had seemed normal for some time and was allowed to go for long walks accompanied by Nurse Phelps. One day, walking along a highway near the sanatorium, the girl, without an instant's warning, had flung herself in front of a passing lorry. Nurse Phelps had sprung after her, hurling her out of danger just in time, but the lorry had struck Nurse Phelps, breaking her back. She had been in Ward 2 for four months.

'She's a darling,' Sue told the girls. 'She never makes a fuss, and she's so gentle and sweet. I don't see how she ever had the courage—' Sue paused, and then continued more slowly, 'They say the instinct for self-preservation is the strongest instinct we have. If that's really so, I don't see why she didn't jump the other way in spite of herself, do you?'

'I don't know,' Connie said. 'I suppose training has a lot to do with it. The "patient first" idea. It has to be sort of second nature, or you'd just look out for yourself.'

The girls were on the roof of Brewster, where the evening air was cool and fresh. Kit was stretched out in a hammock, Connie perched on the parapet where she could look out across the darkening city, and Sue sat cross-legged on the floor. Kit spoke suddenly.

'I don't believe training can give it to you,' she said. 'I believe it's something in yourself.'

'Well, how do you know you have it?' Sue asked.

'You can't know, unless something happens. I think it's either there or it isn't. If it's there it will make you a better nurse—it will come out in little things that aren't heroic at all.'

'Do you mean,' Connie said, 'that if it isn't in you, then you'd never become the really ideal nurse?'

'I don't know—I think so.'

'Well,' Sue turned her head to let the wind blow against her face, 'what is an ideal nurse, anyway? Why should one want to be one?'

Kit grunted. 'Search me!'

'Because,' Connie said seriously, 'what's the good of half doing a thing—of being mediocre? You might as well have some goal of perfection even if you can't reach it. It's—it's more fun, if you like.'

'All right,' Sue returned. 'What's your idea of the perfect nurse, Kit? Let's have a few pearls of wisdom.'

Kit turned on her side and stared at her friends musingly.

'Since we're going in for this,' she said at last, 'I think that the ideal nurse is one who understands what kind of physical comfort will give her patient most peace of mind—little things like colour in the room, the furniture arranged so that it's restful to look at—when to talk and when not to—flowers on the tray, and all that.'

'But that's purely mechanical nursing,' Connie interrupted.

'It isn't unless you do it mechanically. The way I mean, you do it with everything in you, and it has quite a different effect on the patient.'

'That's all very well,' Connie said. 'But it isn't enough. What about the patient's interests and emotions?'

'When you're sick you aren't interested in anything much.'

'Don't be an idiot, Kit! Of course you are! And anyway, if you're interested and amused you aren't thinking about your symptoms all the time.'

'Well, I don't think people like a nurse meddling with their inner lives, all they want is to be made perfectly comfortable.' Kit turned to Sue. 'What do you think, Bat?'

Sue ran her fingers through her hair.

'I don't know,' she said slowly. 'I should say you were both right and both wrong. Seems to me you've left out the most important thing.'

'What's that?' Kit and Connie said with one voice.

'The patient's attitude.'

'Attitude?'

'Certainly. When people are sick they need something to steady them—some—some idea. It depends on the person. Maybe it's just being a good sport, or a noble martyr, or—or thinking they'll get well twice as quickly if they put their mind to it.'

'But, my lamb,' Connie said, 'you can't make people think anything you want them to.'

'Maybe not,' Sue admitted. 'But you can help them think the

way *they* want to. Nobody likes being frightened, or bored, or terribly nervous. They always try to hang on to something, and if you pay attention and find out what it is you can encourage them along that line.'

'But—'

'Now wait, Kit. Let me finish. If they haven't anything to steady them they're miserable, no matter how good a bath you can give, or how many stories you tell them. If they have something to steady them, *then* the other things just make being ill that much easier. Don't you see?'

'Yes, I see,' Kit said. 'I hadn't thought of it that way. Maybe you're right. Only I don't think everybody can do it.'

'I didn't say they could. You asked me my idea of the perfect nurse, and I'm telling you.'

'Oh, all right. Well, let's go to bed. I'm too tired to think, anyway.'

They went to bed, but Sue didn't forget the discussion, and a few days later, on the ward, she found a patient on whom none of their theories would work.

The patient was a middle-aged Italian woman with a compound fracture of the hip. After her operation she had been put into one of the private rooms because her continual wails disturbed the other patients.

Sue explained the situation to the girls.

'What can you do?' she asked. 'She doesn't want anything done for her—it's a struggle to make her bed. She doesn't speak any English, so you can't go into her emotions, or interests, or ideas. She isn't in any pain now—we had the interpreter over to ask her where it hurt. The interpreter told her please not to yell so, and she said she would if she wanted to. So that's that.'

'Doesn't sympathy do any good?' Connie asked, still clinging to her theory.

'My dear, one little pat on the hand and she bellows like anything. She adores an audience.'

'Well, I don't know then. I guess you can't do much.'

The nurses on the ward were equally helpless. All day long and night, at regular intervals, Mrs Riccino's voice wailed:

'*Oh, Mamma mia! Mamma mia!*'

Neither hot drinks, morphine, nor tender care had any effect.

'Does that woman never sleep?' little Mrs Wenesky asked bitterly. 'Maybe yet some of us would like to.'

'She'll be quiet in a few days, Sophie,' Sue promised, without much conviction. And she added quite untruthfully, 'Her operation hurts, you know.'

'Ach, so! An' didn't my operation hurt? But did Sophie make like the zoo noises?'

'No, you were splendid, Sophie dear.' Sue looked down at the plump, freckled little woman. 'You'll be going home soon, Sophie, won't you? You've hardly any limp at all, now.'

Sophie's round face grew rounder.

'You betcher, Nurse Barton. *Lieber Gott!* Listen to her! What is it that she says yet?'

'*Mamma mia!*' Mrs Riccino shrieked.

'It means "Mother",' Sue explained. 'The interpreter says it's what the Italian peasants call the Virgin Mary. Mrs Riccino is a Catholic, you know.'

'It's help she wants? I wish somebuddy would help her keep quiet a little. Maybe I do something!'

'No, no, Sophie! You keep out of there,' Sue said firmly. She knew Sophie's propensity for practical jokes. They delighted the ward, but Mrs Riccino's room was no place for doubtful experiments.

Sue had relief duty that evening and she wondered if, when the ward was quiet, she might be able to do something with Mrs Riccino. She could try Connie's sympathetic theory again, at least.

Through the rush of the evening work Sue heard the tireless voice shrieking on. Mrs Riccino had an almost inexhaustible energy and splendid lungs. The other patients commented on both lungs and energy with great freedom, and there was an atmosphere of irritability throughout the ward.

When everyone was settled for the night Sue ventured into Mrs Riccino's room. A dim light was burning above the bed, faintly outlining the woman's mountainous bulk and dishevelled dark head. Encouraged by Sue's appearance she took a deep breath and produced a shriek of such volume and power that Sue was deafened.

She caught one of the tense hands in both her own and spoke a few soothing words. For an instant she thought that Connie had been right. Mrs Riccino clutched Sue's hands tightly—gratefully, Sue thought at first. Then the woman's features contorted, and, for the benefit of this new audience, she uttered a series of such blood-curdling yells that Sue would have fled from the room had she been able to do so. But Mrs Riccino's grip on her hands was vice-like. Speech was useless. No ordinary sound could break through the tumult.

Sue stood there helpless, inwardly calling down maledictions on the head of the innocent Connie. In her efforts to hush Mrs Riccino she did not see a slight movement by the half-open door, and was not aware that someone else was in the room until Mrs Riccino broke off a shriek in the middle and stared with glassy eyes at the foot of her bed.

Sue turned, startled, to see rising slowly from the floor in the gloom a white and nunlike figure. The head was swathed in white, in which the face made a dim, pink triangle. The room was too dark to see the figure clearly, but in spite of this Sue had no difficulty in recognizing Sophie Wenesky. She wore a long white gown wrapped tightly around her. Her hands were crossed on her breast and her eyes turned upward in saintly contemplation.

A wave of anger choked Sue. Sophie had been told to keep out of Mrs Riccino's room. She should have been in bed. In addition she was making a joke of Mrs Riccino's religion.

'You—' she began furiously, and was interrupted by Mrs Riccino's voice, reduced to a whisper.

'*Madre di Dio! E venga!*'

Sue understood that, and for a brief and blinding moment saw in the dim white figure what Mrs Riccino saw—not fat Sophie Wenesky, but the Divine Mother.

The clasp on Sue's hand relaxed. Slowly and with difficulty the Italian woman crossed herself. Her lips moved, but no sound came from them. Even in that dim light Sue could see the look of simple belief on the swarthy face, and there was a glory in the dark Italian eyes that made Sue catch her breath.

Mrs Riccino's rosary, with its tiny ebony cross, was under the

73

pillow. Sue drew it out as quickly as she could and slipped it into the trembling hands of its owner.

'*Ave Maria—*'

Sue reached up quickly and turned off the light. In the sudden darkness she crept to the foot of the bed, clutched Sophie by the neck, and pushed her through the door, closing it after her.

In Mrs Riccino's room there was blessed silence.

Sue waited a moment. Then:

'Sophie! You come into the linen room and take off that operating-room gown and headpiece!'

'Ach! Sure, Nurse Barton,' said the unrepentant Sophie. 'You ain't mad at me, are you?'

'I certainly am. You might have frightened the poor woman into fits. Don't you ever do a thing like that again!'

The laughter faded from Sophie's eyes, leaving them round and frightened.

'Ach! I were only in fun, Nurse Barton. I didn't mean nothing. Please don't tell on me.'

When Sophie had gone to bed Sue returned to Mrs Riccino's room and put on the night light again. The dark face smiled up at her, quiet and relaxed. The woman was still too dazed for speech in any language, but when Sue brought her an egg nog she seemed pleased. She smiled again when Sue turned the pillow and gave her an understanding pat on the shoulder.

'You—good,' she managed.

Sue went off duty happy. Her theory had been right—even if it had taken a miracle to prove it.

The ward, next day, was all agog over the change in Mrs Riccino. The patients concluded, after much discussion, that she had become exhausted by her own uproar. Comments from Sophie were conspicuously absent. The nurses were too busy to wonder long, and accepted the change gratefully, for there was no further trouble with Mrs Riccino.

She lay placid and happy in her hard cast all through the hot August days, while the sun beat down on the ward roof out of a brassy sky. She wanted Sue, and Sue alone, to take care of her, but apart from that she had no preferences and no complaints.

Sue was growing very tired. The work on Ward 2 was exhausting, for the orderly could not be everywhere at once, and though the nurses were forbidden to lift the patients they frequently did so. The heat was enervating, and Sue was aware of an occasional nagging pain in her side, which had begun the day after she had tried to move one of her patients from his bed to a wheel-chair, without help.

She had quite forgotten that she had been almost a year in training until one morning the Supervisor of Nursing called her aside and said:

'Your vacation will begin on September first, Nurse Barton.' She smiled at Sue's suddenly brightened face. 'I'm sure you need it. You look tired.'

Sue was incoherent with excitement. Three whole weeks at home with Mother and Dad and Ted. Three weeks of breakfast in bed and sitting up as late as she pleased!

Later that day, going over to her room, she found Kit and Connie equally incoherent. Connie's vacation would begin on the same date, and Kit's a week later.

Sue wired home that she was coming, and from that moment was unable to keep her mind on her work. The few remaining days went by in a confusion of packing and day-dreams. And then one noon she came off duty and didn't go back. Connie was leaving at the same time, and Kit saw both girls off. As Sue's train pulled out of the station she saw Kit's face, suddenly woebegone—but after all, Kit wouldn't be alone long. She'd be going home herself in a few days.

Sue's thoughts leapt ahead of the train, to the three who were waiting for her.

Sue slept almost continually for three days after she arrived home. The first night she had talked until midnight, telling stories of the hospital, while her father and mother listened, proud and pleased, and fifteen-year-old Ted sat grinning with delight and trying not to look impressed. But after that she found that she was even more tired than she had realized, and wanted nothing in the world except sleep. It was a full week before she began to be herself again.

Then there were dances and teas and dinners. Sue's friends, to her surprise, assured her that she hadn't changed a bit. Just the same old Sue, they said. Sue wondered at them, for she was not at all the same girl who had gone away a year ago. She had learned how to work; she had had responsibility; and above all she had learned something about human nature, including herself. No she was not the same old Sue.

At first her friends had asked her about the hospital, but there was no way that she could make them see it as it really was. The concept of it was so different from the reality that no explanation would suffice.

'Didn't you hate scrubbing floors? Are the staff nurses awful? Isn't it a relief to have fun again after being shut in for a year? Did you faint at your first operation?'

'I haven't seen an operation yet,' Sue had returned shortly.

'Haven't seen an *operation*? What do you do then?'

It was no use. Sue found it easier not to speak about the hospital, and little by little it faded from her mind until there were days when she didn't think of it at all. There was nothing to remind her of it until one day, in the beginning of her third week at home, she answered the telephone absent-mindedly.

'Ward 2, Nurse Barton speaking,' she said crisply.

A gasp from the other end of the line drew her attention to what she had said. She laughed and apologized. When she had hung up, her mother came to stand in the doorway. There was a startled look on her gentle face. Her blue eyes, always so warm when they rested on Sue, were bewildered now.

'Why, Sue!' she said. 'I—you—you sounded so grown-up then, and far away. I hadn't realized—'

Sue sprang to her feet and threw her arms around her mother, her firm young cheek against the soft one that her baby hands had used to pat.

'Mummy, darling! I'm never far away from you. Don't ever think it!'

From that moment, however, the hospital took possession of Sue's mind. She began to wonder what had been happening in her absence; what changes had taken place; when classes would begin; where she would go on duty. It would be pleasant to slip into uniform—winter uniform now—and hear the swish of her shoes on tile and linoleum. The airy feeling of the corridors came back to her sharply, with the smell of floor wax, soapsuds, and ether.

'I'm actually homesick for the hospital,' she thought.

She was quite rested now, though the little nagging pain in her side was not entirely gone, and her mother complained that she was too thin.

'Do you think you ought to go back so soon darling?' she said the day before Sue's departure. 'Are you sure you're well? Why not stay another month?'

Sue's head was buried in her trunk, and she laughed silently at the picture of Miss Matthews's face on receiving a letter from Sue, casually announcing that she would not be returning for a while.

'I'm afraid I must go back, Mummy,' she said, emerging from the folds of a dress to smile at her mother. She wondered if it were disloyal of her to want to return—to be so eager to do so. Home would always be the dearest place in the world to her. It was a very special place. But her real life was in the hospital now, and it was time to return to it.

The next afternoon, watching the telegraph poles glide past the train window, she remembered how terrified she had been making this same journey a year ago. It was strange now to think of that apprehension, and when the train steamed into the city and Sue descended into the station, she felt that even it belonged to her personally.

In the hospital the first thing was to report to the Training School Office. Everywhere were faces she knew. Even the telephone girls greeted her warmly, and in the office the supervisors were all smiles.

She would have her old room, and in the morning would go on duty in the Emergency Ward.

She was back in her own world once more.

Connie arrived an hour or two later, and burst into Sue's room breathless with excitement.

'I've got the next room but one to yours,' she cried, hugging Sue. 'Won't it be fun!'

They talked for hours, both at the same time, until the ten

o'clock bell interrupted them with its ruthless command for silence and lights out.

Sue was pleased at the thought of Emergency Ward duty. Except for the Amphitheatre it was the most exciting place in the hospital. All day and all night the ambulances clanged up to the entrance—from the railway yards—from the water front—from the slums—bringing victims of accidents, of attempted murder, of attempted suicide, of fights and holdups.

The ward itself was a vast white place, honey-combed with small operating rooms, recovery rooms and dressing rooms. There was one large ward for overnight patients. Nurse Bayer, the staff nurse, a slim, dark girl, told Sue that the E.W. either had more patients than it could handle or none at all.

'It never rains but it pours,' she said.

The other nurse on duty there was Francesca Manson, and Sue was relieved to find that she was a good worker. Her manner with the patients was sharp and impatient, but she was never actually unkind, and she did what had to be done quickly and well.

'She'd never sacrifice herself for anybody,' Sue told Connie. 'I can't think why she wants to be a nurse.'

'Why don't you ask her?'

'I believe I will.'

A day or two later Sue put this query to Francesca as tactfully as she could.

Francesca hesitated a moment before replying. At last she said:

'You won't understand it—you're too soft. But I'm going to tell you anyway. I don't like the patients, and I never will. But I do like organizing. I'd like to be the head of a big thing like the Red Cross—something that is always expanding—where I'd deal with things like warehouses, and equipment, and the establishment of nursing centres, and never see a patient.'

So Francesca, too, had her dream, though it was incredible to Sue that anyone should dislike the patients.

Sue found them endlessly interesting, from the millionaire's little girl who had been thrown from her pony and broken her leg, to the huge Negress whose husband had hit her over the head with a lamp.

Human beings, it seemed, were capable of very strange behaviour. There was the young girl who had been brought into the hospital unconscious—the result of a slight difference of opinion with her sister. The sister, in the heat of the argument, had thrown a piano stool at her. The girl had been unconscious for three days.

'Why on earth didn't you bring her in before?' the resident officer on duty inquired of the family.

They seemed surprised. They hadn't thought of it, they said.

A woman arrived in the ambulance one morning, covered with bruises and with a broken wrist. A huge, burly man accompanied her. He was very much concerned, and said that he must have been a little drunk or he wouldn't have beaten her so roughly.

The resident officer launched into a severe lecture on the subject of wife beating, only to be interrupted by the woman, who sat up on the stretcher, her eyes blazing.

'You got no call to talk to my man like that! He's got a right to beat me if he wants! I'm his wife, ain't I? You leave him be!'

A boy of sixteen with a crooked nose came to the Emergency Ward asking to have his nose broken and reset so that it would be straight. His girl liked him all but his face, he explained earnestly.

Late one afternoon when the ward lights had turned the white walls to ivory, and Sue and Francesca, having for once no patients, were standing at the desk talking, the ambulance drew up at the door, and the stretcher-bearers brought in a very old and wrinkled man. He was shivering with a violent chill, and had collapsed on the street.

He was carried into one of the little operating rooms and laid on a heated table. Francesca had vanished.

Dr Reeves, the junior resident officer, was on duty.

'It looks like a malaria chill,' he said. 'Get him comfortable, Nurse Barton, and then I'll see him.'

Sue took the old man's temperature and pulse and produced hot-water bottles and blankets. When she removed the ambulance blanket she noticed that her patient had a wooden leg, the old-fashioned, inexpensive kind, known as a 'peg stick'.

His eyes were closed and he seemed exhausted. Sue made him as comfortable as she could and was about to call Dr Reeves when she saw that the wizened eyelids had lifted, and a pair of faded blue eyes were fixed on her face. The operating-room light, on its long arm, glared full upon him.

Sue swung the light away.

'Is that better?' she asked gently.

'Yes, miss, thank ye.' His voice was the weak pipe of the very old.

'The poor helpless thing,' Sue thought. She'd talk to him a little —make him feel that someone was interested in him.

'Have you had a chill like this before?' she asked.

'Yes, miss. It's the malaria fever. It come, an' my leg went, all at the same time.'

'How did you lose your leg?'

'I lost it at Balaclava, miss.'

'Balaclava?' Sue said vaguely. The word awoke a thin echo of memory. What had she known about Balaclava? The sixth-form room at school came back to her with its smell of rubbers, and bananas, and steam heat. She heard again, down the years, a boy's earnest voice reciting:

> 'When can their glory fade? . . .
> Honour the Light Brigade. . . .'

Sue bent over quickly.

'Were—were you in the Crimean War?'

'Yes, miss.'

'*Not* in the Light Brigade?'

'I were but twelve, miss—a drummer boy. But I saw the Charge.'

'Excuse me just a minute!' Sue rushed out to the desk. 'Dr Reeves!' she gasped. 'Do you remember the Charge of the Light Brigade?'

Dr Reeves looked up from the order book.

'Whoa, there! What's the rush? You're all out of breath. Sure I remember it—who doesn't?' he chanted:

> 'Into the jaws of Death,
> Into the mouth of Hell,
> Rode the six hundred—'

'Listen!' Sue cried. 'It's in there—I mean—that old man—he lost his leg at Balaclava! He saw the Charge of the Light Brigade!'

'*What!*'

Dr Reeves sprang to his feet and started for the operating room. Nurse Bayer, who had been listening, hurried after him, followed by Sue. Francesca, coming out of one of the recovery rooms, sensed the excitement and quickened her steps.

The three nurses and the young doctor clustered around the tired old figure lying on the table.

Dr Reeves spoke.

'Nurse tells me you were at the Charge of the Light Brigade.'

The faded eyes peered up at him.

'That I was. But 'twas a long time ago. I was a young feller, then. I'm—ninety-two now.'

'Yes of course. Could—could you tell us about it?'

But the old eyes had closed. There was a long silence. Then they opened and wandered over the white walls of the operating room.

'Twarn't like this,' he said, and paused. Presently he began again, speaking with an effort.

'Seems like—'twas worse—at night—the heat—like a—hot, wet blanket—stiflin' us—we—we laid on—th' floor—in th' dirt—an' bugs—hundreds of us—an'—an' sometimes they was—a cool breeze—it come—off th' mountains—an' when it come—th' boys all—kinder stirred like—towards it. . . .'

The thin voice died away. The eyes closed again.

Neither Dr Reeves. nor the nurses moved. After a moment a wrinkled hand plucked at the blanket. There was a light in the suddenly opened eyes.

'Then *she* come—she—I—'

Sue spoke, a queer tenseness in her voice.

'Who did you say came?' she asked clearly.

The old man moved impatiently.

'W'y—she—our lady—Miss Nightingale—'

'*Oh!*'

Not one of the four knew which of them had uttered that exclamation. The eyes of the three nurses were wide and startled.

'Did you see her, yourself?' Sue asked at last.

'Sartin sure—I seen her. I seen her—on her knees—in th' dirt beside us—dressin' our wounds—hours at—a—a stretch—lovely young thing—she was—slim—an' gentle. Once—'

He faltered and stopped.

'Yes?' Sue encouraged, and waited patiently.

When the old man spoke again he seemed to have forgotten the thread of his story, but he was still back in those other days, a mangled boy again, lying on the floor of the barracks below the Silver City of the Turks.

'Th' nights,' he said. 'Them awful nights. She—come then—too—with her lantern—an' water—an' th' rats—run before her—like—like's if the floor—was movin'—she—she woulda give—her life—for us—she most did—an' we woulda died for her—God's grace go—with her.'

The eyes closed again and remained closed.

Dr Reeves laid quick fingers on the wrinkled wrist.

'No,' he said. 'He's asleep. We'd better let him rest.'

They withdrew quietly. Dr Reeves and Nurse Bayer went back to the desk. Francesca turned to Sue with shining eyes.

'Think of it—what one woman did! There was an organizer for you!'

'Yes,' Sue returned absently. She had scarcely heard what Francesca was saying. She was thinking of a lovely young thing, 'slim she was, an' gentle. She would have given her life . . . she almost did. . . .'

There it was again.

The Crimean War had destroyed Florence Nightingale's health. She had never regained it.

But there had been another occasion before that early in the career of the greatest of all nurses, when she had caught a red-hot falling stovepipe in her arms to prevent it striking a patient. She had been badly burned.

Sue clasped her temples with both hands and stood still in the middle of the corridor.

'Oh, *dear!*' she thought. 'I'd never dare! I know it.' She shuddered. 'To be burned—deliberately—to be terribly hurt—I *couldn't!* No matter how much I wanted to. I couldn't! I'm a coward. I ought not to be a nurse!'

HESTER'S SUMMER

Gordon Cooper

When Hester awoke the next morning she wished for a moment she could have been back in the loft at Silver Falls instead of in the bedroom in Pond Street. She had enjoyed her holiday and she knew several weeks must pass before she would again be able to go home. It seemed strange to realize she was not required to be at the infirmary until eight o'clock in the evening, an hour when most people would have come to the end of their work. There was no need to hurry over breakfast, and after she had helped Mrs Thorne with the washing-up, she made her bed, tidied her room and then settled down to study. Through the weeks she and Gretel had made notes and drawn diagrams during Miss Tyler's lectures, and in addition to reading the new nursing manuals which had been sent out from England, the two probationer nurses also borrowed some of the books which were kept in the superintendent's room. Hester's period of night duty would not be allowed to interrupt the sequence of lectures, and she had been told she must still appear in the lecture-room punctually at three o'clock on Tuesday afternoons. At midday Mrs Thorne called up the stairs to say that dinner was ready, and afterwards Hester drew the curtains in the back bedroom and settled down to rest. She thought it unlikely that it would be possible to sleep in the daytime, but she closed her eyes and it did not seem very long before Mrs Thorne came into the room with a pitcher of hot water and told her it was nearly seven o'clock.

'Supper's ready and waiting, Hester,' she said.

'Thank you, Mrs Thorne,' Hester replied, and at twenty minutes to eight she set out for the infirmary. In her basket there was a woollen shawl for when it grew cold. She was to work on the women's ward, and she wondered if she would appear young and inexperienced to adult eyes. She went into the side-room and put on her cap and apron. When she went into the ward Nurse Ridley was sitting at the table, and a younger nurse was re-arranging the pillows of one of the patients.

'Nurse Fielding, isn't it?' said Nurse Ridley.

'Yes, Nurse,' said Hester.

'Listen carefully, then,' the senior nurse said coldly, and she slowly read the ward report.

'Are there any questions, Nurse?' she asked, when she replaced the book on the table.

'No, thank you,' said Hester.

'The night superintendent will be making her rounds several times during your duty,' said Nurse Ridley. 'Make sure that my ward is neat and tidy at all times.'

'Yes, Nurse Ridley,' Hester said.

'If you've finished gossiping, Nurse Clewer,' said Nurse Ridley in a voice which carried to the far end of the ward, 'you can go off duty,' and the junior nurse came hurriedly to the table.

'I wish you goodnight, then,' said Nurse Ridley to Hester.

'Goodnight, Nurse,' replied Hester. Nurse Clewer smiled shyly at her and followed Nurse Ridley into the side-room.

Hester stood by the table, looking round the ward and realizing that it was the first time that she had been placed in charge of a group of patients. There were nine women in the ward. She took a deep breath to steady herself and then went to the first bed on the left-hand side of the room.

'I haven't seen you before,' said an elderly lady. Beneath her cap her hair hung in two long silvery plaits.

'I've been working on the children's ward,' said Hester. From the ward report she knew this was Mrs Mackenzie who was suffering from heart trouble.

'Smartish-looking, too,' said Mrs Mackenzie. 'Not from round these parts, are you?'

'My home's in Silver Falls,' said Hester.

'That's right out in the forest, isn't it?' said Mrs Mackenzie, and Hester laughingly said although the forest was very near, there were farms, small-holdings, cottages, a church and a school-house in the township.

'I didn't realize Silver Falls was such a big place,' Mrs Mackenzie confessed.

In the next bed was Mrs Bond. 'We had a nice bit of beef for supper tonight,' she said. 'It's one thing about being here in the infirmary— it's a treat to eat a meal you haven't had to get yourself. It's my legs, maid,' she went on. 'The doctor said I was to come in for a rest.'

Hester went to every bed, linking each capped and night-gowned figure with the details written in the report which had been read to her by Nurse Ridley. One of the women appeared to be only a little older than she herself was, but in one of the cottages in Minerstown her husband and small child were being cared for by a neighbour. After Hester had made her rounds, aware of a friendly, appraising glance from everyone except Mrs Clay, the most seriously-ill patient, her charges settled down for the night. It was just after nine o'clock when the night superintendent made her first visit. She entered the ward so quietly that Hester, who was sitting at the table with the yellow light of the lamp shining on the report book, did not hear her approach, and she looked up in surprise to see the superintendent standing by her side. Miss Ballard was a tall, middle-aged woman, with the same calm manner as that of Miss Tyler. 'Good-evening, Nurse,' she said.

'Good-evening, ma'am,' said Hester, and she immediately stood up while the night superintendent read the report. Hester glanced round the ward and was thankful that everyone appeared to be sleeping, but Miss Ballard walked to Mrs Mackenzie's bed, paused for a moment, and then passed on to Mrs Bond. After she had been to each bed, she beckoned to Hester to follow her into the side-room.

'Everything seems very quiet and peaceful, Nurse,' she said. 'I believe that this is your first night duty?'

'Yes, ma'am,' Hester said.

'Ring for me if anything untoward occurs—however small,' said

Miss Ballard, and then the night superintendent went out into the passage as noiselessly as she had entered the ward. It seemed strange to Hester to be the only person awake, and as she sat at the table she wondered what would happen if she fell asleep. Once she was aware that she was nodding and that her breathing was becoming slow and measured, so she paced quietly up and down the ward. In the early hours of the morning she was glad of the warmth of her woollen shawl, and she thought gratefully of Nurse Reed. Mrs Ridgeway in the sixth bed woke up and began to cough, making a harsh, choking sound, and Hester hurried to her side with a mug of water, anxious that none of the other patients should be disturbed.

'Is everything all right?' said Miss Ballard, appearing suddenly at the other side of the bed.

'Yes, thank you,' Mrs Ridgeway said hoarsely. 'My throat was so dry, I woke up nearly parched. I reckon I'll be all right now, though.' She settled to sleep again, and Hester smoothed the sheets and blankets, consious that the night superintendent was watching her. Miss Ballard, however, said nothing, but gave a small nod of encouragement and went on her rounds. The rest of the early morning passed uneventfully, and then it was time to begin the routine work of the ward. Hester lit the fire in the stove in the side-room and put the kettles on to boil for when it would be time to take bowls of water to each patient. By seven o'clock everyone was ready for breakfast, and soon after Nan arrived from the kitchen with porridge and bread and butter, and Hester made a large pot of tea.

'Nice and strong, Nurse, please,' said Mrs Bond, when Hester began to fill the mugs.

Remembering Nurse Ridley's words and her cold, unbending manner, Hester hoped nothing would prevent her from having the ward neat and tidy when the senior nurse came on duty. She collected the trays as soon as breakfast was over, and stacked the crockery in the side-room in readiness for Nan. She was replacing the trays on one of the shelves when Nurse Clewer came into the side-room to hang up her bonnet and cloak.

'Good morning,' she said. 'Was it a quiet night?'

'Yes,' said Hester thankfully, and Nurse Clewer nodded understandingly.

Hester went back to the table in the ward and quickly read her report through once more, anxious that it should be clear and concise. When Nurse Ridley appeared she wished Hester good morning, glanced round the ward and then read the report.

'Everything appears to be satisfactory,' she said grudgingly. 'You can go now.'

'Thank you, Nurse,' said Hester, and as she went into the side-room she heard the senior nurse say, 'Come along, Nurse Clewer. We haven't got all day. There's plenty of work to be done as you very well know.'

It gave Hester a strange, holiday feeling to be walking back to Mrs Thorne's house in Pond Street soon after eight o'clock in the morning. The sights and sounds were no different from those she saw and heard when she was on day duty at the infirmary, but because her own work was over for the day, she could glance sympathetically at those for whom the working day was just beginning. As she passed the general stores, boys were unfastening the shutters, and crates and barrels were being dragged out on to the sidewalks by the store-keepers. A group of children stayed for a moment to watch a cheap-jack as he arranged his wares enticingly on his handcart. The boys eyed the knives and leather belts, while the girls looked longingly at glittering necklaces and gleaming ear-drops, until an older girl with a responsible air grasped the hands of the smaller brother and sister and hurried them along the sidewalk towards the school-house in Main Street. At the dairy store, churns of milk from the outlying farms and small-holdings were being unloaded from waggons, and farmers' wives carried baskets of eggs into the store.

'How did it go?' asked Mrs Thorne, when Hester reached the house in Pond Street.

'All right, I think,' Hester said.

'It's no more than what I thought,' said Mrs Thorne, 'I expect you're ready for a cup of tea. The kettle's on the boil.'

Not every period of night duty passed uneventfully. There was the time that old Mrs Clay died peacefully at half-past-two in the morning, and the occasion when Dr Feltham and the night superintendent stayed at the bedside of a miner's wife until she at last regained consciousness. But whatever happened, Hester was expected to have the breakfast things cleared away, and the ward ready for when the day nurses came on duty. Nurse Ridley's accusing eyes seemed to miss nothing, and Hester often wondered what it would be like to work under her unsympathetic supervision. One evening Mrs Mackenzie announced that she was going home the next day. 'I'm grateful for what's been done for me in here,' she said, 'but I'll be glad to get back to my own little place. You must come over and see me when you get the chance. That is, if ever you have the time. I've never been afraid of hard work, but you nurses seem to be on the go every minute of the day. That Nurse Ridley's a one. She may be a worker, but her tongue's so sharp she'll cut herself in two one of these days. The way she speaks to young Nurse Clewer makes a body fair tremble. Still, it takes all sorts to make a world. Don't forget, now, Twenty-three Pollard Street.'

'Thank you,' Hester said. 'I'd like to come.'

'And I'll be more than pleased to see you,' said Mrs Mackenzie. 'I might even have a slice of spice-cake in the pantry.' She watched Hester as she moved on to the next bed. Some people are easy to take to, she thought, which is more than can be said for Nurse Ridley.

At the end of Hester's second week on night duty Mrs Bond said, 'You've got a new patient tonight, Nurse—in the bed in the corner. There was quite a bit of excitement here this afternoon. A Red Indian woman was brought in. I don't know what's wrong with her, and of course that Nurse Ridley wouldn't say, even if I dared to ask her, but I think she's pretty bad. I suppose she must be, because she didn't want any supper. It was a nice bit of fish, too. Years ago my old pa used to tell us about the Indians when he was logging up near the frontier, and some of his tales used to half scare us out of our wits. I remember once I woke up screaming because I thought that some Indians were burning our house down, and Ma came in and scolded me for waking everybody up. That's way back, now—more than fifty years ago— when times were different. All the same, I never thought that one day I'd ever be in a room with an Indian sleeping in a bed not more than a hand's turn away from me.'

'There's nothing for you to worry about, Mrs Bond,' Hester said. Nurse Ridley had read the day report to her, and she was already aware of the new admission. The Indian woman opened her eyes when Hester went to her bedside. Her black hair hung in two long braids. She was wearing a high-necked white infirmary nightgown, but a buckskin dress and leggings were neatly folded on top of the locker. In her report Nurse Ridley stated that a new patient had been brought into the ward at half-past-three that afternoon, and was examined by Dr Feltham. What was not recorded was that she had made a long journey down from the hills in a horse-drawn litter made from hides and branches. She seemed very restless and watched Hester's movements as she smoothed the top sheet and tucked in the blankets, and when Hester placed a hand on her forehead, she drew back against the pillow as if unwilling to be touched. 'Try to sleep,' Hester said soothingly, and when she made her next round she was glad that the Indian woman lay with her eyes closed. Miss Ballard made her first visit to the ward and after she read the report she went to each patient, pausing for a few moments, and then, after wishing Hester a quiet duty, she went on her way. Hester sat reading a chapter of the nursing manual with the lamp close by her. Just after two o'clock Mrs Bond called out, and Hester went quickly to her, but she was still fast asleep and appeared only to be dreaming. As Hester looked down the lined, pleasant face, she was aware that someone had come into the ward, and she turned, expecting to see the night superintendent, but instead of Miss Ballard a man was standing by the table. In the dim half-light he seemed very tall and mysterious, and then with a flash of fear Hester realized that he was an Indian. She remained quite still, thinking of the sleeping women in the ward, and remembering what Mrs Bond had said about the old frontier days. Then slowly she walked towards him, holding her lamp high. He was wearing the loose-fitting buckskin clothes of his tribe, and round his forehead there was a frontlet decorated with quills and beads. He stared impassively at Hester, and as she came nearer she saw that there was a knife in his right hand.

'Have you come to see your wife?' she asked. Her throat was dry and her voice trembled in the silence. The man said nothing, and she realized that in all probability he would not have understood what she had said to him.

'This way,' she said, beckoning, and he took one step forward. She waited until he had reached her, and then she walked slowly with him to where his wife lay sleeping, her hair dark against the pillow. There

The Indian woman opened her eyes and Helen went to her bedside.

was no change in the man's inscrutable face as he looked down at the figure in the bed. It seemed to Hester that he stood there for a long time without moving, and she was aware of the weight of the lamp she carried.

'You must go now,' she said as firmly as she could, and then, with a sudden movement the man took a necklace of shells from the pocket of his shirt and placed it on the coverlet. He looked at Hester and nodded, and moved away from the bed, and with a sense of relief and thankfulness she went with him past the other beds in the ward. She intended to take him to the front door of the infirmary, but in the passage there was an open window through which the visitor had made his entrance. As they reached it, he touched her lightly on the shoulder, and she whirled round to face him, her hand at her throat and her face pale with fear. The Indian bowed, and then climbed over the window-sill and disappeared. Hester placed the lamp on the floor and with shaking hands fastened the window. She hurried back to the ward and sat down at the table, feeling cold in spite of the folds of the woollen shawl. The women were still sleeping. The man had disturbed no one. After a while she went to the bedside of his wife. She picked up the necklace and held it for a moment. The shells were cool against her hand, and she thought that they might form a kind of talisman which the Indian woman would recognise when she awoke. As she placed the necklace on the top of the locker, she thought again of the dark visitor, remembering how he had stood tall and alien with a knife in his hand, and she wondered where he would be spending the rest of the night. When Miss Ballard came into the ward, Hester told her of what had happened.

'There's no harm done, ma'am,' she said.

'For which we must be thankful,' said the night superintendent. 'All the same, he must keep to the normal visiting-times, just as everyone else does. Still, I don't imagine you'll be disturbed again, Nurse. I'll speak to the porter about the window.'

'Thank you, ma'am,' Hester said.

'Make yourself a cup of tea,' said Miss Ballard. 'In the infirmary we care for our nurses as well as for our patients.'

The rest of the early morning passed without incident and when Hester went to the corner bed the patient was awake, looking round the ward and staring up at the beams of the ceiling as if trying to remember where she was.

'Good morning,' Hester said, and she took the necklace from the locker and gave it to the Indian woman. She recognized it immediately, and as her fingers closed round the shells, the perplexity faded from her eyes.

'Your husband brought it for you,' Hester said, and the woman smiled as if she understood.

'Do you know, Nurse,' said Mrs Bond, when Hester took her a bowl of warm water, 'I must have been thinking about Indians just before I went off to sleep. I had such a strange dream. Once I thought there was an Indian right in this room, standing here as large as life. It seemed so real at the time. You were standing by his side, holding the lamp. I reckon it must have been the new physic Nurse Ridley gave me. But even if it makes you dream, it gives you a good appetite as well. I'm just about ready for my breakfast.'

The next evening Hester walked along the passage to the ward, making sure all the windows were securely fastened. As she made her first round, Mrs Bond whispered to her that the Indian woman's husband had appeared during visiting-time. 'A tall, stern-looking man,' she had said. 'He was just like the one in my dream. Wasn't it strange? I shouldn't be surprised if he was a chief or a headman.'

When Hester went to the bed in the corner, a shy smile warmed the smooth, round face of the patient. She was holding the necklace of shells and she glanced down at it, and then looked up at Hester, and Hester wondered if she knew her husband had brought it for her in the early hours of the morning, or if she thought she had been wearing it when she first came to the infirmary. With the passing of the days, gradually the pain and apprehension faded from the Indian woman's face as she began to respond to the treatment prescribed by Dr Feltham. On the morning that she was able to leave, in acknowledgement of the skill of the doctor and the nurses, her husband brought a gift of three striped blankets which were gladly accepted by Miss Tyler. Wearing the dress and leggings, the Indian woman bowed to the grim-faced Nurse Ridley and then rode away with her husband up into the hills. Hester looked at the empty bed when she went on duty, and remembered the moment when she had glanced down the ward and saw the man standing by the table with a knife in his hand.

One morning breakfast was late, and Hester glanced at the clock on the table, anxious that nothing would prevent her from having the ward in readiness for Nurse Ridley and Nurse Clewer. She took each patient a mug of tea, hoping Nan would soon be coming down the passage.

'It's all at sixes and sevens in the kitchen,' the maid said, when at last she arrived with the porridge. 'I overslept, the fire wouldn't draw, and two pitchers of milk were on the turn. We've had to send down to the dairy for some more. There's no speaking to Cook, she's so much out of sorts. I can see it's going to be one of those days when nothing goes right. There you are, Nurse—better late than never.'

'Thank you, Nan,' Hester said. Although she smiled at the tale of woe, she wondered if she would be able to have the breakfast things cleared away before the day nurses came on duty, but Mrs Musgrove, who had been a patient in the infirmary for seven weeks and was going home later in the day said cheerfully, 'I'll give you a hand, Nurse Fielding. You dish up, and I'll take it round to everybody.'

'Thank you,' Hester said, but she was not sure what would happen if anyone came into the ward and saw Mrs Musgrove carrying breakfast trays to each bedside. As if knowing her thoughts, the tall, brown-haired woman said, 'What the eye don't see, the heart won't grieve over. I shall be up far earlier than this tomorrow morning when I'm back home with my husband and children, so there's no need to worry.'

The other patients in the ward were anxious to help Hester and breakfast was eaten as quickly as possible. Nan came to carry everything back to the kitchen and Hester replaced the trays on one of the shelves in the side-room. At ten minutes to eight everything was ready for Nurse Ridley and Nurse Clewer. There was an excited feeling of triumph in the ward, and in her bed in the corner Mrs Musgrove lay back and smiled.

WRONG FOOT

Paula Milne

Jean MacEwan regarded her face in the mirror, and decided, not for
the first time, that she didn't think much of it. To most people
it would have been considered a pretty face, but to its owner
familiarity had, as Noel Coward said, bred contempt. Well, perhaps
contempt is a little strong, Jean thought, putting her head on one side
and squinting at her reflection in the grimy mirror. Perhaps boredom
was nearer the mark. She wondered if other people got bored with
their face. Hers distinctly irritated her. It was a deceitful face. Pretty,
with round cheeks and delicate features, but still deceitful. It gave an
impression of demureness; of placidity and contentment. In reality
Jean knew herself to be none of these things.

Her nursing tutor back in Glasgow had once written of her in a
progress report: 'Jean MacEwan, despite her somewhat fragile appearance, is an ambitious, highly efficient nurse. She has the natural
authority born out of an innate sense of self-confidence. When she
has proved she can temper this confidence with compassion, she will
go far.'

And go far she did, though not necessarily in the way her nursing
tutor imagined. After qualifying, she spent three years general nursing
in various hospitals in her native Scotland, and then applied for the

position of casualty Sister at St Angela's hospital. She had seen the application in one of the national nursing newspapers, and had answered it with little or no expectation of success. When she was granted an interview she still didn't allow her hopes to rise. At only twenty-five she was, after all, very young for such a post, and London casualty units were notoriously tough for even the most experienced Sisters. But she got the job. That is, she got the chance of a crack at it. She had been given a three months probationary contract.

So she had packed her bags, kissed her parents goodbye, and come down to London. She had arrived at Euston, grimy and exhausted on the Friday afternoon, and set about the irksome task of finding a flat, to find that there were none advertised either in the evening papers or on noticeboards. By six o'clock her patience, and her legs, gave up. She found the local YWCA hostel in the phone book and fixed herself up with a temporary room. The following morning she visited the hospital to collect her uniform. It was the first time she had returned to it since her interview, and she was once again struck by the grimness of the place. It loomed above her, large and intimidating, and she was assailed by doubt as to whether she really could be happy in such bleakly anonymous surroundings. She shrugged the doubt from her mind, telling herself it wasn't the building that was important anyway, it was the people inside it.

Jean's mouth suddenly felt dry. It was Monday morning and the start of her first day at St Angela's. She realized she was very nervous, and was rather surprised. Nerves was not a condition she generally succumbed to, and she chided herself for indulging in it now. She *must* give the impression of confidence, even if she didn't feel it, for how else could she expect others to have confidence in her?

She pulled on her regulation mackintosh, and buttoned it up. After a final, cursory inspection of herself, she picked up her handbag and left the sanctuary of her room to face the day.

Jean's appointment was for nine o'clock, with one of the senior administrative nurses. After a brief, somewhat formal, welcome to St Angela's, she was directed to the casualty unit, where she was told the outgoing ward Sister, a Sister Clarke, would be waiting to start the handover.

The casualty unit looked a bit like a casualty itself. It consisted of a large, impersonal, open plan area, with various curtained-off cubicles on each side, and populated by several banks of chairs, where the patients sat while waiting for attention. The walls, Jean observed, as she entered and paused to look round, were covered in large, lurid posters. *Don't take your car for a drink!* one said bluntly, depicting a crashed car and an empty whisky bottle lying in the gutter beside it; *Smoking can damage your health!* announced another, showing an ashtray, brimming with charred cigarette ends. *Give Blood,* instructed yet another, showing a grateful patient being pumped with an inviting-looking pint of fresh blood. Jean's eyes roved round the unit, taking in the battered chairs, the graffiti-scarred walls and the floor tiles, shiny with wear. Student nurses and auxiliaries were weaving about self-importantly, sorting out blankets, stretchers and wheelchairs. On one of the chairs, oblivious of the bustle around him, sat a dishevelled, unwashed young man. His face was obscured by a mass of hair, and his body was partially obscured by a kind of make-shift harness, upon which hung all the apparatus of a one-man band. Tied round his head was a grimy, blood-stained handkerchief. He was playing a mouth organ, the sound of which echoed bleakly round the walls, and for no accountable reason, filled Jean with irritation.

At the far end of the unit, she could see a kind of glass cage, which she assumed to be the Sister's office. Squaring her shoulders slightly, she headed towards it.

The office was a testimony to organized chaos. Bits of paper and charts were taped to the glass walls. The desk was piled high with files and clipboards, mountains of paperwork cluttered every available surface. She went in.

A man, obviously a doctor, was in the office, talking into the telephone. 'I appreciate that,' he was saying wearily down the mouth-piece. 'But five days still constitutes a working week does it not? Even in pathology.' He paused, as the party at the other end started vigorously to defend themselves. 'I know you're overworked,' he interrupted at last, '*I'm* overworked. But I still manage, God knows how, but I *do* manage to get my job done.'

He glanced briefly at Jean while he waited for the answer.

'I haven't much choice but to wait, have I?' he went on irritably. 'In the meantime I'll send someone for the first batch, so have them marked up and ready will you?' He hung up and started to scribble a note on a pad in front of him.

As Jean opened her mouth to introduce herself, the doctor cut her short. 'Right, Nurse—' he had scarcely lifted his eyes from the pad—'take this over to pathology will you? It's just down the corridor. I've some results need collecting. And on your way back, drop into X-ray, and see if a Mr Markham's plates are ready. I need them for a nine o'clock appointment.' Still without looking at her, he tore off a slip of paper and held it out to her. Jean stared at it silently.

'Quick as you can,' he said impatiently, waving the paper at her. 'There's a rush on.'

'I'm afraid there must be a mistake,' Jean said hesitantly, 'I've arranged to meet Sister Clarke here so she can . . .'

'Well Sister Clarke will just have to wait, won't she?' he replied bluntly, turning to look at her for the first time.

'Can't one of the junior nurses go . . . ?'

'They could,' he stared at her steadily, 'if I asked them, but I asked you. And I'm not in the habit of asking twice, Nurse.'

'Sister,' Jean corrected him, with some satisfaction. 'I take over from Sister Clarke at the end of the week. We start the handover today.'

He continued to regard her for a moment, then he rose, his manner abruptly changing gear, apparently all contrition for his earlier attitude. He put out his hand.

'Forgive me,' he said. 'I knew you were due in today, but it went clean out of my . . .' A trace of a smile played round his thin lips. 'Welcome to St Angela's, Sister . . . ?'

'MacEwan,' Jean replied, taking his hand.

'Doctor Sullivan. Casualty Registrar. We'll be working together a good deal.' He perched on the desk, looking at her. 'From Scotland, right?'

'Glasgow.'

'Got yourself somewhere to live yet?'

'I've got a room in the YWCA for the time being,' Jean replied. 'Until I can get somewhere.'

'Why not try looking on one of the hospital notice-boards? People always seem to be advertising their flats on them.'

'I'll do that,' Jean said gratefully, suddenly warming to him. 'Thanks.'

Sullivan rose from the desk, and moved to the door. 'Well, now we've got the formalities out of the way, perhaps you'd like to pop round to pathology and get those specimens?' His voice was still pleasant, but his manner had somehow imperceptibly hardened. 'It's quite clearly signed, so you shouldn't have any problem.'

Jean stared at him in surprise. He shot her a swift, cold smile. 'And when Sister Clarke decides to grace us with her presence, I'll tell her you're here. All right?'

His hand, still holding the pathology slip, was pointedly held out towards her. Jean looked at it for a moment, and then back at his face. Slowly she reached out, took the slip of paper from his hand, and left the room.

Outside, she took a deep breath. A student nurse, bustling past her, mistook the look on her face for anger. But Jean was not so much angry, as rueful. As if she knew she had lost valuable ground, which would be difficult, if not impossible, to recover.

Student nurse Jay Harper watched Jean MacEwan leaving the casualty unit, and speculated as to whether this frail-looking creature could really be their new ward Sister. Next to her, David Preston, a student nurse in his third year, was preparing an instrument trolley. Jay closed the curtains separating them from the main casualty area, and turned to help him.

'You wait,' David was saying, 'ten to one she'll be some starchy Scots spinster who'll have us all running round in circles, doing everything by the book.' He put an opthalmoscope on the trolley. 'I mean, why give the job to someone on the outside anyway? Plenty of people here would have jumped at it.'

'Sphyg . . .' Jay held out a hand, and he placed a blood pressure machine into it.

'She was probably quids in with the SNO,' he continued, warming to his theme. 'The old pals act. They were probably at school together.' He smiled maliciously. 'Sharing girlish secrets behind the gymnasium.'

'What *are* you on about, Dave?'

'Our new Cas. Sister. Jean MacEwan or whatever she calls herself.'

'Make a habit of it do you?' Jay asked, rather more bluntly than she intended. 'Condemning people before you've even met them?'

'I don't like change, love. Particularly at management level. And when she starts fiddling around with the duty rotas, you won't be quite so keen either.'

'Who says she's going to do that?'

'She's the new broom isn't she?' David replied. 'And I don't have to spell it out about new brooms, do I?'

Jay turned to look at him. 'Let's face it, Dave,' she said, lowering her voice so that the patients waiting outside couldn't hear her, 'it isn't so much her being a new broom you object to, as the fact she's a woman.'

'Rubbish,' David managed to sound genuinely injured at the accusation.

'Is it?' Jay asked. 'Well, how come ever since Sister Clarke announced her retirement you've been going on about how it's the ideal job for a male nurse?'

'Because it is.'

'Meaning a woman can't do it just as well?'

He gave her one of his luxurious smiles. 'You said it.'

Jay put a stethoscope on the trolley and drew back the curtain. 'Well you're wrong,' she said, 'dead wrong.'

'We'll see, eh?' He was still smiling confidently.

'And you're wrong about something else,' Jay added, as she started to wheel out the trolley.

'Oh?'

'Jean MacEwan.' Jay nodded to where Jean was just re-entering the casualty unit. 'Starchy Scots spinster, isn't that what you called her?'

Unaware of David's eyes curiously assessing her, Jean made her way over to a woman in a Sister's uniform, whom she took to be Sister Clarke. She was talking to one of the junior nurses, and Jean waited until she'd finished before briefly introducing herself. Sister Clarke, a large, matronly woman in her late middle age, gave her a few perfunctory, but obviously genuine, words of greeting, and then launched into an enthusiastic run-down on the workings of the casualty unit. Judging by the reverent way she referred to doctors, and Doctor Sullivan in particular, Jean suspected she was the kind who accepted the hospital hierarchy without question. Sister Clarke continued to explain the way the unit operated, and Jean's eyes idly wandered over to the young busker, seated among the other patients. He was taking a furtive gulp from a beer bottle, which, when he became aware of her eyes on him, he quickly stashed away in a pocket under his harness of instruments.

'Do you get many of them?' Jean asked, interrupting Sister Clarke in mid-flow.

'Many of what?'

Jean nodded towards the busker. 'His type. I wondered if you got a lot of them?'

Sister Clarke shot her a curious glance. 'Our share I suppose. . . .'

'You're more tolerant than we were in Glasgow,' Jean replied. 'We showed them the door pretty sharp in the casualty unit up there.'

'They've the same right to medical care as anyone else, surely?' Sister Clarke asked, giving Jean a searching look.

'Assuming they're not just malingering,' Jean said. 'Or after a bed for the night.'

Sister Clarke gave her another sidelong glance, and then said simply: 'Well, that's for the doctor to decide isn't it?' She started to move towards the office. 'We'll run through the admission procedure, if you're ready?'

Inside the office, Sister Clarke gestured Jean to a chair while she sorted out some examples of admission cards.

'So, have you met him yet?' she asked, bringing a collection of cards to the desk, and sitting down next to Jean. 'Our Doctor Sullivan?'

'Briefly.'

Something in her tone made Sister Clarke glance over at her once again.

'He wasn't so much interested in getting acquainted,' Jean explained, 'as packing me off on an errand.' She looked through the glass wall of the office, into the casualty unit, where she could see Sullivan talking to a patient. 'I hope you don't have too many like him down here.'

'Like what?'

'Doctors who treat nurses like skivvies.'

'Is that what he did?'

'As good as.'

'He's not so bad really.' Sister Clarke started to lay the admission cards out on the desk in front of them. 'He's demanding of course, believes in giving respect where it's due. . . . But when you've shown him you can do the job, he'll be fine.'

'Until then I'm guilty until proved innocent I suppose,' Jean asked, somewhat surprised at the sudden sourness in her voice. 'I'm used to doctors treating nurses, particularly sisters, as equals, as part of the medical team. If he wants to play the "Great I Am", fine. So long as I don't have to listen to him!'

An awkward silence ensued. Sister Clarke was nonplussed. She had met nurses with progressive views before, but none who were prepared to air them quite so passionately. She decided to change the subject.

'Let's press on shall we?' she said. 'We've got a lot to get through, and I'm due at a Sister's meeting. . . .' She picked up a stack of admission cards. 'Now then, the white cards we use for . . .'

At that moment the door opened, and Sullivan entered. 'Ah, Sister Clarke,' he said, his eyes flicking briefly over Jean, and then back to Sister Clarke. 'Get on to Bed State will you? See if Male Medical has a vacancy. I've a suspect cholecystitis I want to admit for observation.'

'Yes, Doctor.' Sister Clarke was already reaching for the telephone.

'And get Doctor Walker down here,' Sullivan added, as he turned to the door. 'There's a cartilage job in cubicle three I'd like a second opinion on.'

'Will do.' Sister Clarke started to dial an internal number.

Sullivan, about to withdraw, suddenly paused and glanced at Jean. 'Perhaps you'd like to help me out for a while, Sister . . . ?' He let the question hover.

'MacEwan,' Jean said flatly.

'After all,' Sullivan went on, smiling thinly, 'if you want to know what a job's all about, the best way is to get into the thick of it isn't it? And you certainly won't learn much tucked away in here, will you?' Without waiting for a reply, he strode out.

Jean took a deep breath, counted to ten, and glanced over at Sister Clarke. But she was talking on the telephone and appeared not to have heard the interchange. Jean, with ill-concealed bad grace, scraped back her chair and left the room. It was only then, as she replaced the telephone on to the receiver, that Sister Clarke acknowledged that she had in fact registered Sullivan's words, and Jean's response to them. She allowed herself a small smile of wry amusement.

Jean spent the rest of the morning in a whirl of activity, ferrying patients through to Sullivan for examination, familiarising herself with all the nurses working under her, and trying to fathom the complex admission procedure paper-work. Some two hours later, while grabbing a snatched lunch of sandwiches and coffee at her desk, she glanced through the glass walls of the office to see that the young busker was still sitting awaiting attention. Having finished off one bottle of beer, he was making a start on his second. As he gulped at it, he became aware of a pair of eyes observing him. He lowered the bottle and saw a middle-aged woman, wearing a flowered hat and matching suit, stonily regarding him from her seat a few yards away. The busker solemnly raised his bottle to her, in a mock toast.

'To all those poor souls less fortunate than ourselves,' he said. 'Your health, madam.' Keeping his eyes defiantly on her face, he put the bottle to his lips and drank. Embarrassed, the woman hastily averted her eyes, and the busker smiled, as if he were the victor in some unspoken battle.

Jean, watching from the office, frowned. The woman's discomfort was obvious and she was annoyed with the busker for causing it. She went out into the unit, where David Preston passed her, wheeling a patient. She called out to him.

'Mr Preston, isn't it?'

David paused and turned back. Jean lowered her voice fractionally. 'Has the doctor seen him yet?' she asked, nodding towards the busker.

David followed her gaze and shook his head. 'Not that I know of. . . .'

'Why not?' Jean replied. 'The sooner the better, I'd say.'

'No good asking me,' David said, and then pointed to Sullivan, who was just entering the office behind them. 'He's the guv'nor, ask him.' Sullivan was on the phone when Jean re-entered the office.

'You *are* the woman's GP, mate,' he was saying down the mouth-piece, glancing up briefly as Jean entered. 'Who said anything about working miracles? I'm just asking you to refer patients early enough, so that we've got a fair chance of doing something for them—' he strummed his fingers impatiently—'if you'd sent her along to us when she first complained of her headaches we might have had a chance to do something for her. As it is . . .' He paused, finally allowing the other man to get a word in edgeways. But not for long. 'You bet I'm going to make it an official complaint,' he cut in, and abruptly hung up, crashing the telephone on to the receiver with such force that the whole desk shook.

'Problems?' Jean enquired politely.

'GPs.' Sullivan retorted, as if that explained everything. 'Spend half their time on their backsides, dishing out tranquillizers, and call it a day's work.'

'If you've got a moment,' said Jean cautiously, 'we've got another problem.'

'They want to try working in here once in a while,' Sullivan continued. 'See how they like it.' He broke off and looked at her. 'What kind of problem?'

'Can't you hear it?' Jean crossed to the door, and opened it, so that the sound of the busker's mouth organ flooded into the office. Sullivan stared at her blankly.

'There's obviously not much wrong with him, is there?' Jean said. 'So I was hoping you could squeeze him in now. The quicker you examine him, the quicker we'll be shot of him. And then perhaps we can have some peace.'

Sullivan said nothing, his pale eyes impassively resting on her. Jean, slightly disconcerted by his scrutiny, closed the door and leant against it.

'He's disturbing the other .patients,' she said pointedly, as if some further explanation was necessary.

'You've had complaints have you?'

'No, but . . .'

'Perhaps it isn't the other patients he's disturbing.' Sullivan said, 'as much as you.'

Jean felt a flood of angry colour coming into her cheeks.

'I don't know what kind of cosy cottage hospital set-up you're used to, love,' Sullivan went on, before she could collect herself sufficiently to speak. 'But you're going to have to get used to his type here, and worse. A lot worse.' He started for the door.

'So you won't see him?'

Sullivan paused and turned back: 'I'll see him, all right, Sister,' he said. 'But since, as you say, there's obviously not much wrong with him, he's going to have to wait his turn isn't he? I don't know about you, but urgent cases come first in my book,' and he left the room, banging the door closed behind him.

Jean bit her lip. She felt angry and humiliated. Angry because of Sullivan's unreasonable attitude, and humiliated because she had allowed herself to respond emotionally to it. The whole day had been a disaster from the moment she encountered him. Why was she acting like this? Why did she let that busker annoy her, and make herself look so stupid and bigoted in front of a man like Sullivan? He obviously thought nurses were dumb anyway, and her performance was only going to endorse his opinion. She would have to prove him wrong, it was that simple. She would have to make him see that she was perfectly capable of making an independent decision. Then perhaps he would stop barking at her like a sergeant major, and start treating her as an equal. Even as the thought passed through her mind, another one followed it. She smiled to herself and squared her shoulders. With a renewed sense of purpose, she left the room.

Outside, she saw David Preston, talking to an ambulance driver. She beckoned to him, and he crossed over to her.

'Directly a cubicle falls free, I want you to put Larry Adler there in it,' she said, indicating the busker. 'And get his wound ready for me to examine will you?'

David hesitated. 'The doctor's still tied up with that haemorrhage case. . . .'

'No need to worry the doctor,' Jean said. 'I'm going to see to him myself.' She started to move away, when David stopped her.

'Doctor Sullivan usually likes to deal with the patients himself,' he began. 'It's a kind of house rule with him. . . .'

'Is it?' Jean replied coolly. 'Well I'm going to have to bend the rules for once aren't I?' She smiled, seeing David's expression. 'I'll take full responsibility, Mr Preston. If that's what's worrying you.'

David looked at her retreating back.

'You bet your sweet life you will, darlin',' he muttered, and then ambled back to resume his conversation with the ambulance driver.

'You did what?'

'I discharged him,' Jean replied. It was an hour later and she was facing a taut-faced Sullivan across Sister Clarke's desk.

'On whose authority?'

'Look . . .' Jean said patiently. 'It was a straightforward cut. It didn't even need suturing. I sent him to X-ray, but they found nothing; so I cleaned it up and sent him on his way. I'm quite prepared to take responsibility for it.'

'Wrong, love,' Sullivan snapped. 'I'm the registrar, and if anything happens to that patient, *I'll* be the one held responsible.'

'Nothing's *going* to happen to him.'

'Since I was deprived of seeing him myself, I can't be sure of that, can I?'

'You're just going to have to trust my judgment then, aren't you?'

'And what happens if we get someone in complaining of a chest pain?' Sullivan demanded. 'Will you take it upon yourself to discharge them too? Maybe send a suspect coronary packing with a few indigestion tablets, because you fancy some more of your amateur diagnosis?'

'I *am* a qualified nurse you know. . . .'

'. . . And *I* am the senior doctor on duty, and as such it's my duty to see *all* the patients, not just a chosen few weeded out by you.'

Jean stared at him angrily. 'I was trying to reduce your work load.'

'My work load, Sister, is my problem.'

'Not when it affects my nurses it's not,' Jean retorted. 'If you insist on seeing every patient,' she went on, feeling that at last she was on solid ground, 'no matter how trivial their condition, it's no wonder we're as behind as we are. Half those patients have been waiting out there since nine this morning. . . . And I suppose you expect my nurses to stay late until you've seen every last one of them?'

'I doubt that'll be necessary.'

'But if it was,' Jean said, determined to press the point, 'you would?'

'Yes,' he replied unflinchingly, 'I would.'

'That's hardly fair on them, is it?'

'I'm not so much concerned with being fair to your nurses, Sister, as being fair to the patients.'

'By keeping them hanging round half the day?'

'By ensuring they get the best possible medical attention. Which means being seen by an experienced, qualified doctor, who knows what he's doing.'

Jean stared at him, almost too angry to speak.

'I repeat,' she said at last, 'I am perfectly capable of dressing a simple head wound.'

'I'm sure you are,' Sullivan said. 'So in future I'll thank you to stick to doing just that. And leave the diagnosis to those trained for the job.' He turned to go, suggesting that as far as he was concerned, the conversation was over.

'I thought part of your job was to delegate?' Jean demanded. 'Well, isn't it? Isn't that what being head of a team means? To encourage mutual trust? There seems to be precious little of it round here.'

Sullivan paused, and turned back. 'I delegate, Sister,' he said harshly, 'if and when someone's proved they can do the job.'

'And how are they ever going to do that if you won't give them the chance?' Jean retorted.

He fell silent, his pale eyes travelling impassively over her face. 'I don't think you're worried about your nurses, or delegating or anything else,' he said. 'I think you're worried because a noisy young drunk was cluttering up your nice new casualty unit, and creating a bad impression for you. So you want shot of him. Out of sight, out of mind.'

'Nonsense!'

'You didn't think to discharge any of the others did you?' he pointed out. 'That boy with the cut hand, or the old girl with the sprained ankle. If it really was my work load you were worried about, how come they didn't get their marching orders as well?'

Jean opened her mouth to reply, when another, vaguely familiar voice cut in.

'Doctor Sullivan?'

They swung round to face the door, where Miss Lewis, the Senior Nursing Officer, was staring at them coldly. She addressed herself initially to Sullivan.

'If you have a complaint to make about one of my Sisters, Doctor Sullivan, may I suggest you go through official channels? Rather than indulging in a slanging match where everyone can hear you.'

Sullivan glanced at Jean, and then back at Miss Lewis. 'I might just do that thing,' he said, and pushed his way past her, through the door.

Miss Lewis turned to Jean. 'Sister MacEwan, isn't it?'

Jean nodded.

'I just came to welcome you in. Not a very auspicious start, is it?'

'He's not the easiest person to get along with, you know,' Jean replied defensively.

'Sister Clarke seemed to manage without too much trouble.'

'Yes, well, Sister Clarke . . .' Jean began, then paused. She glanced at Miss Lewis and thought better of what she was about to say. 'She and I seem to look at things rather differently,' she ended up, somewhat lamely.

'"Things" in this case being the job?'

'Aspects of it, anyway.'

'And more specifically Doctor Sullivan?'

Sensing a trap, Jean made no reply.

'If you're having difficulties in your working relationship, Sister, and judging by what I just heard, you are, it's better to get it out into the open now isn't it? Before any more damage is done.'

Jean frowned. 'Damage?'

'It's hardly the best example to set your junior nurses is it?'

'I don't know that it's much worse than bowing and scraping to someone simply because they happen to be both male and a doctor,' Jean said heatedly. She shot Miss Lewis a quick look, afraid she might have gone too far. 'I'm sorry,' she added, 'but that seems to be the treatment he's used to.'

'Or the way you want to see it,' Miss Lewis said. 'Since this is your first day, I'm surprised you've had time to see what kind of treatment he gets. Let alone jump to conclusions about it.'

'It's certainly the impression I got.'

'And what about the impression you're giving? Or don't you consider that important?' Miss Lewis glanced at the open door behind her, and moved to close it. 'Within hours of setting foot in the place, you've managed not only to alienate one of your colleagues, but to do it in such a place and manner so as to adversely affect the students working under you. Students to whom you are responsible, Sister, and who look to you to set an example.' Jean was about to reply, but Miss Lewis rattled on, unabated. 'And don't fool yourself they're not aware of it. Friction like this very quickly percolates down, and before you know it, sides are being taken and the entire working team is affected.' She drew a breath, and looked Jean squarely in the face. 'Well, fortunately for you, not everyone attaches the same importance to first impressions. Otherwise I might well not have let this matter rest here, believe me.' She placed a hand on the door knob, and paused. 'There are times,' she said, almost as an afterthought, 'when we all resent the status of doctors, Sister. But the real trick is not to give them the satisfaction of knowing it. It's called tactics,' and she left the room, leaving Jean with her unspoken words of protest still on her lips.

Jay Harper pulled the cubicle curtain closed and turned to confront David, who was struggling into his overcoat.

'Well could *you* have stood up to Sullivan the way she did?'

'No. . . .' David smiled languidly. 'But then I wouldn't have got myself into that situation in the first place.'

'In other words, you'd have played safe, stuck to the rules and done as the doctor ordered?' Jay paused, and then went on more reasonably. 'Don't you ever get sick of it, Dave? Dancing in attendance to them? "Yes, Doctor, no Doctor, anything you say, Doctor". Well, don't you?'

David sighed. 'Look, if we all started doing as she did, by-passing the doctors, questioning them, where would it end? Hospitals are run on discipline, break that down and there'd be chaos.'

'Sounds like a handy excuse to me,' Jay said sullenly. 'For not defending ourselves.'

'You've had your chance, Jay,' David said irritably. 'Hundreds of them. I've not heard you doing much about it. And you know why? Because you know damned well it would end up like today's little effort. With you being hauled up in front of the SNO with a complaint hanging over you.'

Jay stared at him. 'D'you really think he'll complain?'

David shrugged. 'You know Sullivan. He's not exactly the type to make idle threats, is he?'

Sister Clarke shot a surreptitious glance at Jean, sitting at the desk. Her face was cupped disconsolately in her hand, and she was absently doodling on the blotter. Sister Clarke reached for her coat, on a hanger behind the door.

'Anyone can get off on the wrong foot can't they?' she said, suddenly feeling sorry for Jean. She looked very young and vulnerable, hunched over the desk.

'And it couldn't have been easy,' she went on. 'That kind of confrontation never 'is.' She paused and then added, 'If it was, I might have done it myself by now.'

Jean glanced at her in surprise.

'Don't think I haven't wanted to,' Sister Clarke said, pulling on her coat. 'And I've had the opportunity, countless opportunities. When he marches in here the way he does, issuing his instructions, I've often felt like . . .' she broke off. . . . 'But when it comes to it I'm just not that sort of person. I never was. I can never find the right words. Or the guts, depending on how you look at it.'

Jean sighed. 'I'm beginning to think it takes more guts to keep quiet.'

'That depends on how you look at it as well, doesn't it?' Sister Clarke replied. 'All the same—' her tone was almost wistful—'it would have been nice to have done it, just *once* before I left. To prove to myself that I could, if nothing else.' She glanced at Jean, slightly embarrassed, and quickly changed the subject. 'I've got my car today. Can I drop you anywhere?'

Jean stood up and reached for her coat. 'It's OK, the bus stop's only round the corner, and I want to go to the shops on my way.' She pulled her coat on, and then shot Sister Clarke an anxious look. 'D'you really think he meant it? Doctor Sullivan? About making a complaint about me?'

'I'm afraid he did. When Doctor Sullivan says he's going to make a complaint about someone, he invariably does it.' She suddenly smiled. 'At least twice a week.'

Jean smiled in relief, and together they headed for the door. As they reached it, Sullivan entered. He glanced briefly at Jean, and then turned to Sister Clarke, holding out a folder of patient's notes towards her. 'Put this somewhere where it won't get lost, Sister. I'll need it first thing in the morning.'

Sister Clarke however, instead of taking the folder, glanced at Jean, and then back at him.

'Perhaps you could see to it yourself this once, Doctor Sullivan,' she said. 'We're just on our way home,' and before he could reply, she left the office. Jean, following her, caught a glimpse of Sullivan's startled face, before she shut the door. She turned to Sister Clarke with a grin.

'Well,' she said, some of her former spirit returning, 'I think you might have just taught him a lesson there.'

Sister Clarke gave her a small smile, and pulled on her gloves. 'I think perhaps we've all learnt something today, don't you, dear?' And without waiting for an answer, she waddled off up the corridor.

THE PEOPLE IN THE CASTLE

Joan Aiken

The castle stood on a steep hill above the town. Round the bottom of the hill ran the outer castle wall with a massive gateway, and inside this gate was the doctor's house. People could only approach the castle by going in through his surgery door, out through his garden door, and up a hundred steps; but nobody bothered to do this, because the castle was supposed to be haunted, and in any case who wants to go and see an empty old place falling into ruins? Let the doctor prowl round it himself if he wanted to.

The doctor was thought to be rather odd by the townspeople. He was very young to be so well established, he was always at work writing something, and he was often quite rude to his patients if they took too long about describing their symptoms, and would abruptly tell them to get on and not beat about the bush.

He had arranged his surgery hour in a very businesslike way. The patients sat in rows in the large waiting-room amusing themselves with the illustrated papers or with the view of the castle, which filled up the whole of one window in a quite oppressive manner. Each patient picked up a little numbered card from a box as he arrived and then waited until the doctor rang the bell and flashed his number on the indicator. Then the patient hurried to the surgery, breathlessly recited his symptoms before the doctor grew impatient, received his medicine, dropped his card into another little box, paid for his treatment (or not, after the National Health Service arrived), and hurried out by another door which led straight back to the main castle gateway.

By this means the incoming and outgoing patients were not allowed to become entangled in halls and passageways creating confusion and holding up proceedings. The doctor was not very fond of people, and the sooner he could clear them all out of his house and get back to his writing, the better he was pleased.

One evening there were fewer patients than usual. It was late in October. The wind had been blowing in from the sea all day, but it dropped before sunset, and what leaves remained on the trees were hanging motionless in the clear dusk.

'Is there anyone after you?' the doctor asked old Mrs Daggs, as he gave her some sardine ointment.

'Just one young lady, a stranger I reckon. Never seen her in the town.'

'All right—good night,' said the doctor quickly, and opened the door for the old woman, at the same time pressing the buzzer for the next number. Then he thought of a phrase for the paper he was writing on speech impediments and twiddled round in his revolving chair to put it down in the notebook on his desk. He was automatically listening for the sound of the waiting-room door, but as he heard nothing he impatiently pressed the buzzer again, and turning round shouted:

'Come along there.'

Then he stopped short, for his last patient had already arrived and was sitting in the upright chair with her hands composedly folded in her lap.

'Oh—sorry,' he said. 'You must have come in very quietly. I didn't know you were in here.'

She inclined her head a little, as if acknowledging his apology. She was very white-faced, with the palest gold hair he had ever seen, hanging in a mass to her shoulders. Even in that dusky room it seemed to shine. Her dress was white, and over it she wore a grey plaid-like cloak, flung round her and fastening on her shoulder.

'What's your trouble?' asked the doctor, reaching for his prescription block.

She was silent.

'Come along for goodness, sake—speak up,' he said testily. 'We haven't got all night.' Then he saw, with surprise and some embarrassment, that she was holding out a slate to him. On it was written:

'I am dumb.'

He gazed at her, momentarily as speechless as she, and she gently took the slate back and wrote on it:

'Please cure me.'

It seemed impolite to answer her in speech, almost like taking an unfair advantage. He felt inclined to write his message on the slate too, but he cleared his throat and said:

'I don't know if I can cure you, but come over to the light and I'll examine you,' He switched on a cluster of bright lights by his desk, and she obediently opened her mouth and stood trustfully while he peered and probed with his instruments.

He gave an exclamation of astonishment, for at the back of her mouth he could see something white sticking up. He cautiously pulled it farther forward with his forceps and discovered that it was the end of a long piece of cotton wool. He pulled again, and about a foot of it came out of her mouth, but that seemed to be nowhere near the end. He glanced at the girl in astonishment, but as she appeared quite calm he went on pulling, and the stuff kept reeling out of her throat until there was a tangle of it all over the floor.

At last the end came out.

'Can you speak now?' he asked, rather anxiously.

She seemed to be clearing her throat, and presently said with some difficulty:

'A little. My throat is sore.'

'Here's something to suck. I'll give you a prescription for that condition—it's a result of pulling out the wool, I'm afraid. This will soon put it right. Get it made up as soon as you can.'

He scribbled on a form and handed it to her. She looked at it in a puzzled manner.

'I do not understand.'

'It's a prescription,' he said impatiently.

'What is that?'

'Good heavens—where *do* you come from?'

She turned and pointed through the window to the castle, outlined on its hill against the green sky.

'From *there*? Who are you?'

'My name is Helen,' she said, still speaking in the same husky, hesitant manner. 'My father is King up there on the hill.' For the first time the doctor noticed that round her pale, shining hair she wore a circlet of gold, hardly brighter than the hair beneath. She was, then, a princess?

'I had a curse laid on me at birth—I expect you know the sort of thing?' He nodded.

'A good fairy who was there said that I would be cured of my dumbness on my eighteenth birthday by a human doctor.'

'Is it your birthday today?'

'Yes. Of course we all knew about you, so I thought I would come to you first.' She coughed, and he jumped up and gave her a drink of a soothing syrup, which she took gratefully.

'Don't try to talk too much at first. There's plenty of time. Most people talk too much anyway. I'll have the prescription made up—and bring it round,' he was going to say, but hesitated. Could one go and call at the castle with a bottle of medicine as if it was Mrs Daggs?

'Will you bring it?' she said, solving his problem. 'My father will be glad to see you.'

'Of course. I'll bring it tomorrow evening.'

Again she gravely inclined her head, and turning, was gone, though whether by the door or window he could not be sure.

He crossed to the window and stood for some time staring up at the black bulk of the castle on the thorn-covered hill, before returning to his desk and the unfinished sentence. He left the curtains open.

Next morning, if it had not been for the prescription lying on his desk, he would have thought the incident had been a dream. Even as he took the slip along to Boots to have the medicine made up he wondered if the white-coated woman there would suddenly tell him that he was mad.

That evening dusk was falling as the last of his surgery patients departed. He went down and locked the large gates and then, with a beating heart, started the long climb up the steps to the castle. It was lighter up on the side of the knoll. The thorns and brambles grew so high that he could see nothing but the narrow stairway in front of him. When he reached the top he looked down and saw his own house below, and the town with its crooked roofs running to the foot of the hill, and the river wriggling away to the sea. Then he turned and walked under the arch into the great hall of the castle.

The first thing he noticed was the scent of lime. There was a big lime tree which, in the daytime, grew in the middle of the grass carpeting the great hall. He could not see the tree, but why was a lime tree blossoming in October?

It was dark inside, and he stood hesitating, afraid to step forward into the gloom, when he felt a hand slipped into his. It was a thin hand, very cool; it gave him a gentle tug and he moved forward, straining his eyes to try and make out who was leading him. Then, as if the pattern in a kaleidoscope had cleared, his eyes flickered and he began to see.

There were lights grouped round the walls in pale clusters, and below them, down the length of the hall, sat a large and shadowy assembly; he could see the glint of light here and there on armour, or on a gold buckle or the jewel in a head-dress as somebody moved.

At the top of the hall, on a dais, sat a royal figure, cloaked and stately, but the shadows lay so thick in between that he could see no more. But his guide plucked him forward; he now saw that it was Helen, in her white dress with a gold belt and bracelets. She smiled at him gravely and indicated that he was to go up and salute the King.

With some vague recollection of taking his degree he made his way up to the dais and bowed.

'I have brought the Princess's linctus, Sire,' he said, stammering a little.

'We are pleased to receive you and to welcome you to our court. Henceforth come and go freely in this castle whenever you wish.'

The doctor reflected that he always *had* come and gone very freely in the castle; however, it hardly seemed the same place tonight, for the drifting smoke from the candles made the hall look far larger.

He lifted up his eyes and took a good look at the King, who had a long white beard and a pair of piercing eyes. Helen had seated herself on a long stool at his feet.

'I see you are a seeker after knowledge,' said the King suddenly. 'You will find a rich treasure-house to explore here—only beware that your knowledge does not bring you grief.'

The doctor jumped slightly. He had indeed been thinking that the King looked like some Eastern sage and might have information which the doctor could use in his study on occult medicine.

'I suppose all doctors are seekers after knowledge,' he said cautiously, and handed Helen her bottle of medicine. 'Take a teaspoonful after meals—or—or—three times a day.' He was not sure if the people in the castle had meals in the ordinary way, though some kind of feast seemed to be in progress at the moment.

From that time on the doctor often made his way up to the castle after evening had fallen, and sat talking to the King, or to some of the wise and revered knights who formed his court, or to Helen. During the daytime the castle looked broody, solitary and crumbling as always, save for some occasional archaeologist taking pictures for a learned monthly.

On Christmas Eve the doctor climbed up with a box of throat tablets for Helen, who still had to be careful of her voice, and a jar of ointment for the King who had unfortunately developed chilblains as a result of sitting in the chill and draughty hall.

'You really should get him away from here, though I'd miss him,' he told Helen. 'I don't know how old he is—'

'A thousand—' she interjected.

'—Oh,' he said, momentarily taken aback. 'Well in any case it really is too damp and cold for him here. And you should take care of your throat too; it's important not to strain it these first months. This castle really is no place for either of you.'

She obediently flung a fold of her grey cloak round her neck.

'But we are going away tomorrow,' she said. 'Didn't you know? From Christmas to Midsummer Day my father holds his court at Avignon.'

The doctor felt as if the ground had been cut from under his feet.

'You're going away? You mean you'll none of you be here?'

'No,' she answered, looking at him gravely.

'Helen! Marry me and stay with me here. My house is very warm —I'll take care of you, I swear it—' He caught hold of her thin, cold hand.

'Of course I'll marry you,' she said at once. 'You earned the right to my hand and heart when you cured me—didn't you know that either?'

She led him to her father and he formally asked for her hand in marriage.

'She's yours,' said the King. 'I can't prevent it, though I don't say I approve of these mixed marriages. But mind you cherish her—the first unkind word, and she'll vanish like a puff of smoke. That's one thing we *don't* have to put up with from mortal man.'

As soon as Helen married the doctor and settled in his house she became a changed creature. The people in the town were surprised and charmed to find what a cheerful, pretty wife their hermit-like doctor had found himself. She left off her magic robes and put on check aprons; she learned to cook and flitted around dusting and tidying; moreover as her newly-won voice gathered strength she chattered like a bird and hummed the whole day long over her work.

She abolished the buzzer in the surgery because she said it frightened people. She used to look through the door herself and say:

'The doctor will see you now, Mrs Jones, and will you try not to keep him waiting, please—though I know it's hard for you with your leg. Is it any better, do you think? And how's your husband's chest?'

'She's like a ray of sunshine, bless her,' people said.

The doctor was not sure about all this. What he had chiefly loved in her was the sense of magic and mystery; she had been so silent and moved with such stately grace. Still, it was very pleasant to have this happy creature in his house attending to his comfort—only she did talk so. In the daytime it was not so bad, but in the evenings when he wanted to get on with his writing it *was* trying.

By and by he suggested that she might like to go to the cinema, and took her to a Disney. She was enchanted, and after that he was ensured peace and quiet on at least two evenings a week, for she was quite happy to go off by herself and leave him, only begging him not to work too hard.

One night he had nearly finished the chapter on Magic and its

Relation to Homeopathic Medicine, and was wishing that he could go up and discuss it with the King. He heard her come in and go to the kitchen to heat the soup for their late supper.

Soon she appeared with a tray.

'It was a Western,' she said, her eyes sparkling. 'The hero comes riding into this little town, you see, and he pretends he's a horse-dealer but really he's the DA in disguise. So he finds that the rustling is being run by the saloon keeper—'

'Oh, for goodness sake, *must* you talk all the time,' snapped the doctor. Then he stopped short and looked at her aghast.

A dreadful change had come over her. The gay print apron and hair ribbon dropped off her and instead he saw her clad in her white and grey robes and wreathed about it with all her magic. Even as she held out her hands to him despairingly she seemed to be drawn away and vanished through the thick curtains.

'Helen!' he cried. There was no answer. He flung open the door and ran frantically up the steps to the castle. It was vacant and dark. The grass in the great hall was stiff with frost and the night sky showed pale above him in the roofless tower.

'Helen, Helen,' he called, until the empty walls re-echoed, but no one replied. He made his way slowly down the steps again and back to his warm study where the steam was still rising from the two bowls of soup.

From that day the townspeople noticed a change in their doctor. He had been hermit-like before; now he was morose. He kept the castle gates locked except for the surgery hour and disconnected his telephone. No longer was there a pretty wife to tell them that the doctor would see them now; instead they were confronted by a closed door with a little grille, through which they were expected to recite their symptoms. When they had done so, they were told to go round by an outside path to another door, and by the time they reached it they found the necessary pill or powder and written instructions lying outside on the step. So clever was the doctor that even with this unsatisfactory system he still cured all his patients, and indeed it seemed as if he could tell more about a sick person through a closed door than other doctors could face to face; so that although people thought his treatment strange, they went on coming to him.

There were many queer tales about him, and everyone agreed that night after night he was heard wandering in the ruined castle calling 'Helen! Helen!' but that no one ever answered him.

Twenty years went by. The doctor became famous for his books, which had earned him honorary degrees in all the universities of the world. But he steadfastly refused to leave his house, and spoke to no one, communicating with the tradespeople by means of notes.

One day as he sat writing he heard a knock on the outer gate, and something prompted him to go down and open it. Outside stood a curious looking little woman in black academic robes and hood, who nodded to him.

'I am Dr Margaret Spruchsprecher, Rector of the University of Freiherrburg,' she said, walking composedly up the path before him and in at his front door. 'I have come to give you the degree of Master of Philosophy at our University, as you would not come to us or answer our letters.'

He bowed awkwardly and took the illuminated parchment she offered him.

'Would you like a cup of coffee?' he said, finding his voice with difficulty. 'I am most honoured that you should come all this way to call on me.'

'Perhaps now that I have come so far I can help you,' she said. 'You are seeking something, are you not? Something besides knowledge? Something that you think is in the castle, up there on the hill?'

He nodded, without removing his gaze from her. The keen piercing look in her old eyes reminded him vividly of the King.

'Well! Supposing that all this time, what you seek is not *inside*, but has gone *outside*; supposing that you have been sitting at the mouth of an empty mouse-hole; what then?' There was something brisk, but not unkindly in her laugh as she turned and made off down the path again, clutching the voluminous black robes round herself as the wind blew them about. The gate slammed behind her.

'Wait—' the doctor called and ran after her, but it was too late. She was lost in the crowded High Street.

He went out into the town and wandered distractedly about the streets staring into face after face, in search of he hardly knew what.

'Why, it's the doctor, isn't it?' a woman said. 'My Teddy's been a different boy since that medicine you gave him, Doctor.'

Someone else came up and told him how thankful they were for his advice on boils.

'My husband's never forgotten how you cured his earache when he thought he'd have to throw himself out of the window, the pain was so bad.'

'I've always wanted to thank you, Doctor, for what you did when I was so ill with the jaundice—'

'You saved my Jennifer that time when she swallowed the poison—'

The doctor felt quite ashamed and bewildered at the chorus of thanks and greeting which seemed to rise on every side. He finally dived into a large doorway which seemed to beckon him, and sank relieved into a dark and sound-proof interior—the cinema.

For a long time he took no notice of the film which was in progress on the screen, but when he finally looked up his attention was attracted by the sight of galloping horses; it was a Western. All of a sudden the memory of Helen came so suddenly and bitterly into his mind that he nearly cried aloud.

'Excuse me, sir, that's the one and nine's your sitting in. You should be in the two and three's.

He had no recollection of having bought any ticket, but obediently rose and followed his guide with her darting torch. His eyes were full of tears and he stumbled; she waited until he had caught her up and then gave him a hand.

It was a thin hand, very cool; it gave him a gentle tug. He stood still, put his other hand over it and muttered:

'Helen.'

'Hush, you'll disturb people.'

'Is it you?'

'Yes. Come up to the back and we can talk.'

The cinema was pitch dark and full of people. As he followed her up to the rampart at the back he could feel them all about him.

'Have you been here all these years?'

'All these years?' she whispered, mocking him. 'It was only yesterday.'

'But I'm an old man, Helen. What are you? I can't see you. Your hand feels as young as ever.'

'Don't worry,' she said soothingly. 'We must wait till this film ends —this is the last reel—and then we'll go up to the castle. My father will be glad to see you again. He likes your books very much.'

He was too ashamed to ask her to come back to him, but she went on:

'And you had better come up and live with us in the castle now.'

A feeling of inexpressible happiness came over him as he stood patiently watching the galloping horses and feeling her small, cool hand in his.

Next day the castle gates were found standing ajar, and the wind blew through the open doors and windows of the doctor's house. He was never seen again.

LITTLE GIRLS TOO

Gladys Williams

It was in October 1872 that Thomas triumphantly completed his 'capture' of the 'Edinburgh Castle', about eleven months after he had received little Martha, his first girl waif.

In the following June this new-style church and social centre was the scene of an unusually joyful, animated gathering. It was a 'Welcome Home' held to celebrate the Doctor's return to London with his bride at the end of their honeymoon.

In the course of his work the Doctor had met Miss Syrie Louise Elmslie, beautiful, vivacious daughter of a wealthy family living at Richmond. To his delight he found that she shared his keen interest in children, his deep religious faith, and his lively sense of humour. He loved her for herself, but he realised, too, that it would be much easier for him to extend his work for girls if he had a wife who shared his enthusiasm and interest.

This Miss Elmslie certainly did, and their union was to prove a happy, lifelong one in spite of the fact that the Doctor had always to give the giant's share of his time and thought to his 'adopted' family. Nevertheless, from this time forward we get glimpses of him relaxing from his arduous, self-imposed labours in his own family circle—returning, for instance, after a strenuous Christmas Day spent at the

'Edinburgh Castle' with his East End friends and the boys of his big and growing 'outside' family, to spend the last precious hours of the holiday quietly with Syrie and their young children. Or we hear of him taking a summer holiday with them in the lovely Welsh countryside, burdened inevitably with written work that he had to bring with him, yet finding time to share the fun of a family picnic, laughing when a guest opened a bottle of mineral waters the wrong way and he was the one who caught the full blast.

Some of his loveliest surviving letters about his large family are those which he sent to his wife, and it is obvious that she, like himself, knew hundreds of these children by name, especially the sick and crippled little ones, and readily remembered all sorts of incidents about them. She was to outlive her husband by many years, and eventually died at the remarkable age of one hundred and two, maintaining right to the end her deep interest in her husband's larger 'family'.

His elder daughter, whom they nicknamed Queenie, grew to be a lovely, talented girl, who shared her father's tremendous interest in books, and eventually married the novelist Somerset Maugham.

By the time of his marriage, the Doctor was no longer an unknown student, a young Irish stranger in London, but very much a voice making itself heard in East London and even further afield. It was already clear that he was not just another good young man who had started a home for boys where it was much needed, but a social pioneer with original ideas and amazing energy.

We have already seen him as eager to sell Bibles in Paris as in London, and as concerned about education in Germany and Russia as in England. Once he had really accepted the idea that child-rescue was to be the great objective of his life, he became intensely interested in what other people were doing in this field in various parts of Europe—from Quarrier in Scotland to Müller in Bristol, from Falk in Germany to Dr Comandi in Florence, and many, many more. He eagerly visited many of these other establishments, as ready to learn from their experiences as to describe them to his own supporters and ask help for them too. His was a wide, generous and unusual spirit.

When, some years later, the Church of England started its own child-rescue organisation (known today as the Children's Society), some anxious souls asked the Doctor if he were not afraid this would lessen the support he himself received. His cheerful reply was that he was thrilled to see the Church of England setting this splendid example, and hoped wide support would be given to it. He pointed out that some church people had felt unable to support his homes because of his non-sectarian views, but now could have no cause to hesitate in assisting child-rescue work done directly by the Church authorities. As for those who had been helping him, he believed they would be more likely to give to both endeavours than desert him. And even if some did, he added, God would always raise up new friends for his children.

By 1873, not only was a sum of £20,000 coming in annually for his mission, but he was directing quite a number of his projects so ably that they were self-supporting. These eventually included not only the first coffee-palace at the Edinburgh Castle, and a second in Mile End Road, the Dublin Castle, but a number of the boys' trading organisations. The Wood-Choppers' Brigade, for instance, by 1875 had its own wharf, chartered its own ships, imported its own cargoes from Scandinavia, and produced an annual income of over £3,000 with each young worker well provided for and getting a good wage. Or, again, there was the City Messengers' Brigade, made up of boys educated to read and write in the Ragged and Sunday Schools, and picked for their reliability and honesty. The Doctor put them into smart uniforms, advertised their services to business houses and the general public, and stationed them at strategic points in the City of London where they could be easily called upon to undertake such commissions as taking urgent messages (in the days before the telephone), delivering important or valuable parcels, distributing trade circulars promptly, or carrying out personal commissions reliably at a fixed rate of charges. These boys made a most honourable reputation for their Brigade, and by this time were jointly earning for themselves over £1,650 a year.

His young brushmakers, bootmakers, tailors, harnessmakers, and the rest—for he was constantly expanding his trade schools—were encouraged to put forward their best efforts by being paid pocket-money while training, and to contribute by their industry to the reduction of running costs.

Now his marriage was going to give him a much better chance to expand his work for girls. At first it had seemed to him that there were many fewer homeless girls than boys, and he imagined that this was because people felt that boys were better able to 'rough it', and that if a family fell on hard times, the boys rather than the girls should be the first to get out and fend for themselves. He knew, too, that girls were often more useful and made less noise in a crowded home, took care of babies and did odd jobs, so that parents often parted less readily with them.

But, as Dr Barnardo got to know social conditions ever more thoroughly, he began to realise there was a great deal more to the problem than this.

All children in those days were regarded as the 'possessions' of their parents—indeed the law of the land took that view—and bad parents and other evil people regarded girls as more valuable 'possessions' than boys. This was because they were weaker, more easily bullied, thrashed and cowed, more effective for begging purposes and less readily suspected as thieves. There might certainly be fewer girls than boys found wandering on their own, but their fate in the hands of evil 'owners'— bad parents or strangers—could be infinitely worse.

In his daily paper, for instance, Dr Barnardo read such stories as these: two little girls, brought before a magistrate charged with being found begging, wept bitterly—explaining that unless they went out begging and brought home money their mothers would beat them and give them nothing to eat. While they begged in one place the mother of one of them went off on a begging round of her own, carrying a baby, returning from time to time to the children to collect what coppers they had gathered in. Most of the proceeds went on gin.

Late one night, crossing Westminster Bridge, a man heard a six-year-old girl pleading in terror with a great hulking fellow who was threatening to throw her over the parapet into the water. This passer-by reported what he had heard to a policeman, who went to investigate. It was discovered that the bully was a professional beggar of notoriously evil habits, an idle, dissolute vagabond who for years had been in the habit of buying children whom he took on tramps round the country for begging purposes. Nothing could be discovered about the parents of the little girl. Perhaps she had been stolen, perhaps she had been sold.

In the year 1878 a six-year-old girl was the subject of a question in the House of Commons, because she had been sent to Newgate Prison. Her offence was passing counterfeit money on the instructions of her mother. The Minister ruled that the magistrate who had sent the child to prison had done a perfectly proper thing, but that it would be rather better for such very young children to be sent to the workhouse instead of prison!

Two girls of nine and seven were charged at Southwark with stealing purses. They had followed a woman shopper into a store and then, while the older child had gone in front and attracted her attention, the younger had crept up behind, slipped a hand into her pocket and taken her purse. Obviously they had been carefully trained as thieves. They had been obeying the orders of a man and woman who were with them at the time but to whom they were in no way related. The seven-year-old, locked up in a cell with a woman charged with another offence, boasted of the ease with which she could steal purses, adding that she'd got one that morning with two half-sovereigns in it and some silver. She'd taken it to the woman she was working for, and been given a whole shilling for herself.

But even worse things than these could happen. A child who was maimed or blind or in pain might prove a still more effective beggar. Picking pockets was only a step to even more serious forms of crime. And in addition a terrible vice trade flourished, and little girls were often forced into this by cruelty or craft before they were even in their teens. Among the poor, diseased, sick and wretched women of the slums the Doctor was to find some of his firmest supporters once these poor souls realised his determination to help little girls too. For only they knew the difference it would have made to them, if, in their own childhood, a merciful hand had been stretched out to them.

It grieved the Doctor unspeakably that for such little girls practically the only alternative to a life of suffering and crime was to be sent to the workhouse. He believed that if workhouse life was bad for boys, it was a hundred times more harmful to girls.

He objected to it because in a workhouse four or five hundred or even, sometimes, double that number of children of the same sex would be herded together. The little girls all had their heads cropped (at a time when long hair was the fashion and every girl's pride), were made to wear ugly, ill-fitting workhouse uniforms, and were referred to by numbers, not names. There was no attempt to keep them apart from the older women paupers, often people of a degraded, animal type who took a vicious delight in teaching the children all the evil they could. Beds were shared, and a girl's natural, self-preserving instinct for privacy utterly disregarded, and her hunger for beauty and affection systematically starved. Though given food and shelter, workhouse girls were not given any instruction in the art of home-making or in any knowledge of the world outside. In this way they became a helpless and natural prey to evil people when they came out. Do you remember how gullible Oliver Twist was, and how the Artful Dodger doubled up with laughing because he was so 'green'? That dangerous ignorance, the Doctor declared, was the hall-mark of the workhouse child, and girls were even more likely than the boys to be ruined by it.

The Doctor and his young bride-to-be made up their minds that the first thing they would do, once they were married, would be to open a home for 'little gels too' as Martha had put it.

A friend, who knew of their wish, placed at their disposal 'Mossford Lodge', Barkingside, Ilford, Essex, a pleasant house situated in what were then beautiful rural surroundings. Another supporter wrote to *The Christian* newspaper suggesting that admirers of the Doctor's work should mark the occasion of his wedding by raising a special fund to equip the home.

As a result it was possible to repeat, on rather a larger scale and in a country setting, very much what the Doctor had done at Stepney Causeway—enlarging the outbuildings at Mossford Lodge to form the first home for Barnardo girls with rooms for about sixty.

Bearing in mind how important and worthwhile it had proved to train the boys in ways of earning an honest livelihood, the Doctor decided that he must work out a similar plan for his girls. But there he came up against another problem. In mid-Victorian days careers for girls were almost non-existent. In the upper circles of society 'ladies' were not expected to work. It was a most unladylike thing to do! If a gentlewoman was forced by misfortune to have to maintain herself, the only genteel occupation was to go as a governess or companion in a wealthy family, and Charlotte Brontë shows us what a lonely, uncomfortable life this could be. Women secretaries, typists, telephonists and civil servants were unheard of, and school teachers only just coming into being. And though there were seamstresses and women factory workers their toil was usually miserably paid and a clean, inexpensive, safe lodging almost impossible to find. The one occupation in which a working girl might lead a reasonably comfortable, secure sort of life, was domestic service, provided she was well-trained and could secure employment with a kindly mistress in a fairly wealthy household. There good board and lodging would be part of the return received for her work, and there was often congenial and kindly company in the servants' hall. It also, of course, kept a girl right away from the old slum life. It is very easy nowadays to be a bit condescending and superior when we talk of domestic service, and to think of such a life only in terms of the over-worked maid-of-all-work in a lower-middle-class home. But if we remember the rather wistful pictures Charlotte Brontë gives of the cosily-knit domestic staffs in the big houses, or some of the dignified and highly respectable housekeepers, like Mrs Rouncewell or Mrs Bedwell, in Charles Dickens's books, or even the saucy little maids who waited on Mr Pickwick, we get a better idea of the pros and cons the Doctor must have weighed up when he thought of providing for the future of this new branch of his growing family.

With his young wife to help him, the Doctor now went confidently ahead, certain that, if he could turn his little girls into clean, well-mannered cooks, parlour-maids, laundry-maids, house-maids and kitchen-maids, every one would easily be able to find employment, and want and homelessness would be right behind them.

Characteristically he started by gathering in the most utterly un-taught and neglected, unwashed and undisciplined little girls he could find. And he did not realise that he was making the big mistake that governments and educationists and others still often make in a masculine-dominated society—namely, thinking of a girl as a kind of 'watered-down' boy, and of a woman as a kind of 'lesser-man', satisfied and happy with the same kind of things that please the male.

But gradually an uneasy feeling grew in his mind that all was not well with his new family. Somehow, where the boys had delighted to spring to attention, taken a pride in spit and polish, and felt a zest in discipline, the girls were not quite 'cottoning on' in the same way. Then one evening he overheard some of them talking in a way that shocked and distressed him. It revealed that, though he was getting surface results, he was not getting the real thing—that marvellous, holy change inside a person that was the whole dynamic and purpose of his work. Indeed, he feared he was doing little or no better for his girls than the work-houses he had condemned.

But where and how had he failed? He puzzled long over the problem. The awful truth was inescapable—girls were *different* from boys and it was no use treating them as if they weren't. He went visiting other homes and reformatories for girls to try to find a clue, but they all seemed to be run much on the same lines as he had visualised and getting much the same results. But there was one exception—a very new establishment run by a lady called Mrs Meredith—the Princess Mary Village Homes at Addlestone. This very feminine establishment instead of housing its girls in one large building, divided them up between a number of separate small buildings where the girls were brought up in small family groups. Could this be the answer?

One night, between waking and sleeping, the realisation seemed suddenly to flash through his mind that this *was* the answer, confirmed by the memory of one of the most beautiful texts from his beloved Bible: 'Yet setteth He the poor on high from affliction, and maketh Him families like a flock. The righteous shall see it and rejoice. . . .' Of course, he could see it now. *Families* were God's way of doing things; the crowding together of hundreds of human beings and governing them by rule of thumb was man's way.

So real and complete was his realisation of what he must do for his girls that it seemed as if he actually saw the future rise up before him, the children's village that he would build, with little homes all grouped round a village green, a mother in every one. There'd be big sisters and little sisters peeping out the windows and running out of the doors; babies sleeping in prams and little children picking flowers in the gardens. Instead of vast long dormitories, there would be little bed-rooms with four or five beds with pretty counterpanes and a looking-glass so that each little girl could keep herself neat. And of course there'd be no uniforms, for each child would have her own clothes and learn to look after them. And instead of great canteens and cook-houses there'd be small kitchens where little girls could stir the Christmas pudding and learn to cook, and get to know how Mother did things and be able to help and copy her.

And there'd be a village school to which all the children from all the families would go, and a children's church for services on Sundays, and in hospital for sick ones. Girls weren't like boys. They had a greater need to be individual people, to have beauty and quiet and privacy, to be creative in a different way from boys, for after all wasn't the making of a happy home of her very own the right and natural hunger of every little girl? And how the industrial revolution had robbed women of the chance to fulfil that hunger! Wasn't the basic cause of the misery and need of these little girls, that they'd never had *homes*?

With Dr Barnardo, of course, to have an idea was to set to work *at once*! He quickly made arrangements to buy thirteen acres of freehold land adjoining Mossford Lodge, and wrote to *The Christian* newspaper announcing his wonderful new plan, appealing for help in getting the first cottages built. Almost as soon as he had written the letter he began to have doubts, and to his intense disappointment, when it appeared nothing happened. He felt extremely troubled. Having made one mistake, he dreaded making a second.

While in this anxious state of mind he had to go on a special journey to Oxford. On the way there he met a deeply sympathetic friend who shared his own confident religious faith, to whom he confided his problem.

'Suppose,' said the friend, 'that you were clearly shown that this scheme is *not* God's will, would you give it up?'

The Doctor considered, and then said, 'Yes, if I were absolutely sure.'

'Then,' said the friend, 'I think it would be right to ask God for a sign because it is His work that is at stake, and I suggest that we both ask that you shall be given some clear sign before you return home from Oxford of what it is His will you should do.'

The Doctor agreed and they made their joint request.

Next morning, while the Doctor was dressing in his hotel room, there was a knock on his door, and in response to his shout of 'Come in' a stranger put his head round the door. He, too, was only partly dressed.

'Is your name Barnardo?' he asked.

'Yes,' said the Doctor.

'Are you wanting to build some cottages for homeless girls?'

'Yes,' agreed the Doctor.

'Well you can put me down for the first one.'

And the stranger withdrew to finish dressing.

For a second the Doctor was too astonished to do anything. Then he hurried after his visitor to get his name and learn more.

The facts were quite simple. This man and his wife had had a beloved only daughter, Myrtle, who had died. They had read in *The Christian* about the Doctor's plan and decided they'd like to keep alive the memory of their own child by providing and naming one of these cottages after her. It had seemed just the right kind of memorial. But they had taken no immediate action, as the man had to go to Oxford. That morning out of curiosity he had asked the Boots at the hotel if anyone of interest were staying at the hotel and the man had brought him the Visitors' Book. Almost the first name he had seen in it was Dr Barnardo's. He decided right away to knock at his bedroom door and make his promise.

He had no idea that, by so doing, he was answering a most earnest and anxious prayer, and actually saving the whole scheme from extinction—and that the story would be told over and over again many years after.

The promise of that first cottage was quickly followed by others. The foundation stones of fourteen were laid that year and the cottages formally opened the following summer. Within three years the Doctor had received enough offers to build all the thirty cottages visualized in his original plans and before he died was to see more than another thirty added. On June 18th, 1879, HRH Princess Mary Adelaide, Duchess of Teck, came to lay the foundation stone of one of the new cottages and opened three more that had been completed.

She was the first of a succession of Royal visitors who were to honour the Village with visits in the years that lay ahead, and she certainly began that wonderful tradition of friendliness and whole-hearted interest that has made these occasions so extremely happy for staff, children and supporters. She went over every cottage, upstairs as well as down, questioned the Doctor exhaustively on his work and his plans, bought a copy of his *Night & Day* magazine from one of the stalls (generously paying £5 for it), listened to the girls singing, watched the boys drill, and took the salute while their band played 'God save the Queen'.

Some of the very little girls had been a bit puzzled as to which of the quietly dressed visitors had been the Princess and which her lady-in-waiting. But a little girl of six settled the point with authority.

'It was the tall lady', she announced, 'who was the Princess because she looked at me and smiled.'

She was, of course, quite right.

It may be that the Princess went home and described the events of the afternoon to her own twelve-year-old daughter, who eventually, as Queen Mary, became, with King George V, a Royal Patron of the Homes following the example of Queen Alexandra, the first royal patron, and played a big part in fostering a tradition of Royal sympathy and support that was carried forward into the third generation by King George VI and Queen Elizabeth, and into the fourth and this modern age by Princess Margaret.

To his great joy, the Doctor found as the days and weeks went by, that in his Village Home he was providing the kind of environment where girls could grow happily and naturally. He found it wise to have a receiving centre in London where very neglected, untaught little creatures could be given some preliminary care and teaching before being introduced into the Village families, but once there, the very surroundings, the close touch with a personal 'mother' and the influence of the other children did wonderful things.

A contributor to *Chambers' Journal* in 1877 contrasted the reception that awaited a lonely, unloved girl there with the impersonal atmosphere of an industrial school. At this village, she explained, a girl 'becomes at once a member of a *family*, with a dozen other girls of varying ages for playmates and sisters. The "mother" gives her a kiss, and tells her to be a good girl, and they will all love her dearly; and in a few days the forlorn little one is transformed into something human and child-like.'

She commented on the freedom and gaiety with which the children talked among themselves, their bright, cheerful curiosity, their uncut hair, their individual clothes. She liked the way in which each 'family' was allowed to be different from the one next door, the freedom given to each 'mother' to manage her own family affairs, and the way individuality of character was encouraged among the children, and each one given opportunity to use what powers she had for the benefit of the rest of the household.

We find the Doctor himself appealing for nice clothes and pretty ribbons for his little girls, asking if groups of his supporters could undertake, perhaps, to make a set of summer frocks for the girls of one cottage. 'Perhaps,' he explained, 'everyone does not know that a *uniform dress* is not used in our family circles, and we do try to keep up the name of the cottage in the dress of its inhabitants. For instance, the children of Cambridge and Forget-me-not always have some blue on their best hats and hoods; those of Rose and Daisy shades of pink and so on, and for this purpose Mrs Soltan (the Governor's wife) will be very glad to receive any number of scraps of coloured silk and ribbons, such as most ladies can turn out of their cupboards, which the clever fingers of the "mothers" use to the best account. I am glad to say that every "mother" takes considerable trouble to make the clothes neat and prettily varied, believing that by thus educating the children's taste they will, in a great measure, be preserved from the dangers of vanity in finery when they go out into service. The full extent of this danger probably none are aware of who have not worked in London, or other large towns, among young servants who have been brought up in workhouses or large institutions. Disgusted with the plain *unvaried* clothing they have hitherto worn, their first desire is to be "smart", and they commonly rush into the extreme of vulgar finery, to obtain which they often fall into dishonest and other bad ways.'

(What would Jane Eyre's Mr Brocklehurst have said to that!)

Girls began to come in to join the Doctor's family of their own free will, just as the boys had done.

There was Irish Bridget, a little newspaper girl whom the Doctor tried in vain for some time to coax into his fold. But she was an independent little creature who used to take up her daily stand outside the Royal Exchange, having run away from a drunken mother, and, managing to hold her own very well in competition with the street boys, was most reluctant to give up her liberty. But one wet, dreary, cold day the Doctor found her holding a sodden mess in her arms, her unsold papers, and in reply to his question, Was she hungry?, she sadly nodded her head. He took her into a neighbouring shop for a hot meal, said nothing until she was fed and warmed, and then pulled out a photograph of one of his girls dressed in her neat frock, snow-white cap and apron all ready to go out to service.

Bridget's eyes grew round. She was enchanted with the picture, and the Doctor had no need to say more.

Looking him straight in the eye she asked, 'Would you *promise* to make me like *that* if I came into your home?'

The Doctor assured her it would only take a year or two, and then she could be more independent than ever before, with a choice of many good situations.

'I'll come,' said Bridget.

Or there was little Mary, whose story was told in a publication called *Good Words* in 1880 by a woman who had noticed, one day, two children following an itinerant sweep past her country house. The condition of the boy was bad, but the girl was just like a dreadful little goblin, dressed in a dirty, discarded, man's hat and coat, with a rag of print tied round her for a dress, her body black all over in a way that suggested that, contrary to the law, she had been used for climbing chimneys.

'Pretty little girl, ain't she,' snarled the sweep, noticing the way the woman had looked at the child, and she had let the family pass. But later, troubled in her conscience, she determined to track down those children, find out their story and try to do something for them.

It took her some months, but eventually she found that the mother, a confirmed drunkard, had deserted the family and not been much missed, and that the father also was a heavy drinker. He had some affection for the boy, but none for the girl, though eventually he agreed to part with both. The woman wrote to Dr Barnardo who agreed to accept both.

Mary, it transpired, was nine years old, had never in her life used a knife and fork, never been bathed, scratched and bit anyone who crossed her will, and used dreadful language. For the first eight days after her arrival at a Village cottage all was pandemonium. She was fascinated by taps and continually turned them on, spraying water all over the room. She hated wearing shoes, and would run out in her

He pulled out a photograph of one of his girls dressed to go out to service.

135

stocking feet into the wet garden and then back into the house, making muddy foot-marks everywhere, and spring into bed. She frightened the smaller children.

But a turning-point came when the exhausted 'mother' one day could no longer keep back the tears. In her old street life, the child had often been brutally punished, only to respond by becoming ever wilder and more unruly. This reaction was something quite new. It baffled and disturbed her. After loudly declaring that she wouldn't ever say she was sorry, she suddenly fell on her knees at her 'mother's' feet and begged to be forgiven. She was gathered up, and hugged and kissed, and once again for another child the Doctor's dream of a divine change, a new outlook, began to come true.

Poor little Mary, alas, did not live very long. Her past ill treatment caused her to develop consumption, she, herself, explaining, as she snuggled down into her beloved little bed, 'If my father had given me a bed I wouldn't be ill like this. But he'd go to the lodging-house himself but wouldn't pay for me, so I had to sleep on the steps outside.'

The Doctor began to learn that, as far as girls were concerned, he must not wait until they were actually homeless and on the streets before he gathered them in. In his early days he had hesitated to receive any boy who had parents living and a vestige of a home. Indeed boys seemed to have such a good time in his home, that he actually had some try to get in by false pretences—running away from home and pretending to him they were orphans.

But good mothers now began to come to him in times of distress because they had heard about his Village and wanted him to receive their little girls before they were ever exposed to the dangers and misery of street life. He realised these mothers were right. Sometimes it would be a mother who had to go into hospital, knowing, perhaps, that she had small hope of recovery. Or it might be a widow, or a woman deserted by her husband, whose efforts to keep the home in existence were failing. Here the Doctor found that sometimes, by taking one or two children, he could lighten a mother's burden enough to enable her to carry on happily with the rest. Many of these little girls had been carefully brought up, and came to him clean, intelligent, well-trained, and right from the very start helped to build up happy families in the Village.

136

More and more, too, he proved the tremendous value of his women helpers, a very large number of whom, in the early days, gave their services with little or even no payment—as indeed the Doctor himself did for not far short of twenty years, supplementing a modest income from private sources with quite a considerable sum made each year by part-time journalistic and literary work. He had in the end reluctantly to realise that it would be wiser to accept a minimum salary from his own organisation and give his whole time and undivided attention to his work for the children.

Many of these early women helpers of his were drawn from the well-defined upper-middle-classes, 'gentlewomen' they would have been called, whose Victorian fathers and brothers expected them to stay quietly at home sketching and doing embroidery work, maintained by allowances very properly made by their male relatives. Instead they preferred to give their lives to the service of the poor, inspired by the same kind of religious outlook as the Doctor himself.

Some became the first 'mothers' to the little girls at the Village, and perhaps it is not surprising that so many of the girls did well, for many of these women must have been gifted, well educated, cultured and far from ordinary people, who naturally bred refinement and good taste in their 'daughters'. Others became what the Doctor called 'deaconesses', but which really meant a sort of youth-club leader, nursing auxiliary, health visitor, relieving officer, child-care worker, schoolteacher, psychiatrist, parish priest and charwoman all rolled into one. The Doctor and his wife found it impractical to live permanently in the Village at Barkingside, for in those days the journey into London took too long and the Doctor's daily presence was essential at Stepney. They lived first in a house at Bow and then moved to Hackney, converting the Bow house into a centre where the deaconesses could live and be ready at any hour of the day, and sometimes of the night, to go out on a wide variety of missions. Nominally they were under the direction of Mrs Barnardo, but one strongly suspects that the Doctor called the tune. These devoted women undertook auxiliary nursing duties in the infirmary which the Doctor added to his Stepney Headquarters. They conducted what we should call youth-club activities and mothers' meetings at the 'Edinburgh Castle' and ran evening classes to teach working men to read and write. They undertook dispensing at a Medical Mission which the Doctor established to enable poor people to get medical care at a nominal charge. They went out—much as Thomas had done in his early days—into the homes of the poor, nursing the sick, comforting the aged, watching for children in danger. They helped serve food at the Doctor's great feasts at the 'Edinburgh Castle', they were on hand to assist with scores of ingenious schemes the Doctor was continually thinking up to relieve distress in an age of unemployment when the State did practically nothing—his First-Aid for Starving Infants, an embryo infant-welfare service; his loan schemes to buy or get out of pawn the tools needed to enable a breadwinner to become self-supporting; his Servants' Registry to help girls get into safe, reliable jobs and help with their clothes; his Boots-on-Loan and Blankets-on-Loan schemes, his old-age pensions to prevent decent old ladies losing their homes in their twilight years. These and many more were made possible by the wonderful work done by his deaconesses.

It is easy for us today to look at pictures of these ladies in their regulation bonnets and severe, plain-looking clothes and have no idea of the tremendous value of the work they did for love—work of a kind for which the State today pays out vast sums of money. We tend to underestimate the courage of these gently-reared women who went fearlessly, much like the Salvation Army lassies, into the roughest quarters of the city, among people more debased and animal-like than we can imagine, where a form of dress that at once proclaimed their purpose was necessary for their protection. But it was Dr Barnardo who had the imagination and insight to realise, at a time when so many men of his generation regarded women as mere drawing-room ornaments, the heights of devotion, ability and usefulness of which they were capable—and to choose women like these, wherever he could—to set the pattern and the ideal for the young feminine life coming under his influence.

He employed them, too, in his Stepney offices. One, who did literary work for him, has described the warmly human, brotherly way he treated them, his thoughtfulness, deep understanding and appreciativeness. He confided to her once that he had found that 'as a rule women are more painstaking and *naturally* more interested in their work than men', adding with a bow 'present company always excepted'!

138

She tells, too, how she first visited him at Stepney at a time when she herself still rather suspected he 'coloured' his stories. There she saw with her own eyes, among those waiting, two little fellows, their filthy rags tied on with bits of string, devouring a plateful of food with a ghastly avidity that called for no explanations; a wailing baby being hushed by a young mother so literally skin and bone she could hardly put one foot before the other; a group of match-sellers, described by their twelve-year-old leader as 'me and my pals', driven to shelter by the bitter winter weather; two little sisters, one lame, and the other with a rag—and such a rag!—tied over a 'bad eye', brought in by a friendly policeman.

'Now perhaps you do believe my stories are not exaggerated?' was the Doctor's amused, astonishing, uncannily accurate greeting.

PRINCE ANDREY'S WOUND

Leo Tolstoy

Prince Andrey, pale and haggard like every one else in the regiment
walked to and fro in the meadow next to the oat-field from one boundary
line to the other, with his hands clasped behind his back, and his eyes
fixed on the ground. There was no need for him to give orders, and
nothing for him to do. Everything was done of itself. The killed were
dragged behind the line; the wounded were removed, and the ranks
closed up. If any soldiers ran away, they made haste to return at once.
At first Prince Andrey, thinking it his duty to keep up the spirits of the
men, and set them an example, had walked about among the ranks. But
soon he felt that there was nothing he could teach them. All his
energies, like those of every soldier, were unconsciously directed to
restraining himself from contemplating the horror of his position. He
walked about the meadow, dragging one leg after the other, making the
grass rustle, and watching the dust, which covered his boots. Then he
strode along, trying to step on the traces of the footsteps of the mowers
on the meadow; or counting his steps, calculated how many times he
would have to walk from one boundary rut to another to make a verst:
or cut off the flowers of wormwood growing in the rut, and crushing
them in his hands, sniffed at the bitter-sweet, pungent odour. Of all the
thoughts of the previous day not a trace remained. He thought of

nothing at all. He listened wearily to the sounds that were ever the same, the whiz of the shells above the booming of the cannon, looked at the faces of the men of the first battalion, which he had gazed at to weariness already, and waited. 'Here it comes . . . this one's for us again!' He thought, listening to the whiz of something flying out of the region of smoke. 'One, another! More! Fallen' . . . He stopped short and looked towards the ranks. 'No; it has flown over. But that one has fallen!' And he fell to pacing up and down again, trying to reach the next boundary in sixteen steps.

A whiz and a thud! Five paces from him the dry soil was thrown up, as a cannon-ball sank into the earth. A chill ran down his back; he looked at the ranks. Probably a number had been struck: the men had gathered in a crowd in the second battalion.

'M. l'aide-de-camp,' he shouted, 'tell the men not to crowd together.'

The adjutant, having obeyed this instruction, was approaching Prince Andrey. From the other side the major in command of the battalion came riding up.

'Look out!' rang out a frightened cry from a soldier, and like a bird, with swift, whirring wings alighting on the earth, a grenade dropped with a dull thud a couple of paces from Prince Andrey, near the major's horse. The horse, with no question of whether it were right or wrong to show fear, snorted, reared, almost throwing the major, and galloped away. The horse's terror infected the men.

'Lie down!' shouted the adjutant, throwing himself on the ground. Prince Andrey stood in uncertainty. The shell was smoking and rotating like a top between him and the recumbent adjutant, near a bush of wormwood in the rut between the meadow and the field.

'Can this be death?' Prince Andrey wondered, with an utterly new, listful feeling, looking at the grass, at the wormwood, and at the thread of smoke coiling from the rotating top. 'I can't die, I don't want to die, I love life, I love this grass and earth and air . . .'

He thought this, and yet at the same time he did not forget that people were looking at him.

'For shame, M. l'aide-de-camp!' he said to the adjutant; 'what sort of—' He did not finish. Simultaneously there was a tearing, crashing sound like the smash of broken crockery, a puff of stifling fumes, and

Prince Andrey was sent spinning over, and flinging up one arm, fell on his face. Several officers ran up to him. A great stain of blood was spreading over the grass from the right side of his stomach.

The militiamen stood with their stretchers behind the officers. Prince Andrey lay on his chest, with his face sunk in the grass; he was still breathing in hard, hoarse gasps.

'Well, why are you waiting, come along!'

The peasants went up and took him by the shoulders and legs, but he moaned piteously, and they looked at one another, and laid him down again.

'Pick him up, lay him on, it's all the same!' shouted some one. They lifted him by the shoulders again and laid him on the stretcher.

'Ah, my God! my God! what is it? . . . The stomach! It's all over then! Ah, my God!' could be heard among the officers. 'It almost grazed my ear,' the adjutant was saying. The peasants, with the stretcher across their shoulders, hurried along the path they had trodden to the ambulance station.

'Keep step! . . . Aie! . . . these peasants!' cried an officer, seizing them by the shoulders, as they jogged along, jolting the stretcher.

'Drop into it, Frydor, eh?' said the foremost peasant.

'That's it, first-rate,' said the hindmost, falling into step.

'Your excellency? Eh, prince?' said the trembling voice of Timohin, as he ran up and peeped over the stretcher.

Prince Andrey opened his eyes, and looked at the speaker from the stretcher, through which his head had dropped, and closed his eyelids again.

One of the doctors came out of the tent with a blood-stained apron, and small, blood-stained hands, in one of which he had a cigar, carefully held between his thumb and little finger, that it might not be stained too. This doctor threw his head up, and looked about him, but over the level of the wounded crowd. He was evidently longing for a short respite. After turning his head from right to left for a few minutes, he sighed and dropped his eyes again.

'All right, immediately,' he said in reply to an assistant, who pointed him out Prince Andrey, and he bade the bearers carry him into the tent.

A murmur rose in the crowd of wounded men waiting.

'Even in the next world it's only the gentry who will have a good time,' said one.

Prince Andrey was carried in, and laid on a table that had just been cleared, and was being rinsed over by an assistant. He could not make out distinctly what was in the tent. The pitiful groans on all sides, and the excruciating pain in his thigh, his stomach, and his back distracted his attention. Everything he saw around melted for him into a single general impression of naked, blood-stained, human flesh, which seemed to fill up the whole low-pitched tent, as, a few weeks before, on that hot August day, the bare human flesh had filled up the dirty pond along the Smolensk road. Yes, it was the same flesh, the same *chair à canon*, the sight of which had roused in him then a horror, that seemed prophetic of what he felt now.

There were three tables in the tent. Two were occupied, on the third they laid Prince Andrey. For some time he was left alone, an involuntary witness of what was being done at the other tables.

Having finished with a Tatar, over whom a cloak was thrown, the doctor in spectacles came up to Prince Andrey, wiping his hands.

He glanced at his face, and hurriedly turned away. 'Undress him! Why are you dawdling?' he shouted angrily to the assistant.

His earliest, remotest childhood came back to Prince Andrey, when the assistant, with tucked-up sleeves, hurriedly unbuttoned his buttons, and took off his clothes. The doctor bent close down over the wound, felt it, and sighed deeply. Then he made a sign to some one. And the excruciating pain inside his stomach made Prince Andrey lose consciousness. When he regained consciousness, the broken splinters of his thighbone had been removed, the bits of ragged flesh had been cut off, and the wound bound up. Water was sprinkled on his face. As soon as Prince Andrey opened his eyes, the doctor bent over him, kissed him on the lips without speaking, and hurried away.

After the agony he had passed through, Prince Andrey felt a blissful peace, such as he had not known for very long. All the best and happiest moments of his life, especially his earliest childhood, when he had been undressed and put to bed, when his nurse had sung lullabies over him, when, burying his head in the pillows, he had felt happy in the mere consciousness of life, rose before his imagination, not like the past even, but as though it were the actual present.

And all at once a new, unexpected memory from that childlike world of purity and love rose up before Prince Andrey. He remembered Natasha, as he had seen her for the first time at the ball in 1810, with her slender neck and slender arms, and her frightened, happy face, ready for ecstatic enjoyment, and a love and tenderness awoke in his heart for her stronger and more loving than ever.

On Saturday, the 31st of August, the whole household of the Rostovs seemed turned upside down. All the doors stood wide open, all the furniture had been moved about or carried out, looking-glasses and pictures had been taken down. The rooms were littered up with boxes, with hay and packing paper and cord. Peasants and house-serfs were tramping about the parquet floors carrying out the baggage. The courtyard was crowded with peasants' carts, some piled high with goods and corded up, others still standing empty.

The voices and steps of the immense multitude of servants and of peasants, who had come with the carts, resounded through the court-yard and the house. The count had been out since early morning. The countess had a headache from the noise and bustle, and was lying down in the new divan-room with compresses steeped in vinegar on her head. Petya was not at home; he had gone off to see a comrade, with whom he was planning to get transferred from the militia to a regiment at the front. Sonya was in the great hall, superintending the packing of the china and glass. Natasha was sitting on the floor in her dismantled room among heaps of dresses, ribbons, and scarfs. She sat gazing immovably at the floor, holding in her hands an old ball-dress, the very dress, now out of fashion, in which she had been to her first Petersburg ball.

Natasha was ashamed of doing nothing when every one in the house was so busy, and several times that morning she had tried to set to work; but her soul was not in it; and she was utterly unable to do anything unless all her heart and soul were in it. She stood over Sonya while she packed the china, and tried to help; but soon threw it up, and went to her room to pack her own things. At first she had found it amusing to give away her dresses and ribbons to the maids, but afterwards when it came to packing what was left, it seemed a wearisome task.

'Dunyasha, you'll pack it all dear? Yes? yes?'

And when Dunyasha readily undertook to do it all for her, Natasha sat down on the floor with the old ball-dress in her hands, and fell to dreaming on subjects far removed from what should have been occupying her mind then. From the reverie she had fallen into, Natasha was aroused by the talk of the maids in the next room and their hurried footsteps from their room to the backstairs. Natasha got up and looked out of the window. A huge train of carts full of wounded men had stopped in the street.

The maids, the footmen, the housekeeper, the old nurse, the cooks, the coachmen, the grooms, and the scullion-boys were all at the gates, staring at the wounded men.

Natasha flung a white pocket-handkerchief over her hair, and holding the corners in both hands, went out into the street.

The old housekeeper, Mavra Kuzminishna, had left the crowd standing at the gate, and gone up to a cart with a tilt of bast-mats thrown over it. She was talking to a pale young officer who was lying in this cart. Natasha took a few steps forward, and stood still timidly, holding her kerchief on and listening to what the housekeeper was saying.

'So you have no one then in Moscow?' Mavra Kuzminishna was saying. 'You'd be more comfortable in some apartment.... In our house even. The masters are all leaving.'

'I don't know if it would be allowed,' said the officer in a feeble voice. 'There's our chief officer ... ask him,' and he pointed to a stout major who had turned back and was walking along the row of carts down the street.

Natasha glanced with frightened eyes into the face of the wounded officer, and at once went to meet the major.

'May the wounded men stay in our house?' she asked.

The major with a smile put his hand to his cap.

'What is your pleasure, ma'mselle?' he said, screwing up his eyes and smiling.

Natasha quietly repeated her question, and her face and her whole manner, though she still kept hold of the corners of the pocket-handkerchief, was so serious, that the major left off smiling, and after a moment's pondering—as though asking himself how far it were possible—he gave her an affirmative answer.

'Oh yes, why not, they may,' he said.

Natasha gave a slight nod, and went back with rapid steps to Mavra Kuzminishna, who was still talking with commiserating sympathy to the young officer.

'They may; he said they might!' whispered Natasha.

The officer in the covered-cart turned into the Rostov's courtyard, and dozens of carts of wounded men began at the invitation of the inhabitants to drive up to the entries of the houses in Povarsky Street. Natasha was evidently delighted at having to do with new people in conditions quite outside the ordinary routine of life. She joined Mavra Kuzminishna in trying to get as many as possible driven into their yard.

'We must ask your papa though,' said Mavra Kuzminishna.

'Nonsense, nonsense. What does it matter? For one day, we'll move into the drawing-room. We can give them all our half of the house.'

'What an idea! what next? The lodge, maybe, the men's room, and old nurse's room; and you must ask leave for that.'

'Well, I will ask.'

Natasha ran indoors, and went on tiptoe to the half-open door of the divan-room, where there was a strong smell of vinegar and Hoffmann's drops.

'Are you asleep, mamma?'

'Oh, what chance is there of sleep!' said the countess, who had just dropped into a doze.

'Mamma, darling!' said Natasha, kneeling before her mother and leaning her face against her mother's. 'I am sorry, forgive me, I'll never do it again, I waked you. Mavra Kuzminishna sent me; they have brought some wounded men in, officers, will you allow it? They have nowhere to go; I know you will allow it, . . .' she said rapidly, not taking breath.

'Officers? Who have been brought in? I don't understand,' said the countess.

Natasha laughed, the countess too smiled faintly.

'I knew you would let me . . . so I will tell them so.' And Natasha, kissing her mother, got up and went to the door.

In the hall she met her father, who had come home with bad news.

'We have lingered on too long!' said the count, with unconscious anger in his voice; 'the club's shut up and the police are leaving.'

'Papa, you don't mind my having invited some of the wounded into the house?' said Natasha.

'Of course not,' said the count absently. 'But that's not to the point. I beg you now not to let yourself be taken up with any nonsense, but to help to pack and get off—to get off tomorrow . . .'

And the count gave his butler and servants the same orders.

After dinner all the Rostov household set to work packing and preparing for their departure with eager haste. The old count, suddenly rousing himself to the task, spent the rest of the day continually trotting from the courtyard into the house and back again, shouting confused instructions to the hurrying servants, and trying to spur them on to even greater haste. Petya looked after things in the yard. Sonya was quite bewildered by the count's contradictory orders, and did not know what to do. The servants raced about the rooms, shouting, quarrelling, and making a noise. Natasha, too, suddenly set to work with the ardour that was characteristic of her in all she did. At first her intervention was sceptically received. No one expected anything serious from her or would obey her instructions. But with heat and perseverance, she insisted on being obeyed, got angry and almost shed tears that they did not heed her, and did at last succeed in impressing them.

The packing went on fast now, thanks to Natasha's supervision; everything useless was left behind, and the most valuable goods were packed as compactly as possible.

But with all their exertions, even late at night everything was not ready. The countess had fallen asleep, and the count put off their departure till morning and went to bed.

Sonya and Natasha slept in the divan-room, without undressing.

That night another wounded officer was driven along Povarsky Street, and Mavra Kuzminishna, who was standing at the gate, had him brought into the Rostov's yard. The wounded officer must, Mavra Kuzminishna thought, be a man of very great consequence. He was in a coach with the hood let down and a carriage apron completely covering it. An old man, a most respectable-looking valet, was sitting on the box with the driver. A doctor and two soldiers followed the carriage in another conveyance.

'Come into our house, come in. The masters are going away, the whole house is empty,' said the old woman, addressing the old servant.

'Well,' answered the valet, sighing, 'and indeed we have no hope of getting him home alive! We have a house of our own in Moscow, but it is a long way further, and there's no one living in it either.'

'Pray come in, our masters have plenty of everything, and you are welcome,' said Mavra Kuzminishna. 'Is the gentleman very bad, then?' she asked.

'There's no hope! I must ask the doctor.' And the valet got down and went to the vehicle behind.

'Very good,' said the doctor.

The valet went up to the coach again, peered into it, shook his head, told the coachman to turn into the yard, and stood still beside Mavra Kuzminishna.

'Lord Jesus Christ, have mercy!' she murmured.

Mavra Kuzminishna suggested the wounded man being carried into the house.

'The masters won't say anything . . .' said she.

But they had to avoid lifting him up the steps, and so they carried the wounded man to the lodge, and put him in the room that had been Madame Schoss's. This wounded officer was Prince Andrey Bolkonsky.

By two o'clock the Rostovs' four carriages, packed and ready to start, stood in the approach. The wagon-loads of wounded were filing one after another out of the yard.

The coach in which Prince Andrey was being taken drove by the front door, and attracted the attention of Sonya, who was helping a maid to arrange the countess's seat comfortably in her huge, high carriage.

'Whose carriage is that?' asked Sonya, popping her head out of the carriage window.

'Why, haven't you heard, miss?' answered the maid. 'The wounded prince; he stayed the night in the house, and is going on with us.'

'Oh, who is he? what's his name?'

'Our betrothed that was . . . Prince Bolkonsky himself!' answered the maid, sighing. 'They say he is dying.'

Sonya jumped out of the carriage and ran in to the countess. The countess, dressed for the journey, in her hat and shawl, was walking wearily about the drawing-room, waiting for the rest of the household to come in and sit down with closed doors, for the usual silent prayer before setting out. Natasha was not in the room.

'Mamma,' said Sonya, 'Prince Andrey is here, wounded and dying. He is going with us.'

The countess opened her eyes in dismay, and clutching Sonya's arm, looked about her.

'Natasha,' she said.

Both to Sonya and the countess this news had for the first moment but one significance. They knew their Natasha, and alarm at the thought of the effect the news might have on her outweighed all sympathy for the man, though they both liked him.

'Natasha does not know yet, but he is going with us,' said Sonya.

'You say he is dying?'

Sonya nodded.

The countess embraced Sonya and burst into tears. 'The ways of the Lord are past our finding out!' she thought, feeling that in all that was passing now the Hand of the Almighty, hitherto unseen, was beginning to be manifest.

'Well, mamma, it's all ready. What is it? . . .' asked Natasha, running with her eager face into the room.

'Nothing,' said the countess. 'If we're ready, then do let us start.' And the countess bent over her reticule to hide her agitated face. Sonya embraced Natasha and kissed her.

Natasha looked inquisitively at her.

'What is it? What has happened?'

'Nothing, . . . oh, no, . . .'

'Something very bad, concerning me? . . . What is it?' asked the keen-witted Natasha.

Sonya sighed, and made no reply. The count, Petya, Madame Schoss, Mavra Kuzminishna, and Vassilitch came into the drawing-room; and closing the doors, they all sat down, and sat so in silence, without looking at each other for several seconds.

The count was the first to get up. With a loud sigh he crossed himself before the holy picture. All the others did the same. Then the count proceeded to embrace Mavra Kuzminishna and Vassilitch, who were to remain in Moscow; and while they caught at his hand and kissed his shoulder, he patted them on the back with vaguely affectionate and reassuring phrases. The countess went off to the little chapel, and Sonya found her there on her knees before the holy pictures, that were still left here and there on the walls. All the holy pictures most precious through association with the traditions of the family were being taken with them.

In the porch and in the yard the servants who were going—all of whom had been armed with swords and daggers by Petya—with their trousers tucked in their boots, and their sashes or leather belts tightly braced, took leave of those who were left behind.

As is invariably the case at starting on a journey, a great many things were found to have been forgotten, or packed in the wrong place; and two grooms were kept a long while standing, one each side of the open carriage door, ready to help the countess up the carriage steps, while maids were flying with pillows and bags from the house to the carriages, the coach, and the covered gig, and back again.

'They will always forget everything as long as they live!' said the countess. 'You know that I can't sit like that.' And Dunyasha, with clenched teeth and an aggrieved look on her face, rushed to the carriage to arrange the cushions again without a word.

'Ah, those servants,' said the count, shaking his head.

The postillion started his horse. The right-shaft horse began to pull, the high springs creaked, and the carriage swayed. The footman jumped up on the box while it was moving. The carriage jolted as it drove out of the yard on to the uneven pavement; the other vehicles jolted in the same way as they followed in a procession up the street. All the occupants of the carriages, the coach and the covered gig, crossed themselves on seeing the church opposite. The servants, who were staying in Moscow, walked along on both sides of the carriages to see them off.

Natasha had rarely felt such a joyful sensation as she experienced at that moment sitting in the carriage by the countess and watching, as they slowly moved by her, the walls of forsaken, agitated Moscow.

Now and then she put her head out of the carriage window and looked back, and then in front at the long train of waggons full of wounded soldiers preceding them. Foremost of them all she could see Prince Andrey's closed carriage. She did not know who was in it, and every time she took stock of the procession of waggons she looked out for that coach. She knew it would be the foremost. In Kudrino, and from Nikitsky Street, from Pryesny, and from Podnovinsky several trains of vehicles, similar to the Rostovs', came driving out, and by the time they reached Sadovoy Street the carriages and cars were two deep all along the road.

When Natasha had been told that morning that Prince Andrey was seriously wounded, and was travelling with them, she had at the first moment asked a great many questions, how and why and where was he going; whether he were dangerously wounded, and whether she could see him. But after she had been told that she could not see him, that his wound was a serious one, but that his life was not in danger, though she plainly did not believe what was told her, she saw that she would get the same answer whatever she said, and gave up asking questions and speaking at all. All the way Natasha had sat motionless in the corner of the carriage with those wide eyes, the look in which the countess knew so well and dreaded so much. And she was sitting in just the same way now on the bench in the hut. She was brooding on some plan; she was making, or already by now had made some decision, in her own mind—that the countess knew, but what that decision was she did not know, and that alarmed and worried her.

'Natasha, undress, darling, get into my bed.'

For the countess only a bed had been made up on a bedstead. Madame Schoss and the two girls were to sleep on hay on the floor.

'No, mamma, I'll lie here on the floor,' said Natasha irritably; she went to the window and opened it. The moans of the adjutant could be heard more distinctly from the open window. She put her head out into the damp night air, and the countess saw her slender neck shaking with sobs and heaving against the window frame. Natasha knew it was not Prince Andrey moaning. She knew that Prince Andrey was in the same block of huts as they were in, that he was in the next hut just across the porch, but that fearful never ceasing moan made her sob. The countess exchanged glances with Sonya.

'Go to bed, darling, go to bed, my pet,' said the countess, lightly touching Natasha's shoulder. 'Come, go to bed.'

'Oh yes . . . I'll go to bed at once,' said Natasha, hurriedly undressing, and breaking the strings of her petticoats. Dropping off her dress, and putting on a dressing-jacket, she sat down on the bed made up on the floor, tucking her feet under her, and flinging her short, fine hair over her shoulder, began plaiting it. Her thin, long, practised fingers rapidly and deftly divided, plaited, and tied up her hair. Natasha's head turned from side to side as usual as she did this, but her eyes, feverishly wide, looked straight before her with the same fixed stare. When her toilet for the night was over, Natasha sank softly down on to the sheet laid on the hay nearest the door.

For a long while Natasha listened to the sounds that reached her from within and without, and she did not stir. She heard at first her mother's prayers and sighs, the creaking of her bed under her, Madame Schoss's familiar, whistling snore, Sonya's soft breathing. Then the countess called to Natasha. Natasha did not answer.

'I think she's asleep, mamma,' answered Sonya.

The countess, after a brief silence, spoke again, but this time no one answered her.

Soon after this Natasha caught the sound of her mother's even breathing. Natasha did not stir, though her little bare foot, poking out below the quilt, felt frozen against the uncovered floor.

A cricket chirped in a crack, as though celebrating a victory over all the world. A cock crowed far away, and another answered close by. The shouts had died away in the tavern, but the adjutant's moaning went on still the same. Natasha sat up.

'Sonya! Are you asleep? Mamma!' she whispered. No one answered. Slowly and cautiously Natasha got up, crossed herself, and stepped cautiously with her slender, supple, bare feet on to the dirty, cold floor. The boards creaked. With nimble feet she ran like a kitten a few steps, and took hold of the cold door-handle.

It seemed to her that something with heavy, rhythmical strokes was banging on all the walls of the hut; it was the beating of her own heart, torn with dread, with love and terror.

She opened the door, stepped over the lintel, and on to the damp, cold earth of the passage outside. The cold all about her refreshed her.

152

Her bare foot felt a man asleep; she stepped over him, and opened the door of the hut in which Prince Andrey was lying.

In that hut it was dark. A tallow candle with a great, smouldering wick stood on a bench in the further corner, by a bed, on which something was lying.

Ever since she had been told in the morning of Prince Andrey's wound and his presence there, Natasha had resolved that she must see him. She could not have said why this must be, but she knew their meeting would be anguish to her, and that made her the more certain that it must be inevitable.

All day long she had lived in the hope that at night she would see him. But now when the moment had come, a terror came over her of what she would see. How had he been disfigured? What was left of him? Was he like that unceasing moan of the adjutant? Yes, he was all over like that. In her imagination he was that awful moan of pain personified. When she caught sight of an undefined mass in the corner, and took his raised knees under the quilt for his shoulders, she pictured some fearful body there, and stood still in terror. But an irresistible force drew her forward. She made one cautious step, another, and found herself in the middle of the small hut, cumbered up with baggage. On the bench, under the holy images, lay another man (this was Timohin), and on the floor were two more figures (the doctor and the valet).

The valet sat up and muttered something. Timohin, in pain from a wound in his leg, was not asleep, and gazed, all eyes, at the strange apparition of a girl in a white night-gown, dressing-jacket, and nightcap. The valet's sleepy and frightened words: 'What is it? What do you want?' only made Natasha hasten towards the figure lying in the corner. However fearfully unlike a human shape that figure might be now, she must see him. She passed by the valet, the smouldering candle flicked up, and she saw clearly Prince Andrey, lying with his arms stretched out on the quilt, looking just as she had always seen him.

He was just the same as ever; but the flush on his face, his shining eyes, gazing passionately at her, and especially the soft, childlike neck, showing above the lay-down collar of the nightshirt, gave him a peculiarly innocent, childlike look, such as she had never seen in him before. She ran up to him and with a swift, supple, youthful movement dropped on her knees.

He smiled, and held out his hand to her.

'You?' he said. 'What happiness!'

With a swift but circumspect movement, Natasha came nearer, still kneeling, and carefully taking his hand she bent her face over it and began kissing it, softly touching it with her lips.

'Forgive me!' she said in a whisper, lifting her head and glancing at him. 'Forgive me!'

'I love you,' said Prince Andrey.

'Forgive . . .'

'Forgive what?' asked Prince Andrey.

'Forgive me for what I di . . . id,' Natasha murmured in a hardly audible, broken whisper, and again and again she softly put her lips to his hand.

'I love thee more, better than before,' said Prince Andrey, lifting her face with his hand so that he could look into her eyes.

Those eyes, swimming with happy tears, gazed at him with timid commiseration and joyful love. Natasha's thin, pale face, with its swollen lips, was more than ugly—it looked terrible. But Prince Andrey did not see her face, he saw the shining eyes, which were beautiful. They heard talk behind them.

Pyotr, the valet, by now wide awake, had woken up the doctor. Timohin, who had not slept all night for the pain in his leg, had been long watching all that was happening, and huddled up on his bench, carefully wrapping his bare person up in the sheet.

'Why, what's this?' said the doctor, getting up from his bed on the floor. 'Kindly retire, madam.'

At that moment there was a knock at the door; a maid had been sent by the countess in search of her daughter.

Like a sleep-walker awakened in the midst of her trance, Natasha walked out of the room, and getting back to her hut, sank sobbing on her bed.

From that day at all the halts and resting-places on the remainder of the Rostovs' journey, Natasha never left Bolkonsky's side, and the doctor was forced to admit that he had not expected from a young girl so much fortitude, nor skill in nursing a wounded man.

Terrible as it was to the countess to think that Prince Andrey might (and very probably, too, from what the doctor said) die on the road in her daughter's arms, she could not resist Natasha. Although with the renewal of affectionate relations between Prince Andrey and Natasha the idea did occur that in case he recovered their old engagement would be renewed, no one—least of all Natasha and Prince Andrey— spoke of this. The unsettled question of life and death hanging, not only over Prince Andrey, but over all Russia, shut off all other considerations.

THE STORY OF DOCTOR DOLITTLE

Hugh Lofting

This is the beginning of the story of how the famous Doctor Dolittle becomes an animal-doctor.

Once upon a time, many years ago—when our grandfathers were little children—there was a doctor; and his name was Dolittle—John Dolittle, M.D. 'M.D.' means that he was a proper doctor and knew a whole lot.

He lived in a little town called Puddleby-on-the-Marsh. All the folks, young and old, knew him well by sight. And whenever he walked down the street in his high hat everyone would say, 'There goes the Doctor!—he's a clever man.' And the dogs and the children would all run up and follow behind him; and even the crows that lived in the church tower would caw and nod their heads.

The house he lived in, on the edge of the town, was quite small; but his garden was very large and had a wide lawn and stone seats and weeping-willows hanging over. His sister, Sarah Dolittle, was house-keeper for him; but the Doctor looked after the garden himself.

He was very fond of animals and kept many kinds of pets. Besides the goldfish in the pond at the bottom of his garden, he had rabbits in the pantry, white mice in his piano, a squirrel in the linen closet, and a hedgehog in the cellar. He had a cow with a calf too, and an old lame horse—twenty-five years of age—and chickens, and pigeons, and two lambs, and many other animals. But his favourite pets were Dab-Dab the duck, Jip the dog, Gub-Gub the baby pig, Polynesia the parrot, and the owl Too-Too.

His sister used to grumble about all these animals and said they made the house untidy. And one day when an old lady with rheumatism came to see the Doctor, she sat on the hedgehog who was sleeping on the sofa and never came to see him any more, but drove every Saturday all the way to Oxenthorpe, another town ten miles off, to see a different doctor.

Then his sister, Sarah Dolittle, came to him and said,

'John, how can you expect sick people to come and see you when you keep all these animals in the house? It's a fine doctor would have his parlour full of hedgehogs and mice! That's the fourth personage these animals have driven away. Squire Jenkins and the Parson say they wouldn't come near your house again—no matter how sick they are. We are getting poorer every day. If you go on like this, none of the best people will have you for a doctor.'

'But I like the animals better than the "best people",' said the Doctor.

'You are ridiculous,' said his sister, and walked out of the room.

So, as time went on, the Doctor got more and more animals; and the people who came to see him got less and less, till at last he had no one left—except the Cat's-meat-Man, who didn't mind any kind of animals. But the Cat's-meat-Man wasn't very rich and he only got sick once a year—at Christmas-time, when he used to give the Doctor sixpence for a bottle of medicine.

Sixpence a year wasn't enough to live on—even in those days, long ago; and if the Doctor hadn't had some money saved up in his money-box, no one knows what would have happened.

And he kept on getting still more pets; and of course it cost a lot to feed them. And the money he had saved up grew littler and littler.

Then he sold his piano, and let the mice live in a bureau drawer. But the money he got for that too began to go, so he sold the brown suit he wore on Sundays and went on becoming poorer and poorer.

And now, when he walked down the street in his high hat, people would say to one another, 'There goes John Dolittle, M.D.! There was a time when he was the best-known doctor in the West Country. Look at him now—he hasn't any money and his stockings are full of holes!'

But the dogs and cats and the children still ran up and followed him through the town—the same as they had done when he was rich.

ANIMAL-LANGUAGE

It happened one day that the Doctor was sitting in his kitchen talking with the Cat's-meat-Man who had come to see him with a stomach-ache.

'Why don't you give up being a people's doctor, and be an animal-doctor?' asked the Cat's-meat-Man.

The parrot, Polynesia, was sitting in the window looking out at the rain and singing a sailor-song to herself. She stopped singing and started to listen.

'You see, Doctor,' the Cat's-meat-Man went on, 'you know all about animals—much more than what these here vets do. That book you wrote—about cats, why, it's wonderful! I can't read or write myself—or maybe I'd write some books. But my wife, Theodosia, she's a scholar, she is. And she read your book to me. Well, it's wonderful—that's all can be said—wonderful. You might have been a cat yourself. You know the way they think. And listen: you can make a lot of money doctoring animals. Do you know that? You see, I'd send all the old women who had sick cats or dogs to you. And if they didn't get sick fast enough, I could put something in the meat I sell 'em to make 'em sick, see?'

'Oh, no,' said the Doctor quickly. 'You mustn't do that, that wouldn't be right.'

'Oh, I didn't mean real sick,' answered the Cat's-meat-Man. 'Just a little something to make them droopy-like was what I had reference to. But as you say, maybe it ain't quite fair on the animals. But they'll get sick anyway, because the old women always give 'em too much to eat. And look, all the farmers round about who had lame horses and weak lambs—they'd come. Be an animal-doctor.'

When the Cat's-meat-Man had gone the parrot flew off the window on to the Doctor's table and said:

'That man's got sense. That's what you ought to do. Be an animal-doctor. Give the silly people up—if they haven't brains enough to see you're the best doctor in the world. Take care of animals instead—they'll soon find it out. Be an animal-doctor.'

'Oh, there are plenty of animal-doctors,' said John Dolittle, putting the flower-pots outside on the window-sill to get the rain.

'Yes, there *are* plenty,' said Polynesia. 'But none of them are any good at all. Now listen, Doctor, and I'll tell you something. Did you know that animals can talk?'

'I knew that parrots can talk,' said the Doctor.

'Oh, we parrots can talk in two languages—people's language and bird-language,' said Polynesia proudly. 'If I say, "Polly wants a cracker," you understand me. But hear this: *Ka-ka oi-ee, fee-fee?*'

'Good gracious!' cried the Doctor. 'What does that mean?'

'That means, "Is this porridge hot yet?"—in bird-language.'

'My! You don't say so!' said the Doctor. 'You never talked that way to me before.'

'What would have been the good?' said Polynesia, dusting some cracker-crumbs off her left wing. 'You wouldn't have understood me if I had.'

'Tell me some more,' said the Doctor, all excited; and he rushed over to the dresser-drawer and came back with the butcher's book and a pencil. 'Now don't go too fast—and I'll write it down. This is interesting—very interesting—something quite new. Give me the birds' A.B.C. first—slowly now.'

So that was the way the Doctor came to know that animals had a language of their own and could talk to one another. And all that afternoon, while it was raining, Polynesia sat on the kitchen table giving him bird words to put down in the book.

At tea-time, when the dog, Jip, came in, the parrot said to the Doctor, 'See, *he's* talking to you.'

'Looks to me as though he were scratching his ear,' said the Doctor.

'But animals don't always speak with their mouths,' said the parrot in a high voice, raising her eyebrows. 'They talk with their ears, with their feet, with their tails—with everything. Sometimes they don't *want* to make a noise. Do you see now the way he's twitching up one side of his nose?'

'What's that mean?' asked the Doctor.

'That means, "Can't you see that it's stopped raining?" ' Polynesia answered. 'He is asking you a question. Dogs nearly always use their noses for asking questions.'

After a while, with the parrot's help, the Doctor got to learn the language of the animals so well that he could talk to them himself and understand everything they said. Then he gave up being a people's doctor altogether.

As soon as the Cat's-meat-Man had told everyone that John Dolittle was going to become an animal-doctor, old ladies began to bring him their pet pugs and poodles who had eaten too much cake; and farmers came many miles to show him sick cows and sheep.

One day a plough horse was brought to him; and the poor thing was terribly glad to find a man who could talk in horse-language.

'You know, Doctor,' said the horse, 'that vet over the hill knows nothing at all. He has been treating me six weeks now—for spavins. What I need is *spectacles*. I am going blind in one eye. There's no reason why horses shouldn't wear glasses, the same as people. But that stupid man over the hill never even looked at my eyes. He kept on giving me big pills. I tried to tell him; but he couldn't understand a word of horse-language. What I need is spectacles.'

'Of course—of course,' said the Doctor. 'I'll get you some at once.'

'I would like a pair like yours,' said the horse, 'only green. They'll keep the sun out of my eyes while I'm ploughing the Fifty Acre Field.'

'Certainly,' said the Doctor. 'Green ones you shall have.'

'You know, the trouble is, sir,' said the plough horse as the Doctor opened the front door to let him out, 'the trouble is that *anybody* thinks he can doctor animals—just because the animals don't complain. As a matter of fact it takes a much cleverer man to be a really good animal-doctor than it does to be a people's doctor. My farmer's boy thinks he knows all about horses. I wish you could see him—his face is so fat he looks as though he has no eyes—and he has got as much brain as a potato-bug. He tried to put a mustard-plaster on me last week.'

'Where did he put it?' asked the Doctor.

'Oh, he didn't put it anywhere—on me,' said the horse. 'He only tried to. I kicked him into the duck-pond.'

'Well, well!' said the Doctor.

'I'm a pretty quiet creature as a rule,' said the horse, 'very patient with people—don't make much fuss. But it was bad enough to have that vet giving me the wrong medicine. And when that red-faced booby started to monkey with me, I just couldn't bear it any more.'

'Did you hurt the boy much?' asked the Doctor.

'Oh, no,' said the horse. 'I kicked him in the right place. The vet's looking after him now. When will my glasses be ready?'

'I'll have them for you next week,' said the Doctor. 'Come in again Tuesday. Good morning!'

Then John Dolittle got a fine, big pair of green spectacles; and the plough horse stopped going blind in one eye and could see as well as ever.

And soon it became a common sight to see farm-animals wearing glasses in the country round Puddleby; and a blind horse was a thing unknown.

And so, in a few years' time, every living thing for miles and miles got to know about John Dolittle, M.D. And the birds who flew to other countries in the winter told the animals in foreign lands of the wonderful doctor of Puddleby-on-the-Marsh, who could understand their talk and help them in their troubles. In this way he became famous among the animals all over the world; better known even than he had been among the folks of the West Country. And he was happy and liked his life very much.

One afternoon when the Doctor was busy writing in a book, Polynesia sat in the window—as she nearly always did—looking out at the leaves blowing about in the garden.

The Doctor looked up and said, 'How old are you, Polynesia? I know that parrots and elephants sometimes live to be very, very old.'

'I can never be quite sure of my age,' said Polynesia. 'It's either a hundred and eighty-three or a hundred and eighty-two. But I know that when I first came here from Africa, King Charles was still hiding in the oak-tree—because I saw him. He looked scared to death.'

MORE MONEY TROUBLES

And soon now the Doctor began to make money again; and his sister, Sarah, bought a new dress and was happy.

Some of the animals who came to see him were so sick that they had to stay at the Doctor's house for a week. And when they were getting better they used to sit in chairs on the lawn.

And often, even after they got on well, they did not want to go away—they liked the Doctor and his house so much. And he never had the heart to refuse them when they asked if they could stay with him. So in this way he went on getting more and more pets.

Once when he was sitting on his garden wall, smoking a pipe in the evening, an organ-grinder came round with a monkey on a string. The Doctor saw at once that the monkey's collar was too tight and that he was dirty and unhappy. So he took the monkey away from the organ-grinder, gave the man a shilling and told him to go. The organ-grinder got awfully angry and said that he wanted to keep the monkey. But the Doctor told him that if he didn't go he would punch him on the nose. John Dolittle was a strong man, though he wasn't very tall. So the man went away saying rude things and the monkey stayed with Doctor Dolittle and had a good home. The other animals in the house called him 'Chee-Chee'—which is a common word in monkey-language, meaning 'ginger'.

And another time, when the circus came to Puddleby, the crocodile, who had a bad toothache, escaped at night and came into the Doctor's garden. The Doctor talked to him in crocodile-language and took him into the house and made his tooth better. But when the crocodile saw what a nice house it was—with all the different places for the different kinds of animals—he, too, wanted to live with the Doctor. He asked couldn't he sleep in the fish-pond at the bottom of the garden, if he promised not to eat the fish. When the circus-men came to take him back he got so wild and savage that he frightened them away. But to everyone in the house he was always as gentle as a kitten.

But now the old ladies grew afraid to send their lap-dogs to Doctor Dolittle because of the crocodile; and the farmers wouldn't believe that he would not eat the lambs and sick calves they brought to be cured. So the Doctor went to the crocodile and told him he must go back to the circus. But he wept such big tears, and begged so hard to be allowed to stay, that the Doctor hadn't the heart to turn him out.

So then the Doctor's sister came to him and said,

'John, you must send that creature away. Now the farmers and the old ladies are afraid to send their animals to you—just as we were beginning to be well off again. Now we shall be ruined entirely. This is the last straw. I will no longer be housekeeper for you if you don't send away that alligator.'

'It isn't an alligator,' said the Doctor, 'it's a crocodile.'

'I don't care what you call it,' said his sister. 'It's a nasty thing to find under the bed. I won't have it in the house.'

'But he has promised me,' the Doctor answered, 'that he will not bite anyone. He doesn't like the circus; and I haven't the money to send him back to Africa where he comes from. He minds his own business and on the whole is very well behaved. Don't be so fussy.'

'I tell you I *will not* have him around,' said Sarah. 'He eats the linoleum. If you don't send him away this minute I'll—I'll go and get married!'

'All right,' said the Doctor, 'go and get married. It can't be helped.' And he took his hat and went out into the garden.

So Sarah Dolittle packed her things and went off; and the Doctor was left alone with his animal family.

And very soon he was poorer than he had ever been before. With all these mouths to fill, and the house to look after, and no one to do the mending, and no money coming in to pay the butcher's bill, things began to look very difficult. But the Doctor didn't worry at all.

'Money is a nuisance,' he used to say. 'We'd all be much better off if it had never been invented. What does money matter, so long as we are happy?'

But Too-Too, the owl, who was good at arithmetic, figured out that there was only money enough left to last another week—if they each had one meal a day and no more.

Then the animals made a vegetable and flower stall outside the garden-gate and sold radishes and roses to the people that passed by along the road.

But still they didn't seem to make enough money to pay all the bills— and still the Doctor didn't worry.

He didn't even worry when Chee-Chee, the monkey, came to him panting and badly out of breath.

'Doctor!' he cried. 'I've just had a message from a cousin of mine in Africa. There is a terrible sickness among the monkeys out there. They are all catching it—and they are dying in hundreds.'

'Dear me!' said the Doctor. 'Then we shall just have to go to Africa.'

'But that takes money,' said Dab-Dab, who was always practical about such things.

'Well, well,' murmured the Doctor. 'Never mind. Perhaps if I go down to the seaside I shall be able to borrow a boat that will take us to Africa. I knew a seaman once who brought his baby to me with measles. Maybe he'll lend me his boat—the baby got well.'

So early the next morning the Doctor went down to the seashore. And when he came back he told the animals it was all right—the sailor was going to lend them the boat.

The sailor even borrowed enough food for them to stock the ship for the journey, and the Doctor and his whole family went off to Africa.

Although the ship was wrecked in a bad storm on the coast of Africa, they all got ashore safely.

It didn't take Doctor Dolittle long to cure the monkeys of their sickness, and they were so grateful they wanted to give him a going-away present. They asked Chee-Chee what the Doctor would like.

'Why not give him a rare animal,' suggested Chee-Chee. 'He could then charge people to see it and never have to be without money again.'

And the chief of the monkeys asked:

'Have they an iguana over there?'

'Yes, there is one in the London Zoo,' replied Chee-Chee.

And another asked, 'Have they an okapi?'

But Chee-Chee said, 'Yes, in Belgium, where my organ-grinder took me five years ago, they have an okapi in a big city they call Antwerp.'

And another asked, 'Have they a pushmi-pullyu?'

Then Chee-Chee said, 'No. No white man has ever seen a pushmi-pullyu. Let us give him that.'

THE RAREST ANIMAL OF ALL

Pushmi-Pullyus are now extinct. That means there aren't any more. But long ago, when Doctor Dolittle was alive, there were some of them still left in the deepest jungle of Africa; and even then they were very scarce.

They had no tail, but a head at each end, and sharp horns on each head. They were very shy and terribly hard to catch. The natives get most of their animals by sneaking up behind them while they are not looking. But you could not do this with the pushmi-pullyu, because, no matter which way you came towards him, he was always facing you. And besides, only one half of him slept at a time. The other head was always awake—and watching. This was why they were never caught and never seen in zoos. Though many of the greatest huntsmen and the cleverest menagerie-keepers spent years of their lives searching through the jungles in all weathers for pushmi-pullyus, not a single one had ever been caught. Even then, years ago, he was the only animal in the world with two heads.

Well, the monkeys set out hunting for this animal through the forest. And after they had gone a good many miles, one of them found peculiar footprints near the edge of a river; and they knew that a pushmi-pullyu must be very near the spot.

Then they went along the bank of the river a little way and they saw a place where the grass was high and thick; and they guessed that he was in there.

So they all joined hands and made a great circle round the high grass. The pushmi-pullyu heard them coming; and he tried hard to break through the ring of monkeys. But he couldn't do it. When he saw that it was no use trying to escape, he sat down and waited to see what they wanted.

They asked him if he would go with Doctor Dolittle and be put on show in the Land of the White Men.

But he shook both his heads hard and said, 'Certainly not!'

They explained to him that he would not be shut up in a menagerie but would just be looked at. They told him that the Doctor was a very kind man but hadn't any money; and people would pay to see a two-headed animal and the Doctor would get rich and could pay for the boat he had borrowed to come to Africa in.

But he answered, 'No. You know how shy I am—I hate being stared at.' And he almost began to cry.

Then for three days they tried to persuade him.

And at the end of the third day he said he would come with them and see what kind of a man the Doctor was, first.

So the monkeys travelled back with the pushmi-pullyu. And when they came to where the Doctor's little house of grass was, they knocked on the door.

The duck, who was packing the trunk, said, 'Come in!'

And Chee-Chee very proudly took the animal inside and showed him to the Doctor.

'What in the world is it?' asked John Dolittle, gazing at the strange creature.

'Lord save us!' cried the duck. 'How does it make up its mind?'

'It doesn't look to me as though it had any,' said Jip the dog.

'This, Doctor,' said Chee-Chee, 'is the pushmi-pullyu—the rarest animal of the African jungles, the only two-headed beast in the world! Take him home with you and your fortune's made. People will pay any money to see him.'

'But I don't want any money,' said the Doctor.

'Yes, you do,' said Dab-Dab the duck. 'Don't you remember how we had to pinch and scrape to pay the butcher's bill in Puddleby? And how are you going to get the sailor the new boat you spoke of—unless we have the money to buy it?'

'I was going to make him one,' said the Doctor.

'Oh, do be sensible!' cried Dab-Dab. 'Where would you get all the wood and the nails to make one with?—And besides, what are we going to live on? We shall be poorer than ever when we get back. Chee-Chee's perfectly right: take the funny-looking thing along, do!'

'Well, perhaps there is something in what you say,' murmured the Doctor. 'It certainly would make a nice new kind of pet. But does the—er—what-do-you-call-it really want to go abroad?'

'Yes, I'll go,' said the pushmi-pullyu who saw at once, from the Doctor's face, that he was a man to be trusted. 'You have been so kind to the animals here—and the monkeys tell me that I am the only one who will do. But you must promise me that if I do not like it in the Land of the White Men you will send me back.'

'Why, certainly—of course, of course,' said the Doctor. 'Excuse me, surely you are related to the Deer Family, are you not?'

'Yes,' said the pushmi-pullyu, 'to the Abyssinian Gazelles and the Asiatic Chamois—on my mother's side. My father's great-grandfather was the last of the Unicorns.'

166

'Most interesting!' murmured the Doctor; and he took a book out of the trunk which Dab-Dab was packing and began turning the pages. 'Let us see if Buffon says anything—'

'I notice,' said the duck, 'that you only talk with one of your mouths. Can't the other head talk as well?'

'Oh, yes,' said the pushmi-pullyu. 'But I keep the other mouth for eating—mostly. In that way I can talk while I am eating without being rude. Our people have always been very polite.'

When the packing was finished and everything was ready to start, the monkeys gave a grand party for the Doctor, and all the animals of the jungle came. And they had pineapples and mangoes and honey and all sorts of good things to eat and drink.

After they had all finished eating, the Doctor got up and said,

'My friends: I am not clever at speaking long words after dinner, like some men; and I have just eaten many fruits and much honey. But I wish to tell you that I am very sad at leaving your beautiful country. Because I have things to do in the Land of the White Men, I must go. After I have gone, remember never to let the flies settle on your food before you eat it; and do not sleep on the ground when the rains are coming. I—er—er—I hope you will all live happily ever after.'

When the Doctor stopped speaking and sat down, all the monkeys clapped their hands a long time and said to one another, 'Let it be remembered always among our people that he sat and ate with us, here, under the trees. For surely he is the Greatest of Men!'

And the Grand Gorilla, who had the strength of seven horses in his hairy arms, rolled a great rock up to the head of the table and said,

'This stone for all time shall mark the spot.'

And even to this day, in the heart of the jungle, that stone still is there. And monkey-mothers, passing through the forest with their families, still point down at it from the branches and whisper to their children, 'Sh! There it is—look—where the Good White Man sat and ate food with us in the Year of the Great Sickness!'

Then, when the party was over, the Doctor and his pets started out to go back to the seashore. And all the monkeys went with him as far as the edge of their country, carrying his trunk and bags, to see him off.

ALFRED, BATES AND BORIS

James Herriot

The wild unspoiled Yorkshire Dales provide the background to James Herriot's vivid memories of the daily ups and downs of a veterinary practice in the 1930s.

'I work for cats.'

That was how Mrs Bond introduced herself on my first visit, gripping my hand firmly and thrusting out her jaw defiantly as though challenging me to make something of it. She was a big woman with a strong, high-cheekboned face and a commanding presence and I wouldn't have argued with her anyway, so I nodded gravely as though I fully understood and agreed, and allowed her to lead me into the house.

I saw at once what she meant. The big kitchen-living room had been completely given over to cats. There were cats on the sofas and chairs and spilling in cascades on to the floor, cats sitting in rows along the window sills and right in the middle of it all, little Mr Bond, pallid, wispy-moustached, in his shirt sleeves reading a newspaper.

It was a scene which was going to become very familiar. A lot of the cats were obviously uncastrated Toms because the atmosphere was vibrant with their distinctive smell—a fierce pungency which overwhelmed even the sickly wisps from the big saucepans of nameless cat food bubbling on the stove. And Mr Bond was always there, always in his shirt sleeves and reading his paper, a lonely little island in a sea of cats.

I had heard of the Bonds, of course. They were Londoners who for some obscure reason had picked on North Yorkshire for their retirement. People said they had a 'bit o' brass' and they had bought an old house on the outskirts of Darrowby where they kept themselves to themselves—and the cats. I had heard that Mrs Bond was in the habit of taking in strays and feeding them and giving them a home if they wanted it and this had predisposed me in her favour, because in my experience the unfortunate feline species seemed to be fair game for every kind of cruelty and neglect. They shot cats, threw things at them, starved them and set their dogs on them for fun. It was good to see somebody taking their side.

My patient on this first visit was no more than a big kitten, a terrified little blob of black and white crouching in a corner.

'He's one of the outside cats,' Mrs Bond boomed.

'Outside cats?'

'Yes. All these you see here are the inside cats. The others are the really wild ones who simply refuse to enter the house. I feed them of course but the only time they come indoors is when they are ill.'

'I see.'

'I've had frightful trouble catching this one. I'm worried about his eyes—there seemed to be a skin growing over them, and I do hope you can do something for him. His name, by the way, is Alfred.'

'Alfred? Ah yes, quite.' I advanced cautiously on the little half-grown animal and was greeted by a waving set of claws and a series of open-mouthed spittings. He was trapped in his corner or he would have been off with the speed of light.

Examining him was going to be a problem. I turned to Mrs Bond. 'Could you let me have a sheet of some kind? An old ironing sheet would do. I'm going to have to wrap him up.'

'Wrap him up?' Mrs Bond looked very doubtful but she disappeared into another room and returned with a tattered sheet of cotton which looked just right.

I cleared the table of an amazing variety of cat feeding dishes, cat books, cat medicines and spread out the sheet, then I approached my patient again. You can't be in a hurry in a situation like this and it took me perhaps five minutes of wheedling and 'Puss-pussing' while I brought my hand nearer and nearer. When I got as far as being able to stroke his cheek I made a quick grab at the scruff of his neck and finally bore Alfred, protesting bitterly and lashing out in all directions, over to the table. There, still holding tightly to his scruff, I laid him on the sheet and started the wrapping operation.

This is something which has to be done quite often with obstreperous felines and, although I say it, I am rather good at it. The idea is to make a neat, tight roll, leaving the relevant piece of cat exposed; it may be an injured paw, perhaps the tail, and in this case of course the head. I think it was the beginning of Mrs Bond's unquestioning faith in me when she saw me quickly enveloping that cat till all you could see of him was a small black and white head protruding from an immovable cocoon of cloth. He and I were now facing each other, more or less eyeball to eyeball, and Alfred couldn't do a thing about it.

As I say, I rather pride myself on this little expertise and even today my veterinary colleagues have been known to remark: 'Old Herriot may be limited in many respects but by God he can wrap a cat.'

As it turned out, there wasn't a skin growing over Alfred's eyes. There never is.

'He's got a paralysis of the third eyelid, Mrs Bond. Animals have this membrane which flicks across the eye to protect it. In this case it hasn't gone back, probably because the cat is in low condition—maybe had a touch of cat flu or something else which has weakened him. I'll give him an injection of vitamins and leave you some powder to put in his food if you could keep him in for a few days. I think he'll be all right in a week or two.'

The injection presented no problems with Alfred furious but helpless inside his sheet and I had come to the end of my first visit to Mrs Bond's.

It was the first of many. The lady and I established an immediate rapport which was strengthened by the fact that I was always prepared to spend time over her assorted charges; crawling on my stomach under piles of logs in the outhouses to reach the outside cats, coaxing them down from trees, stalking them endlessly through the shrubbery. But from my point of view it was rewarding in many ways.

For instance there was the diversity of names she had for her cats. True to her London upbringing she had named many of the Toms after the great Arsenal team of those days. There was Eddie Hapgood, Cliff Bastin, Ted Drake, Wilf Copping, but she did slip up in one case because

170

Alex James had kittens three times a year with unfailing regularity.

Then there was her way of calling them home. The first time I saw her at this was on a still summer evening. The two cats she wanted me to see were out in the garden somewhere and I walked with her to the back door where she halted, clasped her hands across her bosom, closed her eyes and gave tongue in a mellifluous contralto.

'Bates, Bates, Bates, Ba-hates.' She actually sang out the words in a reverent monotone except for a delightful little lilt on the 'Ba-hates'. Then once more she inflated her ample rib cage like an operatic prima donna and out it came again, delivered with the utmost feeling.

'Bates, Bates, Bates, Ba-hates.'

Anyway it worked, because Bates the cat came trotting from behind a clump of laurel. There remained the other patient and I watched Mrs Bond with interest.

She took up the same stance, breathed in, closed her eyes, composed her features into a sweet half-smile and started again.

'Seven-times-three, Seven-times-three, Seven-times-three-hee.' It was set to the same melody as Bates with the same dulcet rise and fall at the end. She didn't get the quick response this time, though, and had to go through the performance again and again, and as the notes lingered on the still evening air the effect was startlingly like a muezzin calling the faithful to prayer.

At length she was successful and a fat tortoiseshell slunk apologetically along the wall-side into the house.

'By the way, Mrs Bond,' I asked, making my voice casual. 'I didn't quite catch the name of that last cat.'

'Oh, Seven-times-three?' She smiled reminiscently. 'Yes, she is a dear. She's had three kittens seven times running, you see, so I thought it rather a good name for her, don't you?'

'Yes, yes, I do indeed. Splendid name, splendid.'

Another thing which warmed me towards Mrs Bond was her concern for my safety. I appreciated this because it is a rare trait among animal owners. I can think of the trainer after one of his racehorses had kicked me clean out of a loose box examining the animal anxiously to see if it had damaged its foot; the little old lady dwarfed by the bristling, teeth-bared Alsatian saying: 'You'll be gentle with him won't you and I hope you won't hurt him—he's very nervous'; the farmer, after an exhausting calving which I feel certain has knocked about two years off my life expectancy, grunting morosely: 'I doubt you've tired that cow out, young man.'

Mrs Bond was different. She used to meet me at the door with an enormous pair of gauntlets to protect my hands against scratches and it was an inexpressible relief to find that somebody cared. It became part of the pattern of my life; walking up the garden path among the innumerable slinking, wild-eyed little creatures which were the outside cats, the ceremonial acceptance of the gloves at the door, then the entry into the charged atmosphere of the kitchen with little Mr Bond and his newspaper just visible among the milling furry bodies of the inside cats. I was never able to ascertain Mr Bond's attitude to cats—come to think of it he hardly ever said anything—but I had the impression he could take them or leave them.

The gauntlets were a big help and at times they were a veritable godsend. As in the case of Boris. Boris was an enormous blue-black member of the outside cats and my bête noire in more senses than one. I always cherished a private conviction that he had escaped from a zoo; I had never seen a domestic cat with such sleek, writhing muscles, such dedicated ferocity. I'm sure there was a bit of puma in Boris somewhere.

It had been a sad day for the cat colony when he turned up. I have always found it difficult to dislike any animal; most of the ones which try to do us a mischief are activated by fear, but Boris was different; he was a malevolent bully and after his arrival the frequency of my visits increased because of his habit of regularly beating up his colleagues. I was forever stitching up tattered ears, dressing gnawed limbs.

We had one trial of strength fairly early. Mrs Bond wanted me to give him a worm dose and I had the little tablet all ready in forceps. How I ever got hold of him I don't quite know, but I hustled him on to the table and did my wrapping act at lightning speed, swathing him in roll upon roll of stout material. Just for a few seconds I thought I had him as he stared up at me, his great brilliant eyes full of hate. But as I pushed my loaded forceps into his mouth he clamped his teeth viciously down on them and I could feel claws of amazing power tearing inside the sheet. It was all over in moments. A long leg shot out and ripped its way down my wrist, I let go my tight hold of the neck and in a flash Boris sank his teeth through the gauntlet into the ball of my thumb and was away. I was left standing there stupidly, holding the fragmented worm tablet in a bleeding hand and looking at the bunch of ribbons which had once been my wrapping sheet. From then on Boris loathed the very sight of me and the feeling was mutual.

But this was one of the few clouds in a serene sky. I continued to enjoy my visits there and life proceeded on a tranquil course except, perhaps, for some legpulling from my colleagues. They could never understand my willingness to spend so much time over a lot of cats. And of course this fitted in with the general attitude because Siegfried didn't believe in people keeping pets of any kind. He just couldn't understand their mentality and propounded his views to anybody who cared to listen. He himself, of course, kept five dogs and two cats. The dogs, all of them, travelled everywhere with him in the car and he fed dogs and cats every day with his own hands—wouldn't allow anybody else to do the job. In the evening all seven animals would pile themselves round his feet as he sat in his chair by the fire. To this day he is still as vehemently anti-pet as ever, though another generation of waving dogs' tails almost obscures him as he drives around and he also has several cats, a few tanks of tropical fish and a couple of snakes.

Tristan saw me in action at Mrs Bond's on only one occasion. I was collecting some long forceps from the instrument cupboard when he came into the room.

'Anything interesting, Jim?' he asked.

'No, not really. I'm just off to see one of the Bond cats. It's got a bone stuck between its teeth.'

The young man eyed me ruminatively for a moment. 'Think I'll come with you. I haven't seen much small animal stuff lately.'

As we went down the garden at the cat establishment I felt a twinge of embarrassment. One of the things which had built up my happy relationship with Mrs Bond was my tender concern for her charges. Even with the wildest and the fiercest I exhibited only gentleness, patience and solicitude; it wasn't really an act, it came quite naturally to me. However I couldn't help wondering what Tristan would think of my cat bedside manner.

Mrs Bond in the doorway had summed up the situation in a flash and had two pairs of gauntlets waiting. Tristan looked a little surprised as he received his pair but thanked the lady with typical charm. He looked still more surprised when he entered the kitchen, sniffed the rich atmosphere and surveyed the masses of furry creatures occupying almost every available inch of space.

'Mr Herriot, I'm afraid it's Boris who has the bone in his teeth,' Mrs Bond said.

'Boris!' My stomach lurched. 'How on earth are we going to catch him'

'Oh I've been rather clever,' she replied. 'I've managed to entice him with some of his favourite food into a cat basket.'

Tristan put his hand on a big wicker cage on the table. 'In here, is he?' he asked casually. He slipped back the catch and opened the lid. For something like a third of a second the coiled creature within and Tristan regarded each other tensely, then a sleek black body exploded silently from the basket past the young man's left ear on to the top of a tall cupboard.

'Christ!' said Tristan. 'What the hell was that?'

'That,' I said, 'was Boris, and now we've got to get hold of him again.' I climbed on to a chair, reached slowly on to the cupboard top and started 'Puss-puss-pussing' in my most beguiling tone.

After about a minute Tristan appeared to think he had a better idea; he made a sudden leap and grabbed Boris's tail. But only briefly, because the big cat freed himself in an instant and set off on a whirlwind circuit of the room; along the tops of cupboards and dressers, across the curtains, careering round and round like a wall of death rider.

Tristan stationed himself at a strategic point and as Boris shot past he swiped at him with one of the gauntlets.

'Missed the bloody thing!' he shouted in chagrin. 'But here he comes again . . . take that, you black sod! Damn it, I can't nail him!'

The docile little inside cats, startled by the scattering of plates and tins and pans and by Tristan's cries and arm wavings, began to run around in their turn, knocking over whatever Boris had missed. The noise and confusion even got through to Mr Bond because just for a moment he raised his head and looked around him in mild surprise at the hurtling bodies before returning to his newspaper.

Tristan, flushed with the excitement of the chase had really begun to enjoy himself. I cringed inwardly as he shouted over to me happily.

'Send him on, Jim, I'll get the bugger next time round!'

We never did catch Boris. We just had to leave the piece of bone to work its own way out, so it wasn't a successful veterinary visit. But Tristan as we got back into the car smiled contentedly.

'That was great, Jim. I didn't realize you had such fun with your pussies.'

Mrs Bond on the other hand, when I next saw her, was rather tight-lipped over the whole thing.

'Mr Herriot,' she said. 'I hope you aren't going to bring that young man with you again.'

DEENIE'S BRACE

Judy Blume

*Deenie suddenly discovers there is something wrong with her posture
—and not just from a beauty point of view. After endless visits to
doctors' surgeries, she is eventually told that she must wear an ugly,
bulging brace from the neck down to her hips for most of her teenage life.*

*This extract describes how Deenie has the brace fitted and how she must
come to terms with this crisis in her life.*

In the taxi, on the way to the hospital, Ma said, 'I don't see why Dr
Kliner can't do it himself. That's what we're paying for, isn't it?'

'Dr Stewart makes all the moulds,' Daddy told her. 'I asked the nurse
about it.'

At the hospital Daddy checked with some woman behind an
information desk and then we went down a long hallway to a door
marked PLASTER ROOM. 'This is it,' Daddy said, knocking. A nurse
opened the door and Daddy told her I was Deenie Fenner and that Dr
Stewart had called. The nurse smiled at me and said, 'We have five girls
to mould today and you're number three.' Then she told Daddy and Ma
they could wait outside and Dr Stewart would tell them when I was
done.

Ma grabbed me, hugged me and cried a little. But Daddy said,
'Deenie's going to be just fine.'

I pulled away from Ma and buried my head in Daddy's jacket. I
whispered, 'Don't go . . . I'm too scared.'

Daddy kissed the top of my head and said, 'There's nothing to be
afraid of. I promise. Just do whatever Dr Stewart tells you and it will all

be over soon.' He lifted my chin so I had to look at him. 'Okay?' he asked.

'Okay,' I said.

The nurse closed the door to the plaster room as soon as I stepped inside. I didn't even have a chance to look around before she pointed to a door and said, 'You can change in there. Take off all your clothes, including your shoes and put on both of these, one over the other.' She handed me two things that looked like very big socks.

The dressing room turned out to be a supply closet and I thought for sure somebody would open the door while I was naked so I tried to keep my back pressed against it the whole time I was getting changed. The things I had to wear were like body stockings. They fit very close and after I had gotten into the first one I looked down and noticed that you could see everything right through it. By the time I pulled the second one over the first you couldn't see as much and I was glad. Not that I have a lot to see but I didn't want Dr Stewart to see anything.

I adjusted the body stockings so they stretched from my neck down to my thighs. Just as I finished the nurse knocked on the door and called, 'Ready, Deenie?'

'I guess so,' I told her, opening the closet.

When I came out I saw that Dr Stewart was already there and so was some other guy dressed in a white coat.

Dr Stewart said, 'Deenie, I'd like you to meet Dr Hubdu and Mrs Inverness, who will both be assisting me.'

Mrs Inverness was the nurse who gave me the body stockings and Dr Hubdu was from some other country. I could tell by his accent.

'Jump right up here, Deenie,' Mrs Inverness said.

I climbed on to an examining table.

'Now lie down . . . put your head back . . . just relax.'

Dr Stewart and Dr Hubdu were busy studying my X-ray, which was flashed on the same kind of screen I saw in Dr Griffith's office. They mentioned a lot of words like *lumbar* and *thoracic* and I didn't know what they were talking about.

I looked around the plaster room trying to figure out what was going to happen. The room wasn't very big. There was a counter with a sink, like in our kitchen. And right in the middle of the room was some kind of strange steel contraption with a rope hanging from a wheel on the ceiling.

In a minute Dr Stewart was measuring me again and calling out funny numbers and names to Dr Hubdu, who wrote everything down. The only words I got were *iliac crest* and *body firm*, whatever they meant.

'Okay, Deenie,' Mrs Inverness said. 'You can come off the table now.'

'Dr Stewart sat down on a stool in front of the contraption with ropes. He motioned to me and I walked over to him. He held up some funny looking thing and said, 'This is a head halter.' While he was talking he slipped it on me. It was made of two strips of white material and some string. One section of material fitted under my chin and felt like a scarf was tied there. The other part fitted around the back of my head and felt like I was wearing a head-band.

As soon as that was on me Dr Stewart attached a wooden bar to the rope coming from the ceiling and somehow he hooked my head-halter to that. I was sure he was going to pull on the rope and leave me hanging in mid-air but just as I was about to ask him what was going on he said, 'We call this *hanging the patient* but you aren't really going to hang, because your feet won't leave the ground.'

I was glad to hear that.

Mrs Inverness said, 'Hold on to the bar above your head, Deenie. With both hands please.'

I reached up and grabbed hold of the bar.

'That's it,' Mrs Inverness said. 'Very good. You hold that the whole time.'

'Dr Hubdu was behind me adjusting another wooden bar which came just under my backside. Dr Stewart told me to lean against it. I did but I guess I didn't do it the right way because Dr Hubdu said, 'Squat a little, please. Now just rest yourself against the bar as though you were sitting on it. That's better.'

Dr Stewart said, 'Lean forward a little. Good . . . just fine.'

Mrs Inverness ran a long piece of felt under my body stockings and down my back. Then Dr Stewart tied a strip of adhesive around my waist and attached each end to the wooden bar I was resting my rear end against.

After that he stood up and opened a small package of rubber gloves. I watched as he pulled them on. While he was doing that Mrs Inverness was busy at the sink in front of me. She was wetting strips of something. As soon as Dr Stewart sat on his stool again, Mrs Inverness handed him the wet strips and he began to wrap them around me. But after the first few he said, 'I'm not happy with this plaster, Nurse. Give me another roll please.' And he ripped off the strips.

As he waited for Mrs Inverness to wet some more he told me, 'When this dries it will become solid plaster. I have to wrap you tight in order to accentuate the hip line and chest. The brace will be made from this mould.'

I didn't say anything.

Mrs Inverness handed him some more strips and after he wrapped a couple of pieces around me he said, 'That's much better.' He wrapped me from my waist down to my hips and then from my waist up to my armpits. All this time Dr Hubdu stood behind me and I could feel his breath on my neck. 'Make sure her back is perfectly straight,' Dr Stewart told him.

'Yes sir,' Dr Hubdu answered. I got the feeling he was just learning about what was going on.

As Dr Stewart wrapped me up he smoothed the plaster with his hands. I didn't like it at all when he had to smooth out the strips across my chest.

'Head up, Deenie,' Dr Stewart said.

'Watch a point in front of you,' Mrs Inverness suggested.

Now both doctors were pressing on me, one at my back, the other at my front and I tried hard to stare at the handle of the cabinet over the sink.

'Stay just like that,' Dr Stewart said, as he moved his hands faster. 'We'll be finished in no time.'

'There are still some creases in the back, sir.' Dr Hubdu said.

'Smooth them out,' Dr Stewart said. 'We can't have any wrinkles.'

I thought about telling Dr Stewart that he was wrapping me too tight. That I really couldn't breathe any more. But that's when he said, 'Deenie's very cooperative, isn't she?'

And Dr Hubdu told him, 'She certainly is.'

I knew Daddy would be proud to hear that so I didn't say anything about feeling like a mummy.

A second later Dr Stewart ripped off his gloves and said, 'That's the worst of it, Deenie. In a minute the mould will be hard and we'll cut you out of it.'

'It's very tight,' I said. 'And it's starting to feel hot too.'

'That's the chemical reaction. It's changing into hard plaster now.'

'I'm glad I don't have to wear anything like this mould,' I told him.

'Some scoliosis patients are put into casts,' Dr Stewart said. 'But your brace will be a lot different. You won't mind it at all once you're used to it.'

Soon Mrs Inverness tapped me and said, 'It's hard, doctor.'

Dr Stewart felt me himself. 'Good . . .' He whipped a ballpoint pen out of his pocket and drew little lines up and down my mould. Then he measured me again and Dr Hubdu wrote everything down, just like before. 'This will help the brace man,' Dr Stewart told me. 'Okay, Deenie . . . I'm going to cut it off you now. My saw makes a lot of noise but you won't feel a thing.'

His *saw*! I thought, he must be kidding!

But he wasn't. He had a regular power saw that made an awful noise and as he stood behind me running it along my back I was so scared that my teeth rattled. I tried hard not to move at all and prayed that Dr Stewart wouldn't miss with his saw and slice me in half.

At last he turned it off. 'Scissors please, Mrs Inverness.' A few seconds after that, he said, 'Spreaders . . .' I didn't know what he was doing back there but he kept pulling at me. Finally he said, 'There we go! Turn to the right, Deenie.'

I did and I was out of the plaster mould. Dr Stewart cut the tapes and took my head-halter off. I was free! That's when I looked down and discovered that I was only wearing one body stocking. Where was the other one? It must have stuck to the wet plaster and ripped right off. If they hadn't given me two of them I'd be naked! As it was I knew they could all see everything and I was so embarrassed I almost died. I tried covering my chest with my arms and bending over to hide my other half. I'm sure my face was purple and I felt like crying.

Mrs Inverness handed me a wet cloth and said, 'This will help wash the plaster off. You can go and change now.'

I ran for the supply closet. I didn't even realize the plaster had dripped on my legs and feet until then. But I didn't care. All I wanted was to get dressed and out of that room.

*   *   *   *

That night I took my new nightie out of my bottom drawer and tried it on. I stood in front of the mirror and moved just enough to make it turn from pink to purple to lavender. Buddy Brader would never get to see it now and nobody would bring me pink roses either. I took the nightie off and packed it back in the Drummond's Department Store box.

I went to the phone and called Midge. Her line was busy so I tried Janet's number but that was busy too. They were probably talking to each other. I waited for a few minutes before I dialled Midge again. The phone rang three times, then Midge answered.

'Hi . . .' I said, 'it's me.'

'Hi Deenie . . . me and Janet were just talking about you. How'd it go today?'

'I'm not having an operation.' My voice was barely a whisper.

'You're not? How come?'

'I don't need one after all.'

'Well, that's great news! Isn't it?'

'I suppose.'

'You sound funny. Is anything wrong?'

'No . . . I'm fine. I just called to tell you since I'm not having an operation I'll return the nightie. Listen . . . I have to run now . . . bye.' I hung up before Midge could say anything else.

I put the Drummond's box into a brown bag and carried it to school with me the next day. I knew it would be safe inside my locker. At lunch Janet said, 'We're really glad you don't need an operation, Deenie.'

I nodded.

'Were they wrong about your spine?' Midge asked.

'Not exactly.'

'But if it's crooked don't they have to do something?' Janet said.

'The doctors are trying to decide about that,' I told them.

'Me and Midge think you should keep the nightie anyway. Your birthday's in January so it can be a birthday present instead.'

'I really don't need it now,' I said. 'I'd rather return it . . . if you don't mind.'.

They looked at each other.

'It's okay with us,' Midge said. 'We just didn't want you to think you *had* to return it.'

After school the three of us went to Drummond's. The same salesgirl was behind the counter. I handed her the box.

'She's not having her operation,' Janet told her.

'So she doesn't need the nightie,' Midge said.

'Well . . . aren't you lucky!' the salesgirl said to me, and she didn't even try to talk us into keeping the nightie or choosing something else in its place.

I tried to smile. I could tell that Janet and Midge knew something was wrong.

I stopped hanging around the cafeteria after lunch. I told Janet and Midge I had a lot of work to make up because I'd been absent so many times. As soon as I finished eating I went to the library where I sat with my books spread out on the table while I scribbled in my notebook or looked out the window.

One day, while I was sitting like that, somebody sneaked up from behind and covered my eyes with his hands.

'Guess who?' It was Buddy Brader. I'd know his voice anywhere.

'I give up,' I said.

He took his hands away and leaned up against the table. 'What're you doing in here, Deenie?'

'Make-up work,' I told him.

'I came in to watch the fish.' Mr Balfour, our librarian, keeps a big tank of tropical fish on the table in the corner and a lot of kids do wander into the library to watch them. 'You know something?' Buddy said, 'You didn't wave to me this morning.'

'I didn't?' Buddy waves to me every day when we pass each other in the hall, on the way to our first-period classes. 'I guess I didn't see you,' I told him.

'You turned away when I was walking by.'

'Well, I didn't mean to. I just have so many things on my mind.'

'Yeah?'

'I mean it . . . really.'

'Not that it matters . . . I only come in here to see the fish anyway.' He started to walk across the room. Then he stopped and turned for a minute. 'See you around,' he said. He must think I don't like him any more! I wish there was some way to let him know the truth.

All that week I kept hoping Dr Kliner would call to say everyone had made a terrible mistake. That there's nothing wrong with me after all and that I definitely don't have scoliosis. Every time the phone rang I jumped but it was never Dr Kliner. I touched my special place practically every night. It was the only way I could fall asleep and besides, it felt good.

We're starting a new programme in gym. Once a month we're going to have a discussion group with Mrs Rappoport. It sounds very interesting because Mrs Rappoport asked us each to write down a question and drop it into a box on her desk. The question could be about anything, she said, especially anything we need to know about sex. She told us not to put our names on the paper. She doesn't want to know who's asking what. It's a good thing too, because I'd never have asked my question if I had to sign my name. I wrote:

Do normal people touch their bodies before they go to sleep and is it all right to do that?

On Tuesday, when we walked into the gym, Mrs Rappoport told us to sit in a circle so we could talk easily. The first questions she discussed were all about menstruation. But I already knew most everything from my booklet. After that she said, 'Okay, now I think we can move on to another subject. Here's an interesting question.' She read it to us. 'Do normal people touch their bodies before they go to sleep and is it all right to do that?'

I almost died! I glanced around, then smiled a little, because some of the other girls did, and hoped the expression on my face looked like I was trying to figure out who had asked such a thing.

Mrs Rappoport said, 'Can anyone help **us** with an answer?'

Susan Minton raised her hand.

'Yes, Susan . . .' Mrs Rappoport said.

'I wasn't the one who wrote the question but I've heard that boys who touch themselves too much go blind or get very bad pimples or their bodies can even grow deformed.'

'Has anyone else heard that?' Mrs Rappoport asked.

Five other girls raised their hands.

Could it possibly be true? I wondered. And if it was true about boys maybe it was about girls, too. Maybe that's why my spine started growing crooked! Please God . . . don't let it be true, I prayed. I felt my face get hot and I had to go to the bathroom in the worst way but I didn't move a muscle. I hoped nobody could tell what I was thinking.

'Well . . .' Mrs Rappoport said, 'I can see you've got a lot of misinformation. Does anyone here know the word for stimulating our genitals? Because that's what we're talking about, you know.'

It got very quiet in the gym. Nobody said anything for a long time. Then one girl spoke. 'I think it's called masturbation.'

'That's right,' Mrs Rappoport told us. 'And it's not a word you should be afraid of. Let's all say it.'

'Masturbation,' we said together.

'Okay,' Mrs Rappoport said. 'Now that you've said it let me try to explain. First of all, it's normal and harmless to masturbate.'

'You mean for boys . . .' Susan Minton said.

'No, I mean for anyone . . . male or female,' Mrs Rappoport told us. 'The myths that some of you have heard aren't true. Masturbation can't make you insane or deformed or even give you acne.'

I wanted to take a deep breath when she said that but I didn't. I just gulped and looked at the floor.

'Does everybody masturbate?' Barbara Curtis asked.

'Not necessarily,' Mrs Rappoport said. 'But it's very common for girls as well as boys, beginning with adolescence.'

Any minute I thought Mrs Rappoport would ask us to raise our hands if we masturbate and I wasn't sure I'd be able to tell the truth. I never knew there was a name for what I do. I just thought it was my own special good feeling. Now I wonder if all my friends do it too?

But Mrs Rappoport didn't ask us to tell her if we did or we didn't masturbate and I was glad. It's a very private subject. I wouldn't want to talk about it in front of the class. She said the important thing to remember is that it is normal and that it can't hurt us. 'Nobody ever went crazy from masturbating but a lot of young people make themselves sick from worrying about it.'

I couldn't help thinking about Buddy. Can he get that special feeling too? I'd like to find out how much Buddy really knows about girls. I hardly know anything about boys. I think we should have discussions every week. They're more important than modern dance!

That afternoon, when I got home from school, there was a note from Ma, saying she was at the A&P with Aunt Rae. I put my books down, poured myself a glass of milk and was just about to sneak a few chocolate cookies from Ma's secret hiding place, when the phone rang.

'Hello . . .' I said.

'Mrs Fenner?'

'No . . . she isn't in right now.'

'This is Dr Kliner's office calling . . .'

When I heard that my heart started to beat very fast. 'Can I take a message?' I asked then had to clear my throat.

'Deenie's Milwaukee Brace is ready and the doctor suggests an appointment on Friday at ten o'clock.'

'This Friday?'

'That's right. And the doctor also suggests a change of clothes for Deenie . . . a size or two larger than her regular things.'

'What for?' I asked.

'Because the brace takes up a certain amount of room and the girls can't get their regular clothes over it.'

'Oh.'

'Have Mrs Fenner call if she can't make it on Friday. I'll be here until six.'

'I'll tell her.'

'Thank you,' she sang and hung up, like she didn't even care about what she had just told me.

I didn't say anything to Ma about the phone call when she got back from the market. I thought about not telling anyone. But I knew if we didn't show up on Friday Dr Kliner's office would call to find out what happened and then Daddy and Ma would know about the first phone call and that would make me a liar. So I told them during supper. It was already past six-thirty.

'Friday's fine with me,' Daddy said. 'I'll ask Joe to work that morning.'

I'd been chewing on the same piece of meat for a while but I couldn't swallow it so I held my napkin to my mouth and spat it out.

'What's wrong?' Ma asked.

'It was all fat,' I told her. I drank some water, then took a big breath and spoke very fast. 'I'm supposed to bring some other clothes to Dr Kliner's office because mine won't fit over the brace.' I looked at the food on my plate and moved some of it around with my fork.

'Don't worry about your clothes,' Ma said. 'You can get all new things . . . can't she, Frank?'

'Sure,' Daddy said. 'Never mind about that.'

'But my jeans are all broken in the way I like them!'

'So you'll break in new jeans,' Daddy said. 'As many as you want.'

'And I never even wore my two new skirts and sweaters. I was saving them for when it gets cold.' I could feel my throat tightening.

'Maybe we can take them back and get the next size,' Ma said.

'You already shortened the skirts,' I said.

'So we won't return them,' Daddy said. 'It's not important.'

'But it's a waste of money,' I told him.

'Never mind,' Daddy said again. 'All that matters is getting you well.'

'I am well!'

'You know what Daddy means,' Ma said.

Later, Helen came to my room carrying a navy skirt and a striped shirt. 'You can wear these tomorrow,' she said. 'They're bigger than your things and they'll probably look better on you anyway.' She put them down on my bed. They still had tags on them.

★   ★   ★   ★

The brace looks like the one Dr Kliner showed us three weeks ago. It's the ugliest thing I ever saw.

I'm going to take it off as soon as I get home. I swear, I won't wear it. And nobody can make me. Not ever! I felt like telling that to Dr Kliner but I didn't. I had to fight to keep from crying.

Just when I thought I was going to be okay Ma started. 'Oh, my God!' she cried. 'What did we ever do to deserve this?' She buried her face in a tissue and made sobbing noises that really got me sore. The louder she cried the madder I got until I shouted, 'Just stop it, Ma! Will you just stop it please!'

Dr Kliner said, 'You know, Mrs Fenner, you're making this very hard on your daughter.'

Ma opened the door and ran out of Dr Kliner's office.

Daddy hugged me and said, 'I'm proud of you, Deenie. You're stronger than your mother.'

I wanted to tell him I'm not. I hate just looking at the brace, never mind the thought of wearing it. But I was glad he thought I was strong so I kept pretending I really was.

'Why don't you see about your wife,' Dr Kliner said to Daddy. 'I'd like a minute alone with Deenie anyway.'

Daddy said, 'Of course, Doctor,' and he left the room.

Dr Kliner pushed a button on his desk and told me, 'Miss Harrigan will be here in a minute. She's going to help you with your brace. But before she comes I want to tell you something. Your mother's attitude towards your condition is fairly common. Usually when the mother feels that way it rubs off on the patient. I can tell you have your father's attitude and I'm glad. Because wearing the brace can be as easy or difficult as you make it. Do you understand what I'm saying?'

I nodded.

'Before you leave we're going to give you a booklet about scoliosis which explains the exercises you'll have to do every day.'

'I didn't know I'd have to do exercises. I thought I wouldn't be able to do anything like that.'

'Just the opposite,' Dr Kliner said. 'There's nothing you *can't* do.'

'You mean I should take gym in school?' That would mean changing in the locker room where all the girls would be able to see my brace.

'Positively. Gym is very important. So is swimming. Can you swim?'

'Yes, but how do I swim with the brace on?'

'That's the one activity you do without the brace. I'd like you to swim at least three days a week for half an hour at a time.'

There was a knock at the door and Dr Kliner called, 'Come in . . . Deenie I'd like you to meet Iris Harrigan.'

'Hello, Deenie,' Miss Harrigan was very tall and really pretty. She reminded me of that girl I sat next to at the modelling agency, the one who wanted to be in commercials. She picked up my brace and said, 'Let's go change.'

I stood up and followed her into the same room where Dr Kliner had examined me.

'You can get undressed in the bathroom if you want,' Miss Harrigan said. 'But take this in with you. It goes over your bra and pants.' She handed me a piece of material.

'It looks like a boy's undershirt,' I told her.

'It is a kind of undershirt. You wear it under your brace. It prevents most skin irritations.'

'I have to wear an undershirt? Like a baby?'

'Well, it's strictly for comfort.'

'Then I don't *have* to wear it?' I asked.

'It's not a *must*. But you'll feel more comfortable.'

'I don't care about being comfortable,' I said. 'I don't want to wear that thing!'

'Okay then,' Miss Harrigan said. 'Try it without.'

'I will.' I went into the bathroom and locked the door. I took off my dress and folded it up. Then I unlocked the door and called, 'I'm ready . . .'

'Come on out,' Miss Harrigan said. She picked up the brace. I'm going to show you how to get into it now. The first time will be the hardest. After today it will be easier every time you do it.'

The brace is made mostly of metal but there are some white plastic parts too. Miss Harrigan explained that the reason the plastic is full of little holes is so the air can get through to my skin. There are two metal strips down the back of the brace and one down the front. But the worst thing is that the strips are attached to a metal collar.

Miss Harrigan helped me into the brace. 'It's too tight around my neck.' I tried to pull it away.

'It has to hold your neck in place,' Miss Harrigan said. 'The whole idea of the brace is to keep your spine in one position and your spine begins at the base of your neck.'

'It hurts!' I told her. 'Please take it off!'

'It doesn't hurt. There's nothing to hurt you at all. Let me adjust the straps for you.'

Miss Harrigan buckled and unbuckled the side straps until I told her I felt more comfortable. There were three more strips of metal on my brace that I didn't notice right away. Two are around my sides and one starts at the front of my neck, goes under my left arm, and winds up someplace in the back, near my head.

'It feels tight under my arms too,' I told her.

'You have to get used to that,' she said.

Besides the metal strips I had a whole section of white plastic around my middle and some kind of pad on part of my back.

'You'd be more comfortable if you'd wear the undershirt.'

'You said I didn't have to.'

'Why don't you take it home anyway, just in case you change your mind.'

'Maybe,' I told her. 'Right now I feel like I'm in a cage and no undershirt's going to change that! And suppose I grow? What happens then?'

'The brace is adjustable but if you outgrow it Dr Stewart will make another mould of you and you'll get a new brace.'

'I don't think I can live through this. I really don't!'

'I know it seems that way. But you will live through it. Lots of girls do.'

'That's easy for you to say. You don't have scoliosis.'

'That's true,' she said, like we were talking about the weather. 'But when you think of the alternatives, isn't wearing a brace better?'

'What do you mean? Better than an operation?'

'I mean better than growing up with a curved spine.'

'I don't know,' I said. 'I'm not sure about anything.'

Miss Harrigan walked over to a desk and opened the middle drawer. She took something out. 'I'm going to show you some pictures, Deenie. Then you can decide for yourself.'

She opened a booklet to some sketches of people with terrible looking bodies, all crooked and bent over.

'Here's an illustration of a person with scoliosis, a side-to-side curve of the spine.'

'Like me?'

'Yes, except you'll never look that way. Aren't you glad?'

'I'd kill myself if I did.'

'No you wouldn't. But we don't have to argue about it because it's not going to happen.' She turned the page. There was a sketch of somebody who looked just like Old Lady Murray.

'I know someone like that!' I said.

'It's an illustration of kyphosis,' Miss Harrigan told me. 'A front-to-back curve of the spine.'

'Is that the same as hunchback?'

'Yes.'

It was hard to believe that I really and truly had something in common with Old Lady Murray.

When we left Dr Kliner's office I was wearing the brace with Helen's skirt and shirt over it. I was kind of scared that Ma would start crying again when she saw me. Instead she said, 'Well, that's not bad at all. You can hardly tell you're wearing it, Deenie.' I knew from the catch in her voice that she was just saying it and didn't mean a single word.

Daddy asked, 'How does it feel?'

'Like I'm in a cage,' I said.

As I was getting into the back seat of the car I whacked my head on the top of the door.

'Are you all right?' Ma asked.

'I don't know.'

'Let me see,' Daddy said, parting my hair. 'There's no blood,' he told us, as he rubbed my scalp.

'I guess I'm okay,' I said. 'I guess I just can't bend my head with this brace on.' As soon as I said that I started to cry. I cried the way I wanted to when I first saw the brace, loud and hard, until my throat hurt. Daddy didn't try to stop me. He just held me tight while he rocked back and forth, patting my head.

Acknowledgements

The publishers gratefully acknowledge permission to reproduce the following stories and extracts:

CHRISTMAS ON DUTY by Monica Dickens. Story taken from *One Pair of Feet* by Monica Dickens, published by Michael Joseph Ltd. © 1942 Monica Dickens.

DEMONSTRATION PATIENT by P.D. James. Reprinted by permission of Faber and Faber Ltd. from *Shroud for a Nightingale* by P.D. James.

STUDENT NURSE from *Sue Barton – Student Nurse* by Helen Dore Boylston. Reprinted by kind permission of Helen Dore Boylston.

THE PEOPLE IN THE CASTLE from *Not What You Expect* by Joan Aiken. Reprinted by kind permission of Joan Aiken.

ALFRED, BATES AND BORIS from *Let Sleeping Vets Lie* by James Herriot. Reprinted by kind permission of Michael Joseph Ltd.

DEENIE'S BRACE from *Deenie* by Judy Blume. Reprinted by kind permission of William Heinemann Ltd.

The publishers have made every effort to trace copyright holders. If we have omitted to acknowledge anyone, we should be most grateful if this could be brought to our attention for correction at the first opportunity.